IFWG Australia
Dark Phases Titles

Peripheral Visions (Robert Hood, 2015)
The Grief Hole (Kaaron Warren, 2016)
Cthulhu Deep Down Under Vol 1 (2017)
Cthulhu Deep Down Under Vol 2 (2018)
Cthulhu: Land of the Long White Cloud (2018)
The Crying Forest (Venero Armano, 2020)
Cthulhu Deep Down Under Vol 3 (2021)
Spawn: Weird Horror Tales About Pregnancy,
       Birth And Babies (2021)

SPAWN
WEIRD HORROR TALES
ABOUT PREGNANCY, BIRTH
AND BABIES

EDITED BY

DEBORAH SHELDON

A DARK PHASES TITLE

Spawn: Weird Horror Tales About
Pregnancy, Birth and Babies

All Rights Reserved

ISBN-13: 978-1-925956-81-8

Anthology Copyright ©2021 IFWG Publishing International

V1.1

All stories are original to this anthology, except the following: (first publishing instance) "A Rose for Becca" by Jason Fischer, in Borderlands 2009; "Hair and Teeth" by Deborah Sheldon, in Aurealis 2018; "Saturday Night at the Milk Bar" by Gary Kemble, in Midnight Echo 2012.

Printed in Palatino Linotype and Cinzel Decorative.

IFWG Publishing International
Gold Coast

www.ifwgpublishing.com

For Allen and Harry

TABLE OF CONTENTS

INTRODUCTION

Death borders upon our birth, and our cradle stands in the grave.
—Joseph Hall, Bishop of Exeter (1564 – 1656)

One reason why we tell stories is to make sense of trauma. And trauma is always hovering nearby. As physical beings that can experience pain, mutilation, deformation, suffering and death at any moment, we're not safe. Not ever. Horror fiction—in particular, body horror—digs into this fear of vulnerability in a way that other genres cannot match.

From conception to coping with a newborn baby, reproduction is the perfect vehicle for body horror because each phase is a transformation. And nestled at the heart of each transformation is the limitless potential for traumatic outcomes. *What could go wrong?* we fretfully wonder. The answer, of course, is *everything*. We're not in control.

As any woman who has given birth can attest, labour takes over like an unstoppable force of nature, dragging you out to sea on its riptide. You could no more direct what's happening than influence the wax and wane of the moon. It's a world away from the intelligent, cerebral, cognitive, higher self of thoughts and ideas. When contractions start to hurt on an exponential Richter scale that quickly zooms beyond comprehension, you understand in a panic that your *own body* doesn't give a solitary goddamn about you anymore. As a person you have ceased to exist, swept aside in this urgent, overwhelming tsunami of biological imperatives. Now you are simply a mammal. In the process of becoming *something else.*

My son was born about twenty years ago. Giving birth after a gruelling thirty-six-hour labour, I felt like I'd been dropped from a great height and broken to pieces on rocks below. The next morning, I limped into the hospital bathroom to take a shower but when I saw my naked, post-partum body in the mirror, I didn't recognise it. What a ghastly sight! Over subsequent months my body returned to its usual shape, yet I've never forgotten the jolting Kafkaesque shock of swift, transformative disfiguration.

And this is what the genre of body horror does so well—that unexpected pivot into the unknown.

In the hours after our son was born, my shellshocked husband had little to say. Also shellshocked, neither did I. Our son lay swaddled and asleep in a hospital crib next to my bed. I looked upon this little stranger with anxiety. My focus had been on the pregnancy. Somehow, the reality of an actual *child* at the end of it all had escaped my emotional understanding. "What do we do now?" I whispered to my husband. He squeezed my hand and said, "Well…I guess we just live our lives." A new future lay ahead of us, unmapped, and we were setting sail like Magellan.

Parenthood is so life-changing that it makes us alien to ourselves. We experience new feelings and fears. Instincts we weren't aware of kick in. Old patterns from childhood resurface—*Oh God, I sound just like my mother.* Baby blues. Changed relationship dynamics. The endless worrying about how to be a "good parent". It's a disorienting metamorphosis, and perfect fodder for horror fiction. One especially important shift we undergo is existential—nothing destroys the illusion of youthful immortality quite like becoming a mum or dad. It's a seismic upheaval of perspective. Having a child puts us on the factory production line of humanity, trundling us inexorably towards decrepitude and death, because in order for our child to grow up, we have to grow old. A sobering epiphany.

Am I being too morbid? Oh, probably. Since I'm a dark fiction writer, the glass is always half empty.

I got the idea for this anthology from my story "Hair and Teeth", first published in *Aurealis* in 2018, reprinted in *Year's Best Hardcore Horror*, and mentioned in Ellen Datlow's "Recommended List for 2019" in *Best Horror of the Year*. "Hair and Teeth" (reprinted here) is about a middle-aged woman who suspects that her relentless vaginal bleeding is not due to menopause but something far more…nefarious. The story's images and themes wouldn't leave me alone. I decided that I wanted to curate an anthology in a similar vein: a book that would resonate with readers by tapping into the terrors we all share in the shadowy depths of our reptilian brains.

In 2019, I pitched *Spawn: Weird Horror Tales About Pregnancy, Birth and Babies* to IFWG Publishing Australia. Gerry Huntman, Managing Director, responded with enthusiasm and suggested commissioning a few bestselling Australian authors, namely, Jack Dann, Kaaron Warren and Sean Williams. The other stories are from an open callout. I welcomed all subgenres without reservation. What I envisaged was a broad mix of styles that would keep the reader on the back foot, wary and cautious, never knowing what to expect with the turn of every page. I think *Spawn* has achieved that vision. I'm grateful to every writer who submitted, including those who didn't get accepted—I hope they'll submit again next time.

The plan is for *Spawn* to be a trilogy of anthologies. The book you're holding in your hands—number one in the series—is unashamedly Australian. As editor, I make no apologies for this parochialism. Writers in the United States meticulously document their own culture in all its beauty and ugliness, and I have great admiration for such passion, wishing that Australia had the same fervour. We have tremendous horror-writing talent in this country, and I want to showcase and champion it. The second volume in the *Spawn* trilogy will be open to Australasian writers, and the third to worldwide submissions.

The stories you're about to read will scare, unsettle, move and upset you. Leave you disquieted and reflective. Uneasy. So, go ahead, put your eye to the kaleidoscope and gaze into this bizarre and eclectic range of tales that will bend, twist, reflect and refract some of your deepest anxieties about birth, life and death.

I'm sorry I can't be there to hold your hand. Then again, I wouldn't be much help anyway—these stories creep the hell out of me.

Deborah Sheldon
Melbourne, 2020

A GOOD BIG BROTHER

MATT TIGHE

Dad says he is going to teach me how to use the gun. Mum has red, watery eyes as she chews on her toast, but she nods when I look at her.

"It's a grown-up thing you need to learn, honey," she says. "And with the baby coming, you are going to need to do some more grown-up things. You will be a big brother soon." She smiles but it's only a little one that doesn't make the crinkles next to her eyes. "Dad will teach you how to be careful."

Dad gives a funny little huff—it is one of his grown-up noises that I don't really understand. It looks like his eyes are a bit red too, but he goes into the kitchen before I can tell if he has been crying like Mum.

"I heard some noises last night," I say.

Neither of them looks at me straight away, but I can tell they are listening by how still they get. That's another thing adults do—they go still when you ask them something hard. Maybe it helps them think of the answer.

"I heard it too, kiddo," Dad says.

"There was a loud bang," I say. It's not what I really want to say, but I can't find the words. It feels too big.

"Yes, honey," Mum says. "But it had nothing to do with us."

"Oh," I say.

I take a bite of my toast. Mum makes the bread, and it is okay, but the toast has honey, which makes it better. We have lots of honey. Dad has beehives up in the top paddock, behind the big trees. Dad likes to put the honey in his tea, and when he does, he smiles and tells Mum she can't have any because of the baby. He likes to tease her like that. Mum always laughs a bit, but I think she is sad that there is no sugar anymore. I don't mind. I like the honey better.

"We will start after breakfast," Dad says, and I think of the gun. I don't like it. I know what guns do. I saw.

We are standing down in the front paddock. There are some big trees here, like up the back, but no bees. My arms are sore from holding the gun. I haven't shot it—Dad says it's too noisy. We are just practising aiming, and using the bolt action.

"Do you understand?" Dad asks again. I don't know how many times he has asked, but it seems like a lot.

I nod. He keeps looking at me, so I point.

"That's the safety."

"And what do we know about the safety?"

"That we must use it, but we can't trust it."

Dad goes to speak again, but I know what he is going to say so I get in first.

"And the gun is always loaded, even when we know it is not. And the only time you point it at something is when you are going to shoot it. And that…"

"Yes?" he asks, his voice soft.

"If I hear the bells, and if you or Mum are not there, I am to get the gun and point it at the gate. Just like you showed me. If I see something move, I shoot."

Dad nods.

"I don't like it," I blurt. I'm holding the gun under one arm, like I'm supposed to, and I touch the dark barrel with one finger. "It doesn't feel right." It's not what I really want to say. I want to say it feels alive—that it feels like something that might twist around and bite me, but that would sound silly.

Dad sighs and kneels down next to me.

"Listen, buddy, I know this is tough. But I have to tell you something that is going to be even harder. Things are different now."

"You mean like how I can't see my friends?" I ask, but his eyes slide away. That's another grown-up thing, but I know what this one means. It means Dad won't say what he is really thinking.

"Kind of," he says, and then he stops for a long time.

The gun is getting heavy. I'm about to ask him if I can put it down when he starts talking again.

"You are going to be a big brother soon," he says. He smiles a little bit, but it looks sad. It looks like the smile he gives Mum when he puts his hand on her round tummy. "And there might come a time when you…" Dad pauses and has a funny little cough. When he looks at me again, his eyes are watery. "You might have to do some things you don't like. If you do, I want you to remember that no matter how bad it feels, if Mum or me say it's okay, then you just have to do it."

"I don't understand," I say.

The gun feels really heavy. It feels much heavier than it should. I wish I could stop touching it.

"Oh, kiddo, I don't think you could understand, not right now. Just remember, if we say it is okay, you need to do it."

Mum tucks me in. She does that every night, like I'm a little kid.

"I'll be a big brother soon," I say, and she nods without looking at me. She is not paying attention.

"Mum!" I say, and she looks at me.

"Hmmm?"

"I said I'll be a big brother soon. You don't need to tuck me in."

She frowns. "Really?" she says. "Why the grumps?"

I bite my lip. Dad wants me to do grown-up things. I've been thinking and thinking about it, and I've decided I want them to know that I know. That it is a grown-up thing, a big brother thing to know, and I know it.

"I saw what happened," I say, all in a rush.

Mum doesn't say anything straight away, but I can see her hands curl up, gripping my blanket very hard. She doesn't ask what I saw.

"Sweetie," she says after a bit. "That wasn't really Mr Reynolds. You know how we talked about that? How people aren't really themselves if they have the virus? If they are sick?"

"It still looked like him," I say, but it didn't. Not really.

I had woken to the bells ringing, and then shouting. Dad had put bars on my window, drilling them in with the big drill back when the electricity worked, but I could still see down the drive, right down to the front gate. Dad had put a big lock on the gate and the fence was high on each side. It didn't used to be, but when things started to get bad, Dad had spent a lot of money to have some men come out and make the fence higher, and put in the gate with thick iron bars. When they had finished Dad had strung bells through the gate, and they jangled if anyone tried to open it, or even if the wind was strong.

I saw the flickering jumping light of Dad's torch, and I heard the bells ringing, and there was Mr Reynolds standing at the front gate. Mr Reynolds lived a little way down the road, a bit closer to town. He was older and lived by himself, but he was nice. He would always smile and wave when we drove past, and he dropped Easter eggs in the letterbox every year. But he didn't look the same and Dad stood right back, yelling at Mr Reynolds to get away, to not try to open the gate. Mr Reynolds did not even seem to hear him. The torchlight flickered over his arms and, with my face pressed against the window, I could see they had the green and grey bumpy look that Dad said meant someone was sick. His face was okay, but there was something wrong with his mouth. It hung open really wide, wider than I thought a mouth could open. He made some funny noises, puffing noises like he was out of breath, and tried to push the gate open. The bells rang again, loud and sharp.

The light jumped a bit and then steadied right on Mr Reynolds. There was a bang and Mr Reynolds's head changed shape, like when you squish modelling clay. It seemed to push out to one side, and something wet sprayed through the torchlight into the darkness. He fell.

It was quiet for a bit. I heard some soft crunching footsteps going down the drive and then Mum's voice.

"Was he infected?" she asked, her voice shaking.

"Yeah," Dad replied. They were silent, and then he spoke again. "Go back inside. I'll get the gloves and move him away."

I heard Mum coming back, and Dad moving around in the dark, huffing and grunting. The noises stopped after a while, but I kept looking out into the dark for a long time.

Mum is looking at me.

"It's okay, Mum," I say. "I know it wasn't really him."

She nods quickly and gives me a little smile, but her hands are still gripping my blanket really tight.

Mum and Dad are fighting, but even I can tell it's really just because Mum is scared. I think Dad is scared too, but he is trying not to be.

"We've been over this," he says.

They are standing outside near the front door. He has his backpack on. The sun is low, and it is getting hard to see his face. They don't notice me.

"We need medicine. Antibiotics, bandages, and other stuff. I'd be happier if we had more nappies."

"God, we can use the old cloth ones! I'll rip up some sheets!"

Dad sighs. "You know the nappies are only something I'll grab if I see them. But we need other things, and who knows when I'll get a chance to go after the birth?"

"The birth could be any moment!" Mum almost shouts, and Dad frowns.

"I know that!" he snaps, and then rubs one hand over his face. "I know that," he repeats quietly. "And you know I would've gone the other night, but after Reynolds..."

Mum's shoulders slump a bit, and she makes a little hiccupping sound.

"It's just so close now. And town is dangerous."

"I know, honey. But I've done the trip, what, a dozen times? It will be okay. There is hardly anyone left anyway."

Mum nods glumly. I wish I could hug her, but they still haven't noticed me. I'll just have to be helpful. I'll have to be a grown-up. I look at her big tummy. She has one hand resting on it lightly. I'll have to be a good big brother.

I am being shaken. I open my eyes, but it is still dark. I think I make a sound, but I'm not sure.

"Honey," Mum says. "Honey, wake up." Her voice sounds funny, like she is sucking in deep breaths between the words.

"Mum?" I ask, and sit up. There is a little bit of orange light from the candle Mum is holding. Her hand is shaking and big shadows jump across the walls of my room.

"Honey, the baby is coming."

I don't know what to say. I know what she means. Mum and Dad have told me what will happen—they call it a "home birth" when they talk about it. I try to think about all that they said as we sat at the table, but I had not listened very much. It was a bit gross.

"Where's Dad?" I say, and Mum sucks in a big breath.

In the flickering light I see her put one hand on her belly, high up, and wince.

"He isn't back." She stops talking and starts panting. After what seems like a long time, she drops her hand and smiles a little. "He won't be long. It's not even dawn yet. And I've got everything ready." She frowns. "The contractions are coming fast."

I don't know what that means, but I don't think she is really talking to me.

I push the covers back and get up.

"What do we do?" I say.

Mum has put extra sheets—old ones—on the floor in the big front room. It is where the wood heater is, where she keeps the water hot. She has a pile of towels and old sheets in a heap nearby. She has been laying there for a long time now, and she is holding my hand tightly. At first it frightened me because the orange candlelight flickered across her face, making her eyes deep shadows and her open mouth a black hole when she moaned. Now she looks grey. Everything does. It is still night, but everything is getting that funny no-colour that comes just before the sun comes up.

"I don't think it will be much longer," she says, her face all sweaty. She tries to smile, but she winces and sucks in a big breath instead.

I really want to cry but I can't. Mum needs me.

She grunts and squeezes my hand. She has been doing that a lot. Earlier I told her she was hurting me and she started to cry—loud, shaky cries. After that I didn't say, even when she squeezed extra hard.

All of a sudden she screams really loud.

"Mum!" I yell. I'm really scared.

"It's okay," she pants. "This is normal."

I don't believe her. This can't be normal.

"It's almost over," she says, and grits her teeth.

I hope she is right.

And then the bells on the gate start jangling.

"Get the gun!" Mum grunts, and then squeezes her eyes shut. "Get the gun and get ready!"

The gun lives by the front door. I know what she means. It is what Dad talked about.

"Can't you do it?" I ask.

The bells jangle again, and I hear the gate rattle.

"I can't!" she yells, and then screams again.

I let go of her hand and run to the door. I snatch up the gun and step out the front.

The sun is not up yet and everything is grey shadows. It is hard to see down the drive. Everything is just soft lines and shapes. Something, or someone, is pushing on the gate. It is supposed to be locked, but I can see it moving, opening.

"Someone is coming!" I try to call back inside, but Mum screams again.

I put the gun up to my shoulder and look through the sight. All I can see is someone moving, grey against grey. There is a puffing, huffing sound, like someone out of breath.

"Mum?" I ask. My voice has gone all wobbly and soft. "What if it's Dad?"

I keep looking through the sight. Everything is blurry, and I think I am crying. Someone is coming. The puffing sound is getting louder.

"Mum?" I ask again, and then I hear crying.

It is not Mum. It is the crying of a baby, and it is very loud. I want to look back, but I know I can't. I keep looking through the sight of the gun. My arms are starting to shake.

I can feel my finger tightening on the trigger. I don't want to shoot, but Mum and the baby are just there. If it was Dad coming, would he have jangled the bells? Would he call out? Should I call out? All I know is I need to be a good big brother. I need to do the right thing.

"Mum? What do I do?" I whisper.

I can't see properly through my tears. A face swims into view in the sight of the gun. I can't see who it is. All I can hear is the baby crying—my little brother or sister.

I hear Mum take a big watery breath.

"It's okay," she says.

It is what Dad said they would say. I pull the trigger.

SINS OF THE MOTHER

TRACIE MCBRIDE

Ava's first baby is a stone.

Its arrival comes with none of the trappings of pregnancy—no lengthy gestation, no morning sickness, no swelling of the belly, no pain or awareness of giving birth. She simply wakes up one morning to find it nestled between her legs in a small puddle of bloody mucus that makes her recoil in disgust. There hasn't even been an act of conception. Ava is saving herself for marriage.

Gingerly, she picks up the stone. It is warm to the touch, its surface more velvety than its hard, dull grey exterior might suggest, and as it rests in the palm of her hand, it trembles minutely with the flutter of a rapid, bird-like heartbeat. Ava makes a home of sorts for it in a large plastic box. She covers the bottom of the box with kitty litter and arranges a nest of clean rags in one corner. She has no idea what or how to feed a stone baby; breastfeeding is out of the question as she is not lactating, and besides, the thing has no mouth that she can see. She experiments with two saucers in the box, one with fresh water and the other with bread soaked in milk. She never sees the stone move, but the next morning both saucers are empty, so she considers the experiment successful and refills them before going to work.

The next baby is born several weeks later in a manner the same as the first. Like the stone, this one is also small enough to fit in the palm of her hand. It would look like a fully formed newborn human were it not for its tiny elephant head. She places the baby in the plastic tub next to its sibling, which has sprouted two stumpy legs and now shuffle-hops around its enclosure. Ava contemplates the two saucers and adds a small bowl of peanut butter.

Her third baby is a spider. Mistaking it for a conventional spider, she nearly squashes it before she notices its human face. She finds a second tub and fits it out similarly to the first. Rather than spend all her spare time catching insects for the thing, she leaves a small morsel of meat in one corner of the tub in the hope of attracting flies. When she returns home from work that night, her spider baby has constructed an intricate web spanning a good third of its enclosure. It sits in the middle of the web with a vapidly satisfied expression, so Ava assumes it can take care of itself well enough and largely ignores it. Even though it is her baby, Ava has mild arachnophobia; the human face only makes it more repellent.

Ava struggles to concentrate on the sermon in church on Sunday. She has not been sleeping well of late. Her babies are growing, their nocturnal noises increasing with their size and keeping her awake at night. Then there is her mounting anxiety. She has no reason to expect that she will continue to spawn mutants in her sleep—but no reason to expect that she won't, either. She has no idea where to go for help, and how would that conversation even go, anyway?

I've given birth to three mutant children this year, and... No, I don't know who the father is, as far as I know there's no father, because I'm a virgin, and... Yes, I know that's impossible, but you see, my real problem is how do I make it stop, and how do I get rid of these cursed babies without condemning myself to Hell?

Ava shakes herself like a dog and tries to focus on the minister. Instead, she finds herself staring at the back of Dan Tremewan's head. Dan sits in the pew in front of her, next to his fat little wife and three chubby little non-mutant children. Ava has long harboured a crush on Dan, a feeling she keeps squashed a long, long way down. But looking at the smooth, tanned skin on his neck, with the faintest hint of stubble where his hair line has been freshly trimmed, fills her with a potent urge to reach out and stroke it.

Lust. She sits on her hands and closes her eyes, but it is too late. Now that she has allowed this droplet to seep into her consciousness, she finds it everywhere. In the warm, calloused hand of the minister as he briefly clasps hers when she exits the service. In the taut fabric of a fellow passenger's jeans as he brushes past her to take his seat on the bus. God help her, she even finds it in the curve and swell of a woman's breasts as the waitress bends forward to deliver her coffee and cake at a local café that afternoon.

Except God has been resolutely unhelpful so far with this mess, ignoring her prayers. Perhaps He is the one inflicting her suffering. Perhaps He means not to test her faith, but seeks to torment her for His own amusement. The thoughts come unbidden and are so blasphemous Ava gasps aloud, drawing glances from the other patrons in the café. She ducks her head and finishes her afternoon tea, her cheeks burning, when all she really wants to do is flee. *God helps those who help themselves*, she tells herself, repeating it like a mantra throughout the rest of the meal and on the short walk home.

She has not given her babies proper names, but her inner five-year-old has named them unofficially. Her first-born is Stone Baby, the second Nosy, and the third is Creepy. She gets home to find one plastic tub tipped on its side, and soiled kitty litter scattered across the carpet in a conspicuous trail to the bathroom. Nosy is merrily unfurling an entire roll of toilet paper onto the floor while Stone Baby watches on. At least, Ava presumes it watches—it may have grown legs, but she can discern no eyes. Creepy's tub is upright but empty. Ava searches fruitlessly under every piece of furniture before she thinks to look up, and finds it sneering down on her from a corner of the ceiling above her bed.

Ava sighs. She had hoped it would not come to this, had hoped they would stay small enough to be contained within the smooth, translucent walls of their tubs, but of course that is an unreasonable expectation. All babies grow up eventually. She has a plan, and as night falls, she enacts it.

Ava gathers up her children and puts them into a backpack—first Stone Baby, then Nosy, then Creepy, who she still cannot stand to touch with her bare hands and thus scoops up with a tea towel. They make soft sounds of distress from inside their dark and stuffy prison. It is a good hour-and-a-half walk to the nearest bushland. Halfway into the hike, the straps on her cheap backpack give out under the weight of her children, forcing her to carry the noisy, squirming bundle in her arms. Despite the night chill, she is sweating by the time she reaches her destination, and every muscle in her upper body aches with the strain. It is part of her penance, and in any case, she cannot take a taxi or public transport for fear of attracting attention.

She takes a torch from a side pocket of the backpack and turns it on to navigate deeper into the bush, following the path of a creek. Even with the light from her torch, she cannot tell how deep the water is. Deep enough to drown a sack of kittens? She imagines the backpack slipping from her grasp, sliding down the bank into the water, Stone Baby dragging them all under…

No. She could not do that. *Must* not do that.

When she judges she is a safe distance from the road, she un-zips the backpack and releases the children. They scurry around in circles at first, confused by their strange new surroundings. Then, as one, as if they are communicating with each other by telepathy, they stop and gaze up at her expectantly.

Assuming they will run after her, she turns and walks away quickly, determined not to look back. Despite her resolution, Nosy's solitary, plaintive *meep* compels her to glance once over her shoulder. The three have not moved. She turns back to the path and picks up her pace.

Ava tries to force her body into obedience. She takes cold baths, shivering in icy water until she loses sensation in her extremities and her lips turn blue. She starves herself, lasting ten days before she passes out at work, coming around to a crowd of co-workers hovering over her, their hands fluttering like agitated birds. She is used to being largely ignored, and the sudden intense scrutiny unnerves her more than the fainting spell. A colleague drives her home, and when the woman presses a chocolate bar on her and insists that she eat it, Ava does not resist. Ava holds a knife to her own abdomen, the tip of the blade nicking her skin, and wonders whether she can simply cut the evil out of her, but the fear of bleeding to death stays her hand. Ava even visits a doctor for birth control. She can't decide which is more shameful: taking medication to thwart God's will or lying to the doctor about a fictitious fiancé. But nothing works. The babies keep coming.

Every month now, instead of her period, a fresh abomination emerges from her body during the night. She has more like Nosy with human bodies and animal heads, including a hawk-headed creature and one with the face of a dog. She has two with bright blue skin—a boy and a girl—the boy with a third eye in the middle of his forehead and the girl having four arms tipped with fingers as sharp as razors. She almost cries with relief one month when her baby, although tiny like all the others, looks like a normal human—until it opens its mouth. It hisses and snaps at her with a mouth full of needle-like fangs, and lashes the air with a long, thin, forked tongue.

It is a matter of trial and error which babies will cohabit peacefully. After several assaults on her siblings, the four-armed girl is moved into solitary confinement, as is the viper-mouthed child. Ava's bedroom floor becomes crowded with plastic tubs. She invests in a sturdy new hiking backpack and continues to trek into the bush every few months or so to release those of her children who have grown big enough. Each trip she takes, she half-dreads, half-hopes to see some of the others; it would ease her conscience to know they have survived.

The day after her thirty-eighth birthday, she awakens to find in her bed the most disturbing creature yet. Pale green in colour, it has two arms, two legs, a pair of leathery wings, and where its mouth should be, a mass of writhing tentacles. Its forehead is creased in a permanent scowl, and it glares at her with narrowed, red eyes. Its appearance is grotesque enough, but there is something else, some extra dimension or malevolent aura that fills Ava with revulsion and dread. She tosses it into a container on its own. For the first time with any of her babies, she punctures a lid to create air holes and seals the tub shut.

That night is a sleepless one. Squidface, as she has silently named it, does not let up with its furious thumping against the sides of its prison, punctuated occasionally with a guttural growl that is preternaturally deep for such a small being. Somewhere around 3:00am, Ava weighs down the lid of the tub with heavy books for added security.

She calls in sick the next day, then does nothing but sit, stare at Squidface's tub, and wait for nightfall. The only other baby in residence, Willow, is a sleepy tree-creature with pale roots for feet and a gentle face set in a trunk that is gnarled like an ancient bonsai. She would be tempted to keep it, except for the awful stink that emanates from its tiny flowers that have bloomed in recent days. Willow's uppermost branches are visible over the top of its tub; big enough to leave home. She cannot wait for Squidface to grow but will dispose of it tonight.

When the time comes, she carefully deposits Willow into her backpack. Departing from custom yet again, Ava tips her newborn, Squidface, into a separate bag. She tries not to look at it as she does so, but it seems this child has doubled in size overnight. Visions of the creature clawing its way out of confinement and latching onto her face invade her sleep-deprived mind. She carries it as far from her body as she can manage.

When she reaches the bushland, she releases the tree-baby first. It tiptoes, swaying about the clearing, probing the earth experimentally with its roots, then stops to stare up at the moon in awe. It should be a comforting scene, but Ava is on edge. The bag containing Squidface trembles with the creature's ominous growls, and unseen things rustle in the undergrowth in response. It feels like the whole forest is vibrating in answer to her child's call.

With a deep, shaky breath, Ava bends to open the drawstring on the bag. Her intent is to loosen it slightly, then flee the scene while its occupant wriggles free. She only accomplishes the first part of her plan before something, smallish and hard and moving fast, hits her in the back of the knees and sends her sprawling. She rolls over, spitting dirt, and tries to push herself up, only to find herself swarmed and pinned to the ground.

All her children are here. There are dozens of them and they have grown, some now as big as medium-sized dogs. They crawl and hop and grasp, they hoot and squeal and chitter, and orchestrating it all, giving shape and order to the chaos, is Squid-face.

A heavy object smashes onto her shins. Ava screams in pain. She cranes her head to see what has hit her. It is Stone Baby, grown to the size and weight of a bowling ball, perched on her shins. Its legs tense and it jumps, landing on her knees and shattering both kneecaps, drawing fresh howls from its mother. Stone Baby continues a leisurely journey up her body, breaking bones and rupturing organs as it goes.

Blood flows from Ava's wounds and her other children set upon her hungrily. They shred her clothing to reach the soft skin beneath. Some lap at the blood like cats, and some tear slivers of flesh with fangs or claws. Chubby infant limbs become painted with gore. Two of the animal-faced babies have a tug-of-war over her left-hand index finger, the battle ending when the dog-faced child rips it free and scampers off into the bush with it. She could fight at least some of them off, crawl away, yell for help, but she does not attempt even a token struggle.

Instead, Ava submits.

Here is the agony she should have felt with every birth. Here is the nourishment her babies craved from her body that she denied them. Here is the sacrifice that every mother owes her children, instead of the neglect and abandonment they have suffered.

One by one, her babies stagger away with sated bellies. Her body is pulp, her heart close to failure, but her face has been left untouched. She is left alone with just her tentacled child, who has so far stood aloof from the feast. It climbs up onto her bloodied chest and leans forward to deliver a kiss.

A kiss that sends tentacles into her mouth to rip out the delicacy of her tongue. An embrace that slithers over her cheeks, skewers her eyeballs and tears them from her head. A kiss that takes the tender gift of her final breath, and in return offers absolution.

BENEATH THE CLIFFS OF DARKNOON BAY

REBECCA FRASER

When Cecily first saw the lighthouse, squat and white-walled against a charcoal-dull sky, she released the breath she felt she'd been holding since setting sail from Bridport. It was a shuddering exhalation of relief and reservation—the former as respite from the nauseous rolling of Bass Strait's ink-black swell, and the latter borne from apprehension. The reality of the lighthouse's isolation settled on her, heavy as the fog that surrounded it.

Darknoon Island rose from the ocean, a granite-spined, mountainous mass surrounded by sheer cliffs that met the sea in rocky shelves, weather-worn boulders, and barnacle-encrusted blowholes. To Cecily, the island looked like a dragon's tooth, all sharp peaks and jagged edges. She tightened her grip on *The Lady Grey*'s gunwale as the sea pitched again, sending a salt-tinged spray to slap her cheeks with icy hands.

"A formidable sight indeed." Edward lurched along the slippery deck towards her. "Impressive-looking structure though, eh, Cec'?"

He threaded arms around her waist and covered her hands on the gunwale with his own. His breath was against her nape, and she leant back as if to absorb his warmth, confidence and enthusiasm for their new beginning.

New beginning, that's what he had called it. She couldn't help thinking of it as their last hope. Why else would she have agreed to such a drastic change of lifestyle? Perhaps, here on Darknoon, they could find themselves again…find a way back to each other. He would look at her the way he used to, before she'd gone and—

21

"Home for the next year." His moustache tickled her neck as he spoke. "Lighthouse keepers. What a lark! Quite the adventure, it will be." He spun her to face him suddenly, searched her face with serious grey eyes. "You don't have any regrets do you, Cecily? No misgivings? It's going to be very different to life in Hobart. It's not too late to call this whole thing off and—"

"No." Cecily's voice was sharper than she'd intended. *Call the whole thing off,* that's what he'd suggested once before. "No," she repeated, softer, stretching her mouth into a smile. *No.*

She linked her hands behind Edward's neck and kissed him. His lips were welcoming, his hand against her coat-clad back firm as it traced a path down the bustling sweep of her skirts to the curve of her posterior. But as *The Lady Grey* cut her way through the foam-flecked surf to enter the crescent moon of Darknoon Bay, Cecily couldn't help feeling that his kisses lacked the intimacy with which they'd once smouldered.

When the last of their trunks and supplies had been lugged, brine-soaked and sand-caked, across the beach and up the slippery, winding climb that led to the lighthouse keeper's two-room cottage, Cecily watched *The Lady Grey* sail from Darknoon Bay. The sight of the cargo ship's sails disappearing like a white-winged moth into the Furneaux Group's scattered island network sent a shiver down her spine to rival the southerly chill.

It would be twelve months before *The Lady Grey* returned.

A fluttering cramp squeezed low in her belly.

"Looks like the last keeper left us a welcome gift." Edward's voice from inside the square-stoned cottage bubbled with the schoolboy excitement she found so disarming. "Come on, Cec', a toast to us!" The hollow *thunk* of a cork leaving its stopper followed his words.

She stepped back inside the cottage. The fire she'd lit in the grate had started to spread heat into the bone-cold corners of the larger, all-purpose room. Leaping flames cast a buttery light across Edward's face.

"Here." He offered her a glass filled with amber liquid. "This'll warm you from the inside out."

She took the glass, smiled as he raised his own theatrically to the ceiling.

"To new beginnings," he declared. "And to adventure." He clinked his glass against Cecily's, brought it to his lips and swallowed a generous mouthful.

"And to love?" Cecily offered. She took a small sip, grimacing as the whisky burned its way down her throat.

"Ah, but of course. And to love." Edward clinked again, took another swallow.

Cecily sipped again. *Why did his toast to love sound like an after-thought?*

"Look." Edward thumped his fist on a leatherbound tome that took centreplace on the wide sassafras table. "The previous keeper's log book. Seems, despite whatever weaknesses he had, old Bradford was a diligent recorder of events."

He opened the book and pushed it towards Cecily. Every entry was an exercise in careful penmanship, methodically outlining the events and duties Reginald Bradford had undertaken during his tenure as lighthouse keeper of Darknoon Bay.

Cecily bent forward to read his last entry. "*March 18, 1836: All is quiet.* I wonder what that means? It's so short compared to his other entries."

She examined the log's earlier records—tightly-filled pages detailing everything from the daily weather through to the routine tasks his position demanded: repairs, painting, cleaning, and keeping the light burning at night to ensure the safe passage of the sealing vessels that worked the Strait's treacherous waters.

"If I were to hazard a guess," Edward said with a shrug, "I'd say a storm must've blown through in the preceding days. I daresay his entry refers to the restoration of calm weather. More importantly though, Cec', this log represents a jolly thorough manual for the task at hand. The training at the Iron Pot lighthouse was adequate, of course, but you can't beat a first-hand account from a long-timer. 'Specially for a fellow's first posting."

"It's a shame, really. About Mr Bradford, I mean."

"The only shame is his, Cec'." Edward reached to tuck a loose strand of hair behind her ear. "A lighthouse keeper has absolutely no business being drunk at his post. When *The Lady Grey* arrived with the next year's provisions, word is the captain found Bradford quite comatose with liquor, slumped at this very table. Disgraceful display of irresponsibility."

Edward quickly replaced the cork in the bottle, as if remembering he'd just drained a good measure of Bradford's whisky himself.

"Right, I'd best get to the lighthouse. Make sure there's sufficient oil and the wicks are trimmed. Be dark soon." He pulled on his coat. "In the meantime, you've got plenty of unpacking to keep yourself busy. You'll have this place feeling like home in no time, Cec'."

Edward took her shoulders, gave her a firm kiss, then stepped out into the violet-pink gloam of gathering dusk.

At first, Cecily applied herself to the task of unpacking with the zeal of any new homemaker; opening each trunk and refolding linen to fit in cupboards, hanging clothes, unwrapping the few keepsakes and books she'd brought with them. She restocked the pantry with the supplies *The Lady Grey* had carried: quantities of flour, oats, sugar, salted meats and other staples. She'd never had to maintain an inventory before, and the weight of responsibility creased her brow with a ripple of diffidence.

Another soft cramp stirred her belly, like a butterfly flapping its wings. This time, she couldn't deny what it was. The familiar sensation of muscles being pulled and stretched, tingling twitches—the harbingers of new life. Cecily put down the box of tea leaves she was about to shelve. She sat at the table, ran her hands over her stomach, and listened to her body. A missed cycle wasn't unusual—her doctor had assured her of that, what with all the stress she'd been under—but there were other signs: tender breasts, the haze of lethargy she'd felt over the past few weeks, the gag of nausea she woke with some mornings.

Cecily thrilled with the realisation she was expecting, but it wasn't at the thought of the sweet-smelling infant she'd cradle in her arms. No, it was Edward's face that filled her heart. How his chin would tremble with emotion as she broke the news to him, his eyes welling at the anticipation of fatherhood. Oh, he'd been so doting before with little William. So proud. She could make him proud again…and then he'd forgive her. Despite his insistence, she knew he could never truly absolve her. How could he? Coffins should never be that small—

Her gasp of pain chased away the thought-chaos stampeding through her mind. She looked down at her hands and unclenched her fists. Blood-blushed crescent moons showed where her fingernails had pierced her palms. She gave herself a little shake and pushed on with the remainder of the unpacking. Despite the screech of the wind outside as it rioted around Darknoon, the words that returned to her as she filled drawers and shelved crockery were Reginald Bradford's: *All is quiet*.

"**W**atch your step, Cec'. You're carrying precious cargo."

Edward helped her navigate the stairs that wound through the interior of the lighthouse, leading to the lantern room some hundred steps up. The lighthouse stood atop Darknoon Bay's easternmost bluff, a silent sentinel, her elevation affording a dramatic view of the wild expanse of water she protected. Cecily loved to step out onto the narrow observation gallery and peer straight down onto the ocean-crashed rocks. The surge and swell, the foam-fury of the waves as they gushed into tidal pools, the booming over rocks, all mesmerised her. When the sun shone, a glisten of sleek seal's hide sometimes revealed itself in the waves.

"Look." Cecily tried to angle herself closer to the railing but her belly, now six months' swollen, made it challenging. "Seals are down there on the rocks."

"Where?" Edward leant over the railing, the wind making a play for his woollen cap.

"I…thought I saw them lying on the rocks. They were all shiny and long. Their heads were tipped back…almost as if they were staring up at us."

"Well, they're not there now, that I can see." Edward laughed. "Now come away from the edge, Cec'. You're making me nervous."

He held out his hand to lead her from the waist-high railing.

She took a final look at the shoal below. Whatever she'd seen was gone. Must have glided back into the ocean with a retreating wave. Seals were incredibly agile, she knew. She'd spent many a windswept day roaming Darknoon's lowlands while Edward slept off the previous night's shift. She'd come to know the flora and fauna of their remote island home—the cunning burrows of mutton birds, the coarsely-tufted saltgrass and fragrant purple-brown heath, the sinuous tail of a disappearing tiger snake—and she'd seen colonies of seals move from the rocks on Darknoon's north side with a speed that belied their shape. So awkward on land, so efficient in water. But this pair, the ones she'd just spotted, had seemed different. Something about their shape, that knowing tilt of their heads...

"Just listen to that, would you?" Edward said, as he led her back into the lantern room occupied by the huge fresnel lens. "That confounded croaking seems to go on all day and at least half the night. Bleeding geese."

He shook his fist as a flock of Cape Barren geese, necks and black wingtips outstretched, flew overhead. Even the bellow of those strong westerly winds, the Roaring Forties, couldn't drown out the screech-honk chorus.

"Do you ever hear anything else at night?" Cecily ventured. She'd been putting off bringing it up in case Edward thought it was starting to happen again. *Was it?*

"Hear anything? Why, all sorts of things. The wind. The crash of the ocean. Birds, of course. The seals can make a terrific din, vocal creatures they are! You'd be amazed at the sounds one hears between sunset and sunrise."

"Anything like music?" She made her words sound airy, inconsequential.

"Music?"

"Yes, or...singing?" The baby inside her gave a shuddering lurch. She breathed through the series of kicks that drummed across her bladder. "Like a lullaby of sorts."

Edward's raised eyebrow was answer in itself. "Nothing like that, my dear. Why...do you?" He searched her face.

What did his eyes hold? Concern? *Fear?* She mentally chastised herself for saying anything. He'd been coming back to her, slowly, like the petals of a spring flower cautiously unfurling after a bitter frost —

She smiled brightly. "I'm sure it's nothing more than the wind through the she-oaks."

"They do make quite the whistling sound when the wind's up," Edward agreed.

"Then that's what it must be."

Cecily clasped his offered hand and took a step down the winding staircase. She changed the subject as they made their way to the bottom of the lighthouse, but while she couldn't see Edward's face as she made frivolous chatter about the book she was reading, she felt the weight of his gaze on her back.

A few nights later, Cecily heard the singing again.
The soft melodic tinkle of voices floated through the dark. She put down the knife she'd been using to trim the pastry from a pie dish, and listened. There it was again — she hadn't imagined it at all. Edward had been on duty for a couple of hours. She opened the door and stared up at the lighthouse. It winked across the Strait, a beacon of light that paled against the night's canvas, where the Milky Way scattered her diamonds across a skein of black velvet.

Surely Edward must hear it too? Lilting and lyrical, the voices seemed to tease from the darkness. Beckoning. She strained to make out the words, only the voices were too faint. She pulled a shawl around her shoulders and stepped outside. The singing pulled her towards the base of the lighthouse, but she clung to the shadows, knowing Edward would be furious if he saw her walking near the clifftop at night.

At the precipice, she crawled as best she could to the edge — the rocky granite cold and wet beneath the uncomfortable bulge of her belly — and peered over the brink. The voices... She felt sure they were coming from far below as if the very ocean itself were singing to her. At that moment, a streak of wind-riding clouds parted to reveal the full face of the moon, and in its glow, she saw black shapes on the weed-slick rocks below, twisting and undulating as if the music was in them...*of* them. Their heads were lifted towards the lighthouse with a coquettish tilt.

She blinked and they were gone. So were the voices. She scanned the boulders and the tips of the waves where moonlight glinted, her eyes darting for any sign of the enigmatic singers *(all is quiet)*, but the ocean held its secrets.

Cecily struggled to her feet and returned to the cottage, shoulders hunched against the wind. She looked back at the lighthouse before pulling the door closed, and there was Edward on the observation gallery, silhouetted by the night sky. He stood braced against the cold, looking out to sea, as if watching, waiting. But for what?

And in that moment, she *knew*.

Of course he'd heard the voices *(damned liar)*, so why would he tell her he hadn't? Was he trying to make her feel as if she were losing her mind? So that he could get rid of her—lock her away, like last time? There'd been someone else he'd been waiting for once before. Oh, yes *(pig)*, a pretty young thing had caught his eye. But Cecily had known how to regain his attention. The voices—those *other* ones—had whispered a most guileful plan. And then *(oh, sweet William)* and then—

She gripped the doorframe, breathing hard.

Her hands cradled her belly, and she crooned to her unborn child. She couldn't lose Edward again. They'd come so far in these past six months. She'd endured Darknoon's brooding loneliness, silenced her terror of carrying and birthing a child away from the mainland, locked the voices in a secure chamber of her mind... Besides, it was impossible his heart could be captivated by another's here. Why, they hadn't seen another soul for going on—

Sirens.

The voices screamed the answer into her mind. She raked her cheeks with her nails. Why hadn't she thought of it before? It was obvious. The evidence unequivocal. She recalled a snatch of conversation she'd overheard aboard *The Lady Grey*. Two crewmen had made mention of exquisite creatures that lured seafarers with their darkly seductive song. Oh, they'd ribbed each other about them, made vulgar comments as they'd passed their hip flask... yet she'd heard the darkly seductive song herself, witnessed the sirens flaunting themselves languidly on the rocks, enchanting her Edward. They were trying to take him away from her just like (*harlot*) someone had before.

What could she do? How could she compete with the intoxicating wiles of a siren?

Then Cecily remembered the log book. Perhaps Bradford had encountered them too, made notes in his elegant handwriting.

She choked back a sob as she dragged a chair to the large bureau that ran along one wall of the cottage. She'd barely paid the log book any attention since they'd arrived. That was Edward's domain, and he made his entries at dawn when he returned from his shift, long before she'd risen. He'd begun storing it on a top shelf of the bureau lately, insisting the hard-to-reach location afforded additional space in their confined quarters that the huge book would otherwise take up.

Cecily had a nasty moment when she teetered on the chair as she reached for the book on tiptoes, her heavy belly distorting her sense of balance. She steadied herself, gripped the log, and stepped down from the chair. With a racing heart, she lay the book on the table and opened it to the page kept by its ribbon marker. She had intended to flick back through the pages to comb Bradford's entries some six months prior, but the sight of her name inked in Edward's boyish script stopped her hand mid-turn.

She read his most recent entries, then read them again. She turned the pages to read his earlier entries, hands shaking with such fury she tore leaves from the spine. Amid Edward's recording of temperatures, occasional maritime sightings and observations of day-to-day lighthouse management, her name leapt from the page with increasing frequency.

May 31, 1836: Cecily's disposition remains outwardly buoyant, yet I detect a familiar melancholy may have disrupted her spirit. Perhaps it is nothing more than settling into Darknoon's challenging lifestyle, or the emotional excitement of the pregnancy. I shall remain vigilant.

That had been written barely two months after their arrival. Cecily's eyes burned as she read on.

June 6, 1836: Cecily spends her days roaming Darknoon, irrespective of the weather. From the window, I sometimes see her lips moving as if talking to someone, then cocking her head as if listening to a reply. Could it be happening again?

She read faster.

July 22, 1836: I have made a terrible error in judgement bringing Cecily to Darknoon Bay. I believed the change of scenery and intimacy of our circumstances would benefit her. Rid her of the "voices" that once plagued her and help erase the dreadful events of the past year—a new beginning. Yet she babbles incessantly to herself, two-way conversations in a voice I no longer recognise, oft punctuated by bursts of maniacal laughter or howling sobs.

Lies. All lies.

August 16, 1836: Cecily's mania is worsening. I fear for my unborn child.

Yesterday's entry read:

September 9, 1836: I must remove poor Cecily from Darknoon and return her to the asylum for the sake of herself and for our child. I will activate the distress signal upon sight of the next passing vessel. There is nothing else to be done.

Cecily's blood turned to ice. *There is nothing else to be done.* Couldn't Edward see what was going on? The sirens had bewitched his foolish heart, skewing his mind with their falsities and fallacies. And now he meant to be rid of her.

She seized the knife lying next to the forgotten pie dish and ran from the cottage in a lumbering gait. Atop the lighthouse she could see Edward, still on the gallery, looking out to sea *(looking for them)*. She crossed the short distance to the lighthouse and started up the stairs, hair coming loose from her bun to fall across her face. Her breath hitched in her chest as she climbed faster, but she barely noticed. Her eyes, wild and wide, were fixed on the top of the spiral staircase. She clutched the railing with her free hand to better haul herself along.

When she reached the lantern room, she took a moment to

stare at Edward's back—take in the square of his shoulders, the auburn curl that had strayed from beneath his cap, the arms she'd felt embrace her a thousand times (*as did she*) resting on the iron rail as he searched the water. Looking for the sirens, no doubt.

"They can't have you."

Edward whirled at his post. His eyes rounded when he saw her. "Cecily! What are you doing up here? It's the middle of the night." He took a step towards her. "Is everything all right with the baby?"

The baby. He cares only for the baby.

"You see them, don't you? Hear their song?" She ducked her head and stepped out onto the gallery. The ocean boomed and crashed below. A fine mist of sea spray settled on her face like a veil.

"What are you talking—" Edward's words cut off as she lifted the knife. Moonlight glinted from the blade. He licked his lips. "Cecily, my love. You are not well. Let's get you back inside, where it's—"

"I can't let them have you, Edward. I can't lose you again."

She rushed towards him, arms outstretched, to let him fold her into his embrace so they could breathe each other in. But he (*liar*) was grabbing her instead, gripping her wrists, holding her at arm's length (*don't let him leave*) and she pushed against him, pushed him back (*don't forget the knife*) and plunged and punctured and pierced.

And then he was slumping backwards against the rail (*do it*) and with a final shove he was up and over the railing.

Falling.

Falling.

"Edward!" She gripped the rail as he plummeted like a grotesque doll, hands clutching wildly at the air until he landed crooked-limbed on the rocks below. "Oh, Edward. Why did you fight me? The knife... I would never hurt you. The knife was for *them*."

She took the steps back down slowly, every footfall making a noise as hollow and empty as she felt. She would go to him. They could still be together. No one else would have her Edward.

The air whipped and whistled as Cecily stumbled over the slippery boulders beneath the cliffs of Darknoon Bay. Her boots were soaked, her clothes sodden, as she ventured deeper into the network of shallow pools formed by centuries of water forging their designs into the rocky shelf. She searched for Edward, moving clumps of shiny kelp as the tidal surge pushed and pulled them, but there was no sign of his body.

The sirens must have already taken him.

Finally, as the thin grey light of early dawn crept across the Strait, she sank, exhausted, into a rock pool. The icy water reached her waist. Her blouse moulded to the shape of her swollen belly. The baby kicked hard, as if protesting against the ferocious cold.

"Don't you worry." She rested a hand on the curve of her belly. "I'll find him. We'll all be together soon."

But how could she follow Edward out to sea? She couldn't breathe underwater like the sirens. *Gills,* the voice whispered helpfully.

If you had gills, you could.

Of course.

She removed the knife from the waistband of her skirt and lifted her chin to expose her throat. Slowly, deliberately, she carved into her flesh with the tip of the knife, cutting four deep stripes on either side. Blood surged from the flaps of skin and trickled down to mingle with the seawater. Cecily closed her eyes and waited for the tide to return her to Edward.

The sun rose. A pair of seals hauled themselves from the ocean and lumbered across the rocks. They approached the lifeless figure in the rock pool with curiosity, snorting and blowing. Their whiskers tickled Cecily's blue-pale face for a moment and then they were gone, leaping into a retreating wave with agile grace.

All was quiet.

MOTHER DANDELION

ANTOINETTE RYDYR

The young girl ran through a field of tall undulating grass peppered with dandelions. As she ran, she disturbed the delicate weeds, causing their seeds to dislodge, fly up on tiny hazy umbrellas to disperse in the wind.

The feeling of joy overwhelmed her and she treasured it as one of her most precious memories. But this was not a memory that she had ever experienced. This was a dream.

A dream not created from her thoughts and echoes of the past but one chosen for her.

"I did not choose this."

Suddenly, she collapsed and lay paralysed, cushioned by the tall grass. She looked down at her legs but they were gone. All that remained were short stumps, neatly healed and criss-crossed with coarse scars.

"I can't feel my legs."

The girl lay on the hospital bed, her mind in a fog. She twisted her head around at an awkward angle, and tried to focus. Her mouth gaped wide, straining to gasp out the words.

"I can't feel my legs!" Her agonised cries were finally expelled and bounced against the pastel green walls. "I can't feel my legs! I can't feel my legs!"

The attendant rushed over to the distraught girl, wiped her

brow with a warm moist towel. "Shh. Hush now. Everything is all right. You are fine."

The girl's breath stuttered as she tried to communicate. "I can't feel my legs," she finally repeated, but in a soft muted tone.

"Of course not, dear. You don't need them anymore." The attendant continued to wipe the girl's flushed face. "Your work here is for the greater good, Mother Dandelion. Humanity is grateful and will flourish again. Because of you."

"Because of you."

The words were lost on the girl, but the soothing effect of the kind voice and the warm towel against her flushed skin calmed her and she drifted off to sleep. The attendant manually pumped an extra dose of sedatives and lucid-dreaming medication into the feeding tubes.

The girl wandered the field of dandelions which merged into a field of amaryllis.

She came across another girl sitting cross-legged in the field of flowers with a book in her lap.

The other girl looked up at her. "My mother used to read to me. Can you read to me?"

"You have the book. You can read for yourself."

"I never learnt to read properly. The schools closed when I was little. Now I'm a flower. But I don't want to be a flower." The girl opened the book to a page revealing an amaryllis. Its fluted reddish-pink petals had been flattened. "I can't read the writing so I press the flower in the book. Then I can look at the pretty picture I made."

The writing on the board read, TOGETHER WE CAN BE STRONG.

Instructor J145 was saying, "We must all make sacrifices for the advancement and betterment of humanity."

During the induction training session, Instructor J145 stood rigid at a lectern and spoke with the conviction of a cleric preaching a sermon. Attendant Dandelion sat riveted to the speaker's words that instructed the carers on their duties and responsibilities. The importance of the RePop Program was impressed upon the students.

"As many of you know and experienced, when the near-extinction event occurred, it progressed rapidly. The world heaved with the stench of death. There was no time to stop it. There was only time to react to it, process it and do its bidding. Mass graves were dug by excavators and land filled with corpses.

"No one has yet found an answer but as it began, it ended, and one day there was no more death. But the world's population had been reduced to less than one percent. Instead of a gradual rebuild, a rapid expansion has been decreed and all efforts are devoted to achieving this objective.

"For this reason, we must forget our previous lives and forgo our individual goals. Now there is only one goal that we must all strive for." Instructor J145 paused for effect, catching the eyes of every one of her students in turn.

"To repopulate the world."

Instructor J145 continued, "Unfortunately, most people have become infertile. To fast track the RePop Program, suitable fertile candidates must be found and inseminated by multiple donors. In vitro fertilisation clinics have been adapted, and egg and sperm banks harvested, to move us forward toward this goal. When the world is whole again, we will be human again and have names again. We must, one and all, work tirelessly together. Together we can be strong."

"We are the frontline troops."

The girl waded through the fields of tall waving grass. White star-shaped flowers began to appear and proliferate. She bent down and touched one. It felt soft and woolly.

Straightening up, she noticed a girl standing in the midst of a sea of the white edelweiss flowers. The same white flowers were printed on her dress. She was looking up at the sky.

The girl approached the girl in white. "What are you looking at?"

"The sky," the girl in white answered simply.

The girl looked up too and was struck by the bright clear cerulean sky that seemed to stretch forever upward. "It's so blue."

"There are no clouds," the girl in white said.

The girl pondered a moment. "It's a sunny day."

The girl in white kept her head tilted as if searching, then said, "There is no sun."

"There is no sun."

The sign above the door of the Flower Ward read TOGETHER WE CAN BE STRONG. The Flower Ward was kept at a balmy temperature which, often times, Attendant Dandelion found to be too cloying and humid for her comfort. But it was not her comfort that was important. The comfort of the mothers was of optimum priority.

So, while the mothers gambolled within their lucid dream states, the carers checked them and tended to their needs. They mopped brows, checked temperatures, washed bodies, emptied waste reservoirs. They rolled them onto their left sides, rolled them onto their backs, then onto their right sides to discourage bed sores.

Careful not to dislodge the electrocardiogram wires attached to Mother Dandelion's chest, Attendant Dandelion slipped her hands under the girl's armpits and slowly turned her on her side. She massaged her neck and shoulders and rubbed moisturiser into her skin. The carer's hand slid down the girl's arm to the scarred stump that ended just above where the elbow would have been. To assist the carers to move their charges, all the mothers had had their arms surgically reduced.

Happy mother, healthy baby.

As she diligently carried out her duties, Attendant Dandelion found solace in the words of Instructor J145.

"We must do what is necessary," Instructor J145 had said. "You will administer drugs to each birth-giver to stimulate fertility and encourage growth. Stimulants that will generate a suitable vessel for multiple births. We must remain resolute. The future of humanity depends on *us*. But we are not heartless. As such, we will provide each birth-giver with lucid dreaming so that they may experience joy. Your devotion to this most important task is paramount. Let this be your mantra: 'Happy mother, healthy baby'."

Rolling her on her back, Attendant Dandelion lifted the semi-conscious girl's head, plumped her pillow and gently laid her head down again. A soft sheer gauze was draped over the girl's eyes to filter the harsh fluorescence and better facilitate a dream state.

The girl in the dandelion dress opened her eyes and found herself in a field of purple anemone flowers. She saw another girl wearing a dress with the same purple flowers printed on it, who was collecting the flowers.

"What will you do with them now that you've picked them?"

"They need to be sorted and put in order. There." The girl in the purple dress pointed.

Turning, the girl in the dandelion dress saw a large metallic table amidst the flowers.

The girl in the purple dress placed the flowers on the table, arranging them by hue in a row from palest to darkest.

The beds in the Flower Ward were arranged in a row. Behind each bedhead was a machine from which extended wires taped to the skin and tubes that punctured the bodies of the inert mothers lying in the beds. Each machine connected to a central integration server, which monitored rhythms and vital signs, and kept daily records of their well-being. It coordinated a regimen of feeding by measuring and administering nutritious content and supplements.

Although the machines ensured that the mothers were kept

hydrated at all times, Attendant Dandelion regularly gave her own charge sips of water, which she could see the girl savoured.

For her next duty, Attendant Dandelion retrieved the breast pump. She massaged and squeezed the girl's swollen breasts while hand-pumping to maximise the flow of milk and ensure that every milk duct was syphoned till empty. The milk was then delivered to the nursery.

Mother Dandelion's eyes began to flutter. As Attendant Dandelion mopped the girl's perspiring skin she leaned in and whispered in her ear. "You're going to have a very special visitor today. Official A898 is coming to inspect our good works. Got to have you looking your best."

Before the older woman became known as Attendant Dand-elion, she was a survivor. She'd scavenged for food amongst the wreckage of civilisation and that's where she found the scrawny girl, huddling from the cold. The girl was approximately twelve years old and alone. Her entire family had been taken by the catastrophic event that had claimed most of the world's population. And she, too, thought that she would join them soon when the bleeding began between her legs.

The older woman took the girl to the hospital to receive care and treatment.

After seeing the nurse, the older woman went to offer up her name but was cut off before she could utter it.

The nurse said, "No, I don't need to know your name. That person is dead. This is a new beginning for both of you."

"For both of you."

The nurse smiled at them, gave the older woman two food coupons and directed her to the cafeteria. The room was stark in its emptiness. The older woman sat the girl down at a table while she fetched the food.

Upon returning, she placed a plate before the girl and one for herself. From the deep pockets of her coat she retrieved two small bottles of orange juice and placed them on the table next to the plates. The girl looked at the food, unsure. For so long she had been used to scrounging for scraps, that she didn't know what cooked food was.

The older woman picked up her food and raised it to her mouth. "Go on." She took a bite and chewed.

The girl followed her lead. She took a bite and a smile spread across her face. Even after she swallowed, she could not stop grinning. "I've never tasted anything so wonderful in all my life! What do you call this?"

"It's a hamburger, dear."

"A *hamburger*. I didn't know something like this could exist. It is the most delicious thing ever."

"I'm very glad you are enjoying it. You will never go hungry again. Neither of us will."

"You're going to stay with me?"

"Yes, always and forever. I will never leave you. I will look after you and always be there to help you."

The girl smiled again. Took another bite of the hamburger. "This is the best day of my entire life."

The older woman smiled warmly at the girl. "Mine, too."

"Mine, too."

Attendant Heliotrope bumped into Attendant Dandelion, snapping her out of her reverie.

All the attendants were excited. They'd never had an Alpha Official visit the Flower Ward before. They rushed about, preparing the mothers, cleaning them and making them look presentable.

"Would you like to borrow some make-up?" Attendant Heliotrope asked.

"Huh?"

Attendant Heliotrope offered a box of used cosmetics while indicating her handiwork. Attendant Dandelion gaped at the girl in the next bed. Her face had been painted with pink cheeks and harsh red lips. The make-up added an obscene severity to the girl's appearance.

"Isn't she pretty?" Attendant Heliotrope gushed.

Attendant Dandelion smiled. "Yes dear, she looks radiant." Although she actually thought that Mother Heliotrope more resembled a clown than a maiden.

"We must be our best today, ladies," Attendant Edelweiss proclaimed. She handed out fresh linen to the carers. Each sheet was screen-printed with the flower corresponding with their charge. The linen was draped over the misshapen bodies of the mothers to make them presentable to the official visitors.

"I'm guessing you're about forty-nine," Attendant Heliotrope asked of Attendant Dandelion.

"Sorry, what?"

"Your age. I'm thirty-five. You look about forty-nine, maybe forty-eight, maybe fifty or thereabouts. Am I right?" Attendant Heliotrope grinned.

Attendant Dandelion's smile tightened to a thin line. "No, you are not right." She continued with her duties.

"Well, aren't you going to tell me?"

"If I do, will you stop bothering me?"

"Sure, didn't mean to pry. Didn't think it was a big deal."

"I'm twenty-nine."

A laugh escaped Attendant Heliotrope but was quickly stifled when she saw the stern features on the other woman. "No! Really? I'm so sorry. Your life must have been hard during the—"

"Forget it. Tend to your charge. Today is an important day."

A distant figure strode across the field of tall grass and blue hyssop flowers. The closer she got, the larger she became. In just a few strides, she reached the girl in the dandelion dress. The giantess stood over ten feet tall. She knelt, then sat down so that the other girl didn't have to strain to look up at her.

"I've walked the field as far as the eye can see, but there is no end. The fields are forever." Her fingers locked around her knees and she drew them to her chest. "I can't find a way out." She sobbed as she rocked back and forth.

"But you're so big and strong, you can do anything," Dandelion said.

"I'm not strong. I've walked the field for too long. I'm weak now. And so tired."

"So tired."

Official A898 and his entourage strode down the hall of the fertility wing. They stopped at the Flower Ward. The sign above the door read TOGETHER WE CAN BE STRONG. Upon entering the Flower Ward, a pungent odour assailed his olfactory senses. Instinctively, his hand shot to his nose, but he had been briefed on what to expect, thus he attempted to maintain his composure.

Attendant Edelweiss approached the group, curtsied and ushered them around the ward.

"This is Mother Amaryllis. She has been with us five months. See how her belly has already started to swell with joy."

The group could see the bulge under the floral printed sheet covering Mother Amaryllis's body. Official A898 nodded with approval.

At the next bed Attendant Edelweiss continued the introductions. "This is my charge, Mother Edelweiss. I have had the honour of caring for Mother Edelweiss for three years."

The group moved to the next bed. Official A898 attempted to convey interest by reading the name sign attached to the railing of the bedhead. "And this is Mother Anemone?"

"Yes, sir. Mother Anemone is a relative newcomer to our happy family."

At the next bed, Attendant Hyssop stood tall and erect and butted in to garner some of the glory for herself. "And this is Mother Hyssop, sir." She whisked away the floral sheet covering Mother Hyssop to present her in all her glory.

Official A898's eyes spun, unable to comprehend the abomination that lay on the bed before him. Again, he stiffened his back and composed himself while Attendant Hyssop espoused the virtues of her charge. Attendant Edelweiss frowned, but Attendant Hyssop would not be deterred.

"Mother Hyssop is a veteran of five years," Attendant Hyssop was saying. "We are very proud of her. We have provided her with an extra-long bed to accommodate the profound joy she brings into the world."

Transfixed by the sight of the monstrous Mother Hyssop, Official A898 forced an upward curl at the corner of his mouth. Mother Hyssop's lower torso no longer resembled that of a human. It had stretched to the foot of the bed and beyond. Her vertebrae had been separated to allow for the extension and expansion of her womb. The monstrous bloat spilled over the edge and culminated in a grotesque rubbery orifice at its far end. A sickly yellow fluid wept from the puffy purple lips. Resembling a large lumpy sack, Mother Hyssop's expanded abdomen pulsated with embryos and foetuses at various stages of development.

Knowing what to expect and observing it in reality were two different experiences, Official A898 thought to himself. His eyes scanned the hapless and helpless form of Mother Hyssop, noted the knotty scars where her legs had once been, and the engorged labial lips bruised dark purple, almost black.

Just as the group approached the next bed, Mother Dandelion gasped, and a blood-stained baby slipped from under her printed sheet and plopped into a catching bucket.

A splash of amniotic fluid splattered onto the toe of Official A898's shiny left shoe.

Time froze. Everyone looked wide-eyed at the yellow spillage dripping down the patent leather. The sound of the infant's scream pierced the air and time suddenly lurched forward. Immediately, attendants bustled about, grabbed cleaning rags, and fussed over wiping the residue from the official's shoe.

The glowing red counter on the machine behind Mother Dandelion's bed flashed three times before advancing one digit to now read *713*.

Attendant Dandelion reached into the cushioned bucket, which was streaked with dried blood and body fluids, to retrieve the infant. She proudly held it up close to the official's face.

"Another perfect baby, sir!" She beamed, hoping the kudos would extend to her. "That's seven hundred and thirteen babies in only two years that Mother Dandelion has birthed."

A waft of noisome stench drifted into Official A898's nose and he winced. He forced a wan smile as he swallowed the acid reflux that had risen and burned his mouth.

Attendant Anemone snatched the mewling baby and rushed off to deliver it to the nursery. Attendant Dandelion momentarily stood with her empty arms raised, still cradling the vanished child.

"We thank you for your service, uh…" He squinted at the half-obscured sign above the bed. Attendant Dandelion dropped her arms to her sides, bowed her head and took a step backwards to allow a clear view. "…Mother Dandelion," he said.

Then Official A898 shook open a sheet of paper, cleared his throat and read the script.

"We have witnessed your fine work here and we are confident that the RePop Program is on track. We thank you for your contribution to the rebuilding of humankind and society as a whole." He addressed the mothers lying on the beds in the middle of the large sterile room. He praised their sacrifice and described at length how their efforts would help humanity rise again after the devastation that caused the majority to perish. "With your help, we shall rebuild."

"Together we can be strong."

Mother Dandelion could hear the voice of someone speaking, but the sound was gargled as if underwater. Like bubbles filled with air rising to the surface and bursting, the words no longer contained any meaning.

Although the gauze covering her eyes had been lifted, she could not discern the blurry shapes standing before her. The only clear reality she could discern was in her lucid dreams.

The official turned on a crisp heel and exited the ward, followed by his entourage.

Although much easier than the births experienced by her mother and her mother's mother and all others before her, Mother Dandelion was breathing heavily from the exertion of labour.

The cluster of foetuses kicking and turning inside her expanded womb were grinding and pressing against her nerves and spinal cord which had, mercifully, been severed. She couldn't feel any pain from the writhing masses within her, but she could sense them.

Her attendant wiped her brow. "You made quite an impression today," she beamed. "You will not be forgotten."

"What is my name?"

"What, dear?"

"I've forgotten my name."

Mother Heliotrope turned her garishly painted face towards the voice. Her eyes were still covered by the sheer gauze. Attendant Dandelion noticed the eavesdropper and drew the curtain separating the two beds.

"Why, you're Mother Dandelion."

"That's not my name," she whispered, half out of breath. "I had another name."

"We all had another name, dearest. But that was in another life. My name is Attendant Dandelion and yours is Mother Dandelion. That's who we are now. That's what matters."

The attendant pumped another dose of sedatives and lucid dreams into the girl and she relaxed.

"Sleep now. You've earned it."

"Sweet dreams."

The girl walked through the field of dandelions till she found the batch of heliotrope. And in this area, she found another girl sitting with her head bowed. She raised her head. Garish pink make-up smeared her cheeks and lips.

"I heard you say you don't know your name. I don't remember mine, either," she said. "If we remember, will we become who we used to be?"

"I don't know." The girl leant down and used the hem of her dress to wipe the pigment from the sitting girl's face.

"You've ruined your dress."

The girl looked down at the dress printed with dandelions. "I think my name is Dandelion."

"Pretty." The other girl looked at the floral pattern on her own dress. "I think my name is Heliotrope. Not as pretty as your name."

Dandelion took the hand of Heliotrope and helped her up. "Come on, there are others here. Let's find them."

And they ran off into the fields of waving grass and flowers.

Attendant Dandelion soothed Mother Dandelion by tenderly stroking her face. She waited till she was certain the girl was soundly asleep before withdrawing for the night.

Directly across the hall from the Flower Ward was a smaller room that served as the living quarters of the carers. It was sparsely furnished and resembled an army barracks with bunk beds and a two-door metal storage cupboard for each woman's belongings. There was a small wet area with a sink, refrigerator and communal kettle. Modest luxuries included a small bookcase of ancient novels with yellow and tattered pages, and individual reading lamps.

Flower Ward attendants would retire to this room once they completed their twelve-hour shifts. They prepared the mothers in the evening by administering sleeping sedatives to induce a sound slumber throughout the night.

But the mothers would never be left alone even as they slept.

The duty roster for the night shifts had been drawn up and each attendant would mind the ward for two hours before waking the next carer in turn. And, of course, the machines continued to monitor vital signs at all times.

In the field of tall grass and flowers, a group of girls came together.

One of the girls reached across and clutched the hand of another, who in turn took the hand of the girl beside her until all were holding hands in a circle.

"We have a choice. We can choose to be strong. Together we can be strong." The girl in the dandelion dress released the grip of one hand, reached down and picked a dandelion. "Together we will make a wish and when I blow away the seeds of this dandelion, it will come true."

She brought the fluffy white head of the dandelion to her lips, took a deep breath and blew the tiny seeds free. They were grabbed by the wind and swirled around. As each girl was lightly touched by a dandelion seed, she sent her thoughts, love and aspirations to fly off and be caught by the gentle breeze and carried up into the endless sky.

The girl in the dandelion dress stood holding the dandelion stem, now devoid of seeds. Soon she collapsed in the tall grass, followed by the other girls who also fell to the ground.

The central machine in the Flower Ward began to squeal an alarm, alerting the attendants that something was wrong. Throughout the fertility ward, the frantic attendants ran around desperately trying to revive their charges, but the mothers' eyes remained closed and would not open.

"Together we are strong."

FAMILY UNIT

SEAN WILLIAMS

The City of Churches' streetlights are laid out in a multi-coloured grid, seemingly to the horizon. The hillside grave-yard has a spectacular view. The house next door, through boarded-up windows, not so much. Seventies brick walls laced with virulent graffiti. Front yard ripe with waist-high weeds. The rank tang of cats' piss.

Inside, a body in the bath. Feet hang over the chipped ceramic lip, head and arms folded up in a knot under the tap. Naked skin blackened and damp like seaweed. There are tattoos. A target circles his left nipple where someone might shoot for his heart. Thinking he has one.

I reel back on my heels.

It's him. Finally, him.

"Luke Sandeman Thorrold?"

"Fuck off." The voice emerges as a thin wheeze from his harrow-ingly emaciated body. His eyes flicker open. By torchlight they're abyssal. "Who's asking?"

"You don't know me."

"Let's keep it that way."

He shifts in the bath, stinking of filth and rot. I have no idea why he's still alive.

I have half an idea.

"Tell me what your brother did."

"You know what Liddy did. Why else would you be bothering me?" His hooded eyes grow sharper, minutely. "Unless he's woken up?"

I take no pleasure in telling him that his brother, Matthew Liddiatt Thorrold, is dead. "Three months ago. Aneurysm."

"Ah…the big one."

"So, it's down to you now. You're the only one who knows."

His eyes drift shut. "And that's why you came. Now Liddy's not around to incriminate."

"I was hunting you already. Aren't you tired of carrying his secret? Look at you. You don't have much time left for forgiveness."

"Fah." The harsh sound comes with a fleck of spittle that alights on my sleeve. "If I wanted a priest, I'd ask for one."

He hasn't asked for food or a doctor either, or even another hit. Whatever strength remains in him is on the verge of collapse. I will have his confession if I have to wring it out of his ruin with my bare hands.

"Liddy was never waking up from that coma, you know," he says, "and soon I'll be out of the picture, too. That'll make them happy."

"You mean your family?"

"Yes. My own flesh and blood. Fuck every last one of them. Let God sort them out."

He gasps a bitter laugh. I feel an echo of it in my own chest.

"Tell me about your brother…and Laura."

"Laura? God, poor Laura. I'd forgotten her name." Words emerge in a stream like gas from a bloated cadaver. "Liddy's first mistake," he says, "was being born to the wrong parents."

They're my parents too (he says) so believe me, I don't say that lightly. There are great downsides to great wealth. Money enabled Liddy's shyness in ways that weren't healthy. His penthouse was a fortress he never left. He had minions to bring him everything and anything he wanted. The family didn't care. I was the only one who saw the damage, his only friend.

Along with money, he inherited genes for autosomal dominant polycystic kidney disease, which run down Mother's side. He could have kept the side-effects at bay if he'd been more active. That wasn't his way, though. His penthouse came with a gym that I don't think he used once. We had it converted to a small medical suite when his weight went up and his health really started to go. That way, he didn't have to leave to visit the hospital.

His perfect day involved eating, drinking and reading rare books he bought on the Internet. A good life for someone with nothing to offer society and who never yearned for it in return.

Except once.

Eventually, his kidneys were in such a bad way that the only treatment left was a transplant.

Liddy and I talked a lot about that. What would it be like to have a piece of a stranger inside him? I would have happily given him one of mine, brother's love and all that, but we weren't compatible. I promised him we'd get the best kidney money could buy.

"But will it come from someone nice?"

What difference would that make?

"Sometimes, when you're not here," I remember him saying, "I get lonely."

Nothing like part of you dying to remind you that one day all of you will be gone.

The specialists dutifully found Liddy a kidney, while I waited anxiously for them to put him back together again, slightly heavier than before. I had responsibilities that took me from his side, family business he wasn't interested in, but I always came back to him, hopeful that this would keep him alive.

And the transplant was successful. Liddy recovered. Our normal lives should have resumed. Could have resumed.

Didn't.

He stops and reaches for the tap above his head. I watch, repulsed; the movement reveals infected sores under his armpits and exposes the full terrain of his ribcage. But for the heroin, he would be in constant pain, like his brother had once been. I've researched polycystic kidney disease: brain aneurysms are just one of many nasty side effects Liddy's brother doesn't suffer from. But that doesn't mean he isn't suffering.

Maybe he deserves to.

It takes him two fumbles to turn on the tap. Water trickles over his greasy hair and face, into his mouth. He swallows twice.

Shutting off the tap and letting gravity reclaim his stick-figure arms, he asks, "How much do you know?"

"I know what the police report says."

"That fabulous work of fiction. Written by lawyers, paid for by the family. My brother was not a murderer."

"What was he, then?"

"Alone. Hooked on a romantic dream. Those old books he read; they never give the fat guy a happy ending."

"Did you try to give him one?"

"Of course. I brought women to visit. He would engage with them, but none got close. Until Laura."

Poor Laura, he had called her earlier. "Go on."

"She was healthy and broke. The exact opposite of Liddy. She needed money and he needed a kidney. She was the 'nice' donor the surgeons found for him."

I'm as shocked as if he'd slapped me across the face. "Laura sold one of her kidneys?"

"You're surprised. Why should you be? It's a paragon of twentieth-century capitalism. The donor makes money; the recipient gets a new life. It's almost biblical in its perversity."

I hear an echo of expensive, private-school education in his diction. That doesn't make what he's saying any easier to absorb. In all my research, I heard nothing of this.

"The police report...the autopsies..." I pull myself back from the edge of a precipice. "Are you confirming that Laura wasn't a prostitute?"

"Yes. Although I did pay her, you know, to come visit him. Not the first time but the second and third. The fourth time, she wouldn't take the money. She knew it wasn't right."

"What wasn't right?"

"Liddy and her. To Liddy, that kidney was a proof of concept. He liked having a piece of Laura inside him; it made him feel close to her. Now he wanted her love as well. But you can't buy love like you can a pound of flesh. The girl had a life of her own; she didn't want to be part of his. I tried to convince him that he ought to respect that. He thought I didn't understand, but I did, I did. I just couldn't do anything about it."

The precipice yawns again. The official story painted a picture of callgirl and client, an entanglement of greedy lust. Perfectly noir and, I now knew, perfectly wrong.

That wasn't Laura.

"Was your brother jealous? Did he think there was someone else? Is that what drove him to kill her?"

"No, no. And I told you, he didn't murder her. Not technically. Aren't you listening?"

I've seen the photos. In my dreams, I walk amid the butchery, searching for her face.

"If your brother didn't murder her, what did he do?"

"Something much worse."

The murder-suicide cover story was a good cover for the family, you'll have to admit. In every barrel, there's one rotten apple, right?

Yes, yes, we're all rotten. After she turned down the money I offered her, Liddy told me to offer more. But this wasn't about the money. No one ever said no to him. His minions didn't because they were paid not to, and then there was me, the doting brother who did whatever he wanted. Normally.

We argued. It was horrible. His anger was so huge and powerful—proportionate to the sheer mass of him—that for the first time he actually scared me. All he wanted was Laura. If I insisted on keeping them apart, he said, then I could fuck right off.

It didn't seem at the time as though I had any other choice. I'll come back tomorrow, I told myself, when he's cooled down. But one day became two, thanks to that new fear, then a whole week, and by then the family had noticed. I had nothing to tell them because Liddy's business was not theirs. Their business was paying his bills, which they did even as the numbers that month skyrocketed.

Shame brought me back to him. I loved him, and I'd abandoned him. God only knew what state he was in after so long stewing over a woman whose love he couldn't possess.

He let me in when I called up. When I saw him sitting in his big recliner, like nothing had changed, I thought it had blown over. He greeted me with welcome cheer. Open that bottle, pour us both a drink, sit here next to me and tell me what's happening!

There was a smell in the penthouse that I hadn't noticed before. A disinfectant smell. And when Liddy reached for his wine, his sleeve rode up and I saw bandages around his wrist. I almost dropped both glasses in shock. Not suicide, surely. Not ever. Not him.

If he had succeeded…because I had left him…

He saw my expression and tugged down his sleeve. I forced myself to toast his good health as though nothing had been revealed, but from behind my mask I watched him even more closely than before. There was a new leanness to his features, a certain boniness to his fingers. He had lost weight.

"Working out?" I asked, but he just laughed it off. Indeed, he seemed broader than ever. Maybe not seeing him for a while had robbed me of my familiarity with his proportions. The weight of his existence. The cost.

I swore never to abandon him again.

We talked for hours. I didn't ask him any questions and Liddy didn't mention Laura or the bandages. It was good to resume our friendship, bruised though it was. We ordered food, opened more wine, blessed the government for their stance on inheritance tax, and cursed the family. I began to imagine us healed.

Too soon, it was time to go. But before I left him, I went to the bathroom. When I walked back along the corridor to return to him, I heard him speaking.

"Be calm, my love, be calm. There's nothing to fear. Bedtime soon. We're safe as houses."

It wasn't his usual voice. He wheedled, as a child might a pet, or—and I hated myself for thinking this—as an inept lover might the object of his desire.

I asked him who he was talking to. He looked guilty but also pleased in an odd way, as though I had given him the opportunity to share a secret.

"Laura," he said.

The last time she and I had spoken, she had been adamant that she wanted nothing more to do with me or Liddy. And here they were, conversing intimately in the dead of night?

One of the minions tracked her down, he told me. After our argument, they "persuaded" her to come back to him. Their success cast my failure in an unflattering light, but that wasn't the worst of it. Every unnerving detail I had noticed upon arriving that night came flooding back with sickening strength as more details joined them. Liddy's phone was nowhere to be seen. And here in his vast apartment, there was no sign of a woman anywhere.

He laughed and patted his stomach.

"She's in here, silly," he said.

I thought I was going to throw up. He'd eaten her?

The same rage I had glimpsed a month ago rose up in him. "I'm not a fucking monster," he told me. "I did nothing she hadn't already signed up for."

Standing with care, taking off his clothes and then his bandages, which covered far more than just his wrist, he revealed himself completely. To me. In trust or as punishment for doubting him? I wonder, even now.

His body was covered in long wounds. Carefully sutured and sterilised, still red in places. Surgical, like the one on his side where the new kidney had been transplanted. Laura's kidney.

How easy it is to mistake need for generosity.

This time, Liddy had taken more than just her kidney. He had taken all of her…into him…into the vastness of his body…

Where, he was most careful to assure me, she still lived.

Pushing propulsively off the disgusting floor, I stagger from the bathroom and into the night. Outside, the air is feverishly cold, but I can smell only decay. I avert my eyes from the suburban black hole that is the cemetery and pace among the weeds, wanting to escape, knowing I have to stay until the end. Worse is yet to come. I know it. I despair of it.

I must hear it.

Not a fucking monster, Liddy Thorrold said. Taking a person and…and subsuming them in such a gross way… How did it work? Did her heart pump alongside his? Did her lungs still breathe in and out? Or were she and he joined more intimately than that, sharing the same blood and air? How conscious was she through all this? What did she feel? What did she see, hear, taste, and smell?

I try not to imagine the pain. The horror. The abjectness.

Inside him.

Be calm, he had told her. My Laura, and the man who didn't think himself a monster.

How could I have known?

What could I have done if I did?

An eternity of agonised self-doubt passes, and I am ready to return for the rest.

The truth is that I need more than just the truth: I need his silence as well.

"I thought you'd fucked off. What do you want now—the details? I can't tell you because I'm not a surgeon, and you can't ask the surgeon because the family cleaned everything up. No witnesses, no evidence. The coroner didn't even notice the original kidney transplant because they found the right number of organs at the scene. Everything was sewn up. Forgive the pun."

"You and your family…you're all fucking monsters."

"At least I have the decency to feel bad about it."

"No. You felt bad for your brother and you worried about him getting into trouble, but you don't give a shit about anyone else. What did you do when you found out that Laura had been… taken? Did you call the police? Did you call her family? They were worried sick, and you…you forgot her fucking name…"

He twists in the bath to study me more closely, his flesh making a damp sound as it separates from the enamel.

"Who are you? Why are you here?"

I cannot meet his stare.

"You say you want the truth, and you're getting it. But your name… Tell me that much in return."

"Benjamin Frear."

"Means nothing to me. Yet Laura meant something to you. What, exactly? We traced everyone, every possible contact."

"It doesn't matter."

"Sure, sure it doesn't." His eyes roll back into his head. "What are you going to do to me, Benjamin Frear, once you have your truth? Are you going to be a monster too?"

I cover my eyes. He has no right to see my tears.

"Finish it," I say. "Get it done, and I'll go."

"You think it'll help," he tells me. "Nothing will help."

It was very difficult to take one person and fold them into another, unstitched and stretched out like a rag doll, then jumbled up so they'd fit. The whole thing defies belief…but there it was. I could see the aftereffects with my own eyes. Furthermore, I could understand how it was possible. Liddy had space inside him once they sucked out some of the fat. His heart was strong. His kidneys weren't, but he had both of hers now. The anti-rejection drugs he'd already been on kept doing what they were supposed to do. And this gave him the perfect excuse to eat for two.

If he was bothered by the thought of what he'd done to her, I never saw it. The opposite, if anything. He would involve her in our conversations, not that she could possibly respond, smothered as she was. He would crack jokes that only she would understand, he said, because she could still hear. Suddenly, he'd stop to show part of her moving inside him.

Did I feel slighted? About him not needing me as much? No, no. Please, don't think that I was the one who killed her.

Did I want to undo what he'd done? Yes. Did I curse the day he made me an accessory to kidnap and whatever else this was? Yes. Did I wish he wasn't a fucking maniac for doing it in the first place? Yes, of course I did. But did I want to hurt either of them? Definitely not.

He was happy.

As time passed, though, it became clear he wasn't healthy. He was carrying two whole bodies now. He grew thinner in his extremities but remained extremely large, and the strain on his body showed in other ways. He was unconversational. He lost his taste for alcohol. Sometimes he barely had the energy to bathe, and I would help, trying not to look too closely at the bulges. The evidence.

I consulted regularly with the medical team, who performed constant tests, knowing their paycheques depended on Liddy staying well. I detected a base level of anxiety that concerned me. How would Liddy react if the drugs weren't enough and his body rejected Laura's? What would he do if given a choice between his life and hers?

Weeks passed. Then months. I ceased attending to family affairs and devoted myself entirely to Liddy. If he was to die, I swore, he wouldn't be— God, I was about to say "on his own". He was never on his own, now. Everything Liddy did, he did with Laura. Including…dying.

In desperation, I sought a second opinion from specialists that didn't know his history. Perhaps there was something the first team had missed; they were, after all, entirely too involved in everything he had done, had maybe conflicting stakes in maintaining his health. I don't know. Fear made me paranoid. What if the family was actively trying to get rid of him, slipping poison into his food? But I ate that food too, and I wasn't sick. Besides, they wouldn't do that to one of their own. They didn't even suspect what he had done. Only I among them knew.

The other team had no reason to lie to me, which made their diagnosis even harder to accept. The first thing they did was ask if I was certain the samples came from my brother. I assured them that they did. Why?

Because every indicator suggested he was pregnant.

The full import only hit me when I was home and reading the documents they provided. The results were difficult to interpret for anyone lacking knowledge of Laura. His bloods were wild with odd levels and imbalances. They showed the genes for polycystic kidney disease, but they also showed the presence of other genes, and hormones that no healthy male should carry in those quantities. The second team discussed the possibility that Liddy was a chimera—a single person made of the fused genes of two eggs, one of whom was female. That sort of thing was not unknown, apparently. But had any chimera fallen pregnant before? From their own twin? That was a different matter.

Me, I knew about Laura, and I knew what must have happened. I wouldn't put anything past Liddy at that point. He must have taken more than Laura's freedom when he kidnapped her. Liddy must have raped her, too. And now, the seed of that crime was growing within him, perhaps killing him.

I'd heard of poetic justice before, but this was the first time I'd seen it in action.

For days, I was at a loss. What should I do? Should I bring in the second team to perform an ultrasound, to see if their suspicions were correct? Could I examine him myself, next time I bathed him, in the hope of finding the baby's location? Assuming it existed. And if it did, what then? Could Liddy possibly support three people? Could I possibly let him try? Could he be convinced to have an abortion?

I now had the responsibility for the lives of all these people. Liddy, which was fine; I'd never turn my back on him again, even if he asked me to. Laura, although that was not something I ever wished for. And now a child? I didn't want their blood on my hands. I didn't want any of it. If I could turn back time, we'd get a kidney the ordinary way and take our chances on it coming from someone "nice" or not. Maybe it would've ended up the same. We'll never know, now, the depths of my brother's crazy.

Really, I had only one option: to tell him. Without accusing him of anything. I didn't want him to get angry again.

Laura is pregnant, I said. It's putting too great a strain on your body. You should get rid of it. Now. Before it kills you.

I knew right away he wasn't going to do anything of the sort. His head was still full of fantasies. He had Laura, and now they were having a child. Jesus fucking Christ. I wanted to slap some reality into him, but instead I explained everything to him again, a different way. He and Laura were tissue-compatible, but he and the baby might not be. At that moment, the placenta was protecting him from the child, but when it was born—inside him, for fuck's sake!—no amount of anti-rejection medication would save him or it.

"You don't know we're not compatible," he said, still resisting reason. His hands pressed one side of his abdomen, and I realised he was touching where he thought the baby was growing. Maybe he could feel it. Maybe he had known it was there all along. He must've been aware of the possibility. And he hadn't told me!

I tried a third time. "Even if you live long enough, the baby's probably not going to survive the birth. Laura might not survive either. You'll be killing them. Can you live with that?"

"I won't have to," he said, promising them the best care our money could provide. We would bring in the medical second team, the one that already knew about the baby. Everything would be all right. The three of them could live on together. That was his dream.

A family unit. Him, Laura, and the child. Flesh and blood.

"You have to make this work," he told me. "This kid will be my heir. It's the only thing I'll leave behind, the only thing that matters." He took my hand. "Promise me."

I did promise him. God save me, I did.

And here we are.

The rest you can probably guess.

For a while, I don't trust myself to speak. My hands are shaking. "You have a screwed-up definition of family."

"Tell me about it. Mother refuses to accept the coroner's verdict, you know. She sued me over my testimony. I'm trying to protect her from the truth, but still I get disowned. You can't fucking win."

He is shaking too, perhaps from cold, or withdrawal, or revulsion.

"Were you there…at the end?"

"No. I wasn't. We crunched the numbers, based on when we thought conception had occurred, but the baby came early. The C-section team wasn't ready. It was the middle of the night, skeleton staff, I was asleep, Liddy panicked…I don't know. Maybe he had second thoughts. Anyway, he sealed himself in the apartment. None of the team had the override code. By the time they got hold of me, it was over."

"Tell me."

He doesn't want to, and who can blame him?

"Liddy had a knife, but he wasn't planning to use it the way the police report says he did. He was obviously going to cut his baby out himself, but before he could do that, he had a massive aneurysm—the first—which knocked him out. Leaving Laura inside his body, in labour. Her options were even more limited. No doubt she had heard everything we talked about in the months leading up to this. She knew what was going on, what was at stake. She knew what was supposed to happen, but it wasn't happening. There was no team, no rescue, no hope unless she made it for herself."

He shakes his head, disbelief mingled with respect.

"She was strong. Maybe she'd been exercising, all those weeks. Maybe that's another reason why Liddy had been so sick. She was inside him, part of him, but she still had her muscles and her will. It took both, I imagine, to bust herself out…burst herself out…so the delivery could finish. If it could. There was always a chance that Liddy and her would both bleed to death, since they were connected. Where would that leave the baby?"

I'm trying not to see those crime scene photos again, but they are imprinted on the inside of my eyelids.

"By the time I got there," he says, "the place was a bloodbath. It looked like a cow swallowed a grenade and then trod on a landmine. Amazingly, Liddy was still alive, in a terrible condition, torn half apart, in a coma, but alive. Poor Laura was dead. Crushed under his unconscious body. What a fucking way to go."

There are no words for the loathing I feel for him and his whole foul family, who allowed this tragedy to go unacknowledged so long. Indeed, covered it up as the rampage of a sick man, who murdered his family and then failed to take his own life.

"And in the carnage," Liddy's brother goes on, "one baby, bawling its lungs out."

My head comes up. "No, that's not right. The baby died. I've seen the report. Two bodies, it says. Laura and the baby. Two, not one."

"There were indeed two bodies," he says, and I can see by a curl in his lip that he's pleased I'm surprised. Chalk up a victory for the dying man. "Because there were two babies."

"How...?"

"Twins. Not spotted in the ultrasound, thanks to the almighty tangle in Liddy's stomach. One drowned in Liddy's blood, the other—delivered alive."

"Jesus." The revelation sets my heart pounding, threatens to tip me over the edge. "The surviving child. What happened to it? Is it still alive? Where is it?"

His lip twists another notch. "Before I answer that question, Benjamin Frear, answer mine, and answer it properly. What were you to Laura? Because sure as shit, no one sits here this long for a story. Were you her childhood sweetheart? Her secret boyfriend? The creep who took advantage of her when she needed the money most, but you refuse to believe she sold herself like the police keep telling you?"

I have my hand across his face before I even know I've moved, mashing his lips and nose into the bones of his skull.

"Shut up. Shut the fuck up."

He laughs, and I press harder. Nothing can stop the liquid sound of his cruel mirth.

Belatedly, I remember hepatitis, AIDS, other diseases I could catch from him, from his teeth, and I yank my hand away.

"Secret lover, then," he says, guessing correctly. "That's why we didn't know about you. And you know what? Now the numbers work out. Liddy didn't rape Laura after all. She was pregnant before he even met her. Thank you for that! This means the babies were yours, not his. You poor fuck. Bet you didn't come here to learn you had a living son!"

"Where is he?"

"Where do you think? In the family. My sister is raising him as her own. Because she thinks he is Liddy's flesh and blood. They can ignore what Liddy did, but they can't ignore that. Flesh and blood. They can't let anyone slip free."

He laughs again, and I wonder who he's really mocking.

"So, what are you going to do now, lover boy? Rescue your child using the evidence in your genes, but in the process expose how his mother really died? Or let him grow up thinking he belongs to the family—to become as rich and corrupt and as disgusting as the rest? What a choice!"

He lurches to grab my arm.

"I don't envy you," he says, "but I thank you. This has made my fucking year. They don't know they've got a cuckoo in their nest, and I'll never tell them if you don't. Just like Liddy didn't. He knew he wasn't the father all along. It's perfect, so perfect."

I yank myself free, frustrated and angry. My goal achieved—to clear Laura's name—now leaves me adrift on even stormier seas.

Do I tell no one? Everyone? Do I abandon her memory? Or my son?

Fleetingly, I consider turning on the tap and holding him under, drowning Luke Sandeman Thorrold in water like the blood of his brother drowned an innocent child.

But that would be like a baptism, a fate too good for him.

"Sun's rising," he says, nodding at the faint light filtering through the grim window. "You'd better go before my feeders arrive."

"Your…who?"

"Minders. Minions. The ones who make sure I eat. This is what I get for failing to kill myself with something definitive, like a gun. Heroin hasn't worked. Neither has starving myself. Flesh and blood, remember? The family might disown me, but they will never let me go."

Enough of that mantra. I am done. I have everything I came for, and more besides. His laughter follows me through the ruined house, fading at last to silence when I am standing outside. The sky is grey. The city lights still sparkle. The headstones of the neighbouring cemetery cast a permanent pall. He's right: I feel no better for knowing what happened to Laura, what she endured to save her child.

Our child.

My son.

A black van pulls up in front of the house. I am already seated behind the steering wheel of my car, compulsively compressing and releasing my hands, as though making fists could change a thing about how I feel.

Screwed-up definition of family?

I can talk.

Finally, I start the car and drive home. If I'm quick, Liv, Scarlet and Sophie won't know I ever left.

THE STILL WARM

PAUL MANNERING

Celine woke into darkness so thick that, for a moment, she feared she had been buried in the cold earth. She inhaled and the rich smell of freshly turned dirt filled her nose. Her throat burning with raw pain, she struggled to sit up, to make sense of her surroundings.

Her head slammed into a hard surface.

She cried out and instinctively raised her hands to her face, scraping her knuckles as she did so. Probing the darkness with fingertips, Celine found wooden boards inches above her face.

I'm in a box…?

The thought brought a fresh burst of panic, and she twisted and writhed, hitting and pounding against the coarse wood.

"Nicholas!" The tightness in her throat reduced her scream to a hoarse whisper.

She remembered looking down at the circle of torches. Nicholas's face shimmering in firelight. Nicholas forcing his way through the crowd. Demanding they not light the pyre.

They were going to burn me…

The terror of that evening froze Celine to the bones. Nicholas—sweet, loving Nicholas—had saved her from the purifying flames.

"We will hang this witch and the Devil's child in her belly!" Nicholas declared.

The moment of hope had been torn away by his words. Bound to the stake atop the unlit pyre, Celine had stared, open-mouthed in shock.

This cannot be… Nicholas loves me…

Many nights, he had whispered to her how much he loved her. His breath warm against her skin. The cold air kept at bay by the closeness of their bodies in his chamber. Celine had been in awe of him. Nicholas was educated, respected, powerful. A young priest whom even the village elders treated with respect and deference. Three months into their secret tryst, she missed her regular menses. By summer's end, the quickening flutter deep in her flesh filled her with hope and dreams of a life with Nicholas and the child they would raise as man and wife.

Nicholas promised to abandon his position in the church. He would be a father and husband instead. God could forgive them this sin. Surely, Celine had prayed, when the Lord looked down upon the miracle they had wrought, there could be no sin?

When it became clear that she was expecting, Celine had refused to name the father of her child—at the priest's insistence. Muttered rumours and dark looks followed her around the village. Wives were suspicious that the young beauty had bewitched their husbands. Her refusal to name the sire only strengthened their growing hatred.

They came for her one morning when Celine felt certain the child was ready to slip from her body at any moment. An angry mob burst into the small stone house, built by Celine's grandfather, the only home she had ever known. To Celine's mother, Elspeth, her daughter's refusal to confess who fathered her child meant they could not expect mercy. This wilful rebellion and embrace of sin made it clear her daughter had indeed lain with the Devil. And so, Elspeth stepped aside when the men of the village came to demand Celine be brought before the elders to answer the charge of witchcraft.

Celine was ushered outside. Spectators had gathered, the accusers of the past months as watchful as crows over carrion. In the fading light of day, Celine looked to each of them in turn. They met her gaze for a moment and then glanced away, eyes hooded, faces scowling.

"Why are you doing this?" Celine cried.

No one answered.

She passed by and the first rock was thrown, striking her

between the shoulders and dropping her to her knees. The shouts and missiles flew. Mud, stones, eggs, fruit. Whatever could be snatched and hurled. By the time Celine was placed in the stocks, both she and the men hauling her were dripping with filth but only Celine was sobbing. She spent a terrible night in the cold, bent over, arms and neck held in the stocks. Waiting for Nicholas to come and rescue her. To demand her release. To declare that he was the father of the child she carried.

Instead, he had been waiting at her trial when she was dragged inside the communal hall next morning. He sat with the town fathers in judgement against her. Nicholas in his priest's robe, praying to God for protection against the harlot and her pact with the Devil.

Celine had pleaded, screamed at them that she was innocent Her accusers were friends, cousins, and neighbours she had known since birth. They all regarded her with fear and loathing. They needed to punish her and absolve themselves. Nicholas looked at her with eyes as cold as river stones, yet in her heart, Celine knew he would not abandon her like this.

Judgement was passed unanimously. She was taken away to prepare for her execution.

No one came to visit during her final hours. Celine gave up begging for mercy. At the end of the day, abandoned by the man she loved, tied to the cleansing pyre, Celine welcomed death.

"She will not burn!" Nicholas had declared, giving her a wretched moment of hope, his eyes feverish in the flickering light of the burning torches. "No, the witch shall be hanged!"

A rope and a tree made the simplest of gallows and the deed was done without ceremony or opportunity for final words, lest they come in the form of a curse upon those present. For her part in the execution, Celine did not protest or struggle. She supposed that Nicholas took this as a sign she accepted her fate. The necessary sacrifice to assuage the sins of the flesh. The Devil would receive his due and God would forgive Nicholas for his trespass…

Now, awake in darkness, the skin of her neck torn and bruised from the noose, Celine began to scream. Her nails splintered and tore as she scratched at the wood of her coffin. No Christian burial for her and the illegitimate child. They would lie in forgotten ground, unconsecrated and forever damned. First, she screamed in horror at her lingering fate, then in the madness of grief at the betrayal by the man she loved, and finally in the deep agony of rhythmic contractions as her swollen belly began to expel the cursed child.

The smell of her fluids filled the tight space and the warmth of broken waters soon chilled against her skin. With no room to spread her legs wide and no space to sit up, Celine endured the searing pain. Her shrieks were barbed and as the air grew thick and foul, she coughed and choked on the blood trickling down her throat. Her eyes stung with sweat and salty tears. She howled and moaned. Slamming her fists and palms against the boards, Celine whimpered like an animal dying torn and bloodied by dogs.

A final gasping groan reverberated through her tight prison and Celine's back arched.

The warm, wet lump slithered against her inner thighs, and a moment later a mewling cry sucked the foul air. Reaching down, she felt the slickness spilling from between her legs and the pulsing viscosity of the cord. She pulled on it, drawing the tiny form up over the hem of her stained dress. Gasping for breath, she slid the newborn to her breast. The baby nuzzled at her nipple and she cradled the child against her flesh. Celine's mind burned in an inferno of curses against Nicholas, and a wonder at the miracle she had delivered.

Father Nicholas woke into darkness so thick that, for a moment, he feared he had been buried in the cold earth. The dream had been the same for the past week. A mewling babe crying for him in the night; the priest on his knees, cassock soaking in the pre-dawn dew as he clawed at the ground, grovelling before the wrath of God that beat down upon him with the intensity of the summer sun.

He rose from his bed and splashed water on his face. The moonlight slicing through the narrow window of his chamber was as pale and sharp as a page of the *Evangelium*. Nicholas shaded his eyes against the glow and shivered in the frigid air.

The sound came again, and he wanted to dismiss it. To state with confidence that the mewling cry was a cat or the calling of some nocturnal bird. The dread that caressed his spine would not allow him that certainty. Driven by an unease he could not adequately define, the priest slid his feet into cold boots before venturing out into the night, the hood of his cassock lifted to shield him against the watchful eye of God.

Nicholas went to the copse near the only road to the village. He had not visited the place in the week since Celine had been hanged from the oldest oak in the stand of trees. Whenever he passed the grove on his way to minister to his flock, he averted his gaze from the scratched markings on the limb where the rope had rubbed the bark raw. Now, under the first full moon since her execution, Nicholas approached the low mound of sod under which the crude coffin lay. Sinking to his knees, the priest made his silent application to God. Begged for His forgiveness and mercy upon the souls of the damned. Hands curled, Nicholas dug into the earth, tearing clumps of grass from the scalp of the grave as he sobbed.

When his tears ran dry and the night grew still, the earnestness of Nicholas's prayers eased into a meditative and reassuring murmur. The sound that roused him was slight and strange, like the soft sigh of sand through an hourglass.

Nicholas lifted his head, pushing back the hood of his robe, ears straining to hear beyond the hiss of his own pulse. It sounded again. A whine such as a sleeping pup might make in the pile of its litter. Telling himself it was a fox or a mouse in the grass, Nicholas prayed more fervently and set his hands on the ground to raise himself up on legs that had gone stiff and tingling from kneeling in supplication.

The ground under his palms shivered and split slightly.

Something pushed upwards, the way a burrowing mole might breach the night air.

Unable to find the strength to stand, Nicholas stared at the dark veins of shadow that spread with the cracks in the earth. The chasm spread wider as probing digits, stained dark with rich earth and no bigger than maggots, wriggled in the ashen moonlight. Nicholas moaned in horror as a small hand reached up and clenched the air in front of his face.

The dark birthing eased for a moment and then, with renewed effort, the creature forced a second tiny fist through the sod. With both hands exploring the night air, the arms pushed upward. Nicholas toppled to his side, scattering dirt as he dragged himself back from the scene, gaping at the creature forcing its way through the uplifted dirt.

Grey skinned, hairless, infantile.

The dread homunculus slid out of the grave and lay squirming on the grass.

Nicholas found his voice and, in Latin, beseeched God to protect him from the Dark One's spawn. The small creature lifted its head and fixed the priest with coal-black eyes, then crawled towards him. The dull, glistening rope of umbilical flesh that anchored it to the dark hole writhed like a thin serpent.

The priest whimpered when tiny fingers gripped the toe of his boot. The demon advanced with grim determination. The black claws, as large and sharp as a cat's, dug into the fabric of Nicholas's robe as the homunculus ascended his prone form. Paralysed with fear, Nicholas babbled in Latin, then Greek, and finally in the tongue of his mother as the newborn pressed its fingers into the soft flesh of his neck. Nicholas felt the cold touch of the baby's lips, then a sharp pain as needle-like teeth pierced his flesh. Blood welled then gushed as the infant suckled on the surging pulse of the priest's terror.

The body was found just after dawn by two boys walking to their shepherding duties. They immediately crossed themselves and the oldest sent his companion to rouse the village. Soon a crowd gathered, and the muttering of their fear rustled among them like a breeze through the trees.

Johan, the most senior of the village elders, arrived in his own good time. His gnarled knuckles tightened on his walking stick when he saw the body. The priest lay on his back, eyes open and staring into the morning sun. Nearby, the unhallowed earth where the witch had been buried a week earlier was torn asunder. Clods lay scattered across the black fabric of Father Nicholas's cassock, his nails and hands stained with his toil.

"'Tis the Devil's work," Elspeth, the witch's mother, whispered.

Johan felt inclined to agree. A narrow hole had been dug into the grave site, evidenced by the soil on the priest's hands.

"Fetch shovels," Johan commanded of two nearby men.

The men hesitated. Only Johan's glower meant he did not have to repeat the instruction.

The soft ground was cut and lifted once again. The rectangle of rough-wood coffin was exposed. A central plank had splintered and cracked. Jagged fangs of broken wood were pushed upwards. Johan murmured a prayer and ordered the men with shovels to rip aside the remaining wood.

The grave's occupant was stained with earth and blood. A congealed mess of red and grey fluids lay over her nether regions. Her broken and bloodied hands cradled the small form of a newborn child to her bare breast.

"Bring them out," Johan ordered.

The two men with shovels gulped, crossed themselves and, reaching into the grave, seized the woman by the cloth of her dress, lifting her with the infant undisturbed on the tray of her torso. They placed the bodies on the ground.

Gesturing the men aside, Johan eased onto one arthritic knee. Celine the witch was clearly dead, her face locked into the carved rictus of the departed. How the child came to be born and laid so sweetly on its mother's chest was not so clear. The dried grey cord that bound it to Celine snaked down into the stained mess under her dress. Johan reached out to whisper a prayer and his fingertips rested gently on the newborn's naked back.

With a cry, he jerked away and staggered to his feet.

"Build a fire!" Johan shouted. "Build a fire on this spot! Burn them. Burn the witch, her child and may God forgive us! Burn the priest's body where it lies!"

"Please, Johan," Elspeth wailed. "Has my daughter not suffered enough?"

Johan turned on her, eyes wide, lips curled to show the blackened stumps of his teeth. "The coffin-born child," he choked, as spittle flecked the stubble of his chin. "The dead babe is still warm."

THE HOT-AND-COLD GIRL

SAMANTHA MURRAY

She has bare feet and her hair is messy, and I first see her when I am seven.

Mother calls her my imaginary friend, but even though no one else can see her, there is nothing at all about her that is imaginary. She looks about my age, maybe a little bit younger, and she doesn't ever speak.

"Why can't you talk?" I ask her that first day, and she twirls a tendril of her hair around her finger and makes me feel a prickle of cold that tingles my fingertips. That's what she does when she doesn't like something. Later, when I suggest we take all of the dolls I used to play with when I was small and make them jump off the footbridge into the rapids of the river, she makes me feel warm like I've just been toasting marshmallows. So that's what we do.

She only comes sometimes, and even though she is pretty bossy, she is also fun to play with.

She comes on the day Lisa and Shay and I dare each other to walk across the bridge railings when the water is high and moving fast. Lisa and Shay have just started letting me hang around with them, and this is the first time they've come over to my house. Lisa takes neat little steps with her arms stretched wide for balance, then Shay does it, although she takes off her shoes first and hesitates before she starts.

It is my turn and I clamber up. I feel all shiny because I think Lisa and Shay are starting to really like me, and I know this bridge, I've walked it before, and I can do it faster than they can.

71

But as I stand up to get my balance, the hot-and-cold girl makes me cold, colder than ever before, so that my fingers and toes are icy and numb and my lips feel chapped. It's a cold like being way down, down under the water where I cannot feel the sun, and my teeth start to chatter. I climb off the railings and see the twist to Shay's mouth and the hard glint in Lisa's eyes.

I don't want to talk to the hot-and-cold girl after that but when I am walking home, she slips her hand into mine and a little spidery trail of warmth runs up my arm until my ears feel fuzzy. It's hard to stay mad.

By the time I am sixteen, the hot-and-cold girl comes less and I don't tend to listen to her as much. She hasn't changed, not a bit, so I am much older than her now, and I don't want to play dolls-in-the-river or dragons-in-the-garden or hide-and-seek. I let my eyes drift past her sometimes as if she is just part of the patterned wallpaper, just a daydream, just imaginary.

I am standing with my friends waiting for Shawn to bring his car around. My long, filmy coat is doing little to keep me warm, but it doesn't matter because I am feeling giddy like I am strung about with lights. Shawn seemed especially keen for me to come along tonight even though he is older, and I turn my back on the hot-and-cold-girl when I see her and ignore her, and keep laughing.

I can't ignore her though when the car pulls up because as my friends pile into the back seat, the hot-and-cold-girl takes my hand and I am so cold I can't breathe.

I shrug her off and reach for the car door. The coldness stabs me right through my stomach and it is so cold that it burns. I tell my friends in stumbling sentences that I'm sick. I see the confusion and disappointment in Shawn's eyes and I want nothing more than to go with them, but I don't.

I berate myself as they drive off, all of my friends together, the sum total of my friends, and it begins to rain, soft gentle hazy misty raindrops landing on my face and I hate the hot-and-cold girl.

The hot-and-cold-girl is nowhere to be seen the next day when I hear that Shawn's car never made it back from the city. His car was going too fast, the road was too slippery, he was too drunk. Just before the outskirts of town, the car had aquaplaned and collided with a tree.

I wrap myself up in my blankets although I am not cold. I feel numb and lonely and I wish the hot-and-cold girl was here to keep me company because all of my friends are gone.

The hot-and-cold girl looks out of place at the bar where I meet Xander for the first time.

"I thought I'd outgrown you," I whisper as I watch her little feet step lightly over the crushed potato chips on the carpet. Her hair is still messy, and I never realised when I was younger how fragile she looks.

I chat to Xander for a while and when he asks for my phone number, I am trying to find a nice way to refuse because he isn't my type, not really, not at all. But then I am suffused with warmth as if I am curled up in front of a fireplace, and I notice how green his eyes are and I think perhaps I should give it a go, maybe just one date.

Xander is a bad choice, my worst-ever choice.

Falling for him is like falling from a bridge down, down, down into the icy water below. Is like racing through the night in a car going fast, so fast, too fast and being caught up in the violence of screeching tyres and puncturing metal and stopping too suddenly. One day Xander shakes me so hard that I bite my own tongue and my mouth fills with the taste of sharp, hot copper. The hot-and-cold girl does not turn up at all and whether the warmth I'd felt when Xander first kissed me and ran his hand down my spine had come from her or just my own treacherous body, I did not know. But I had followed it, that trail of warmth, as if it would lead me into the sunshine, into happiness. And instead it had led me here.

When I next see the hot-and-cold girl, I am looking in my bathroom mirror at the dark circles under my eyes and wondering how I look so old. Xander is gone and I am nine parts heartbroken and one part relieved, and I am alone holding the stick I've just peed on.

Except I am not alone because the hot-and-cold girl is there looking back at me from out of the mirror and she looks happier than I've ever seen her.

The broadness of her smile feels like a quick stab of betrayal. Xander wasn't good for me. He cheated on me and he was harsh with me. Somehow, he made me see myself differently, and feel young and stupid and always at fault, broken and unworthy. He left me with a heart all splintered and shivered into sharp cutting pieces that stick into me every time I move, so much so that I am half-surprised not to see blood trailing down the insides of my arms and legs and pooling darkly on the bathroom tiles.

The hot-and-cold girl had always looked out for me, like my own barefooted guardian angel. How could she have steered me in Xander's direction? How could she have made me think he was warm and good and right? I look at both of us in the mirror and the misery rises up again to twine itself around my despair.

"I'm not even nineteen yet, I can't have a baby," I say to her, but she sends me such warmth it is like a flower of heat is unfolding in my chest, radiating outwards to every part of me. And all of a sudden, I realise.

"This is you, isn't it?" I say, brandishing the two little pink lines at her.

And I am so warm, I feel like I might start to glow.

But way, way down, beneath the contentment that is invading my body, there is a small part of me that thinks, *look at how much she can do without being born, what will she be able to do when she's really here?* I'd always thought she looked out for what was best for me, but perhaps she had been only looking out for what was best for herself, and only sometimes were those the same thing. And that little part of me, tucked right down under the radiating happiness that is not coming from me, that little part is scared.

"**I**t's a girl," I tell people as my stomach blooms with the hot-and-cold girl, when it's meant to be too early to tell. They smile at me indulgently sometimes, and sometimes their smiles are laced with pity or judgement or both, and I don't smile back.

"Do you have a name yet?" I am asked, as my internal organs shift around to make room for the hot-and-cold girl, as she strips the nutrients from my blood, as my body prioritises this new passenger ahead of me and gives everything to her first because she is the important one now, not me.

"No," I say shortly. I don't like the question, it feels wrong. The hot-and-cold girl has never had a name.

"No," I say, when my mother offers me cake and tea, wearing her perpetually half-disappointed, half-concerned look. The hot-and-cold girl will only let me eat particular things at particular times, but that makes sense because after all she has been telling me what to do from the beginning.

At night back in my old room at my mother's house, I put my hand on my enormous belly as it rolls and contorts in alien and somewhat repulsive ways as the hot-and-cold girl kicks and punches me from the inside, pressing sharply into my bladder. My lungs are compressed upwards and my breathing is shallow. *I liked it more when you were imaginary*, I say, but it doesn't even make it out as far as a whisper.

"**I**t's too late for an epidural," the doctor says, her voice calm. *But it hurts*, I tell her, or try to say. I'm not sure my words make it outwards because it's like everything has been sucked inwards, like the whole world has gasped, like I'm at the centre of an imploding star.

And it hurts.

Does it hurt as much as drowning? As much as falling off the bridge and striking my head on the stones beneath? Does it hurt as much as being caught up in the wreckage of a car with my dead friends in it, all tangled metal and hot blood and rain?

This hurts more, it must do.

Dreamily, I think with longing of the deaths that could have been mine. My hair floating languidly in the river, or when everything was silent again in what had been the car and the beams from the headlights shone against the rain falling down.

But I am here, instead, and all is pain and brightness and screaming.

For only a moment I see the hot-and-cold girl in the corner of the room, smiling, but I think this time I really have only imagined her because she is not over there. She is right here and they are placing her in my arms.

I still haven't named the hot-and-cold girl and she is five days old. She is tiny and perfect and she never cries.

My phone rings as I am about to feed her, and I get distracted and start talking to my mother. A jolt of electric coldness shoots through one of my nipples so intensely that I bite my lip and draw blood. Of course, she's hungry. I put her to my breast and she latches on immediately. I look down into her clouded ordinary baby eyes, and wonder what to do.

Love her.

It's the only answer I can find, the only answer I have, the only thing I can do. And I do already, helplessly and overwhelmingly and blindly. I do. But there is a part of me that doesn't want to. And that part of me is as cold as ice.

EXPEL THE DARKNESS

ROBYN O'SULLIVAN

Carmen opened her eyes, instantly alert. No dreamy, drowsy state between asleep and awake. Just sudden, sickening awareness—not of her surroundings but of fear. A chilling emotion that knotted her stomach and gripped her heart.

She lay motionless and tried to get a sense of where she was. Though she strained her eyes, she could see nothing in the darkness. Her mind had surrendered to the fear. She had to wrench it back, focus on her surroundings. She was in her bedroom, lying on the bed. But she couldn't feel it beneath her. She was suspended in a black space. The darkness spread into every corner, insinuating itself into every tiny cavity.

Carmen shivered, yet sweat pricked her armpits and dampened her face. She wanted to run her fingers across her upper lip but her arm wouldn't move. The fear intensified, concentrating itself in the pit of her stomach. Could the blackness around her be expanding, or was it the threat of danger looming in the darkness? She couldn't think clearly.

The sound of her husband's breathing broke through the fear. She focused on the rhythmic rate of his slow breaths, matching it. *Inhale, exhale*. Awareness of her body and its strength returned. She would rid herself of the fear, expel the darkness.

Carmen slid off the bed, dropped to the floor, and began crawling towards the door. First one hand forward then the other. Her long black hair fell down and her breasts and pregnant belly swayed heavily. She dragged her knees across the rough seagrass matting until her fingers touched the cool terracotta floor of the hallway. Continued on her hands and knees down the hall to the bathroom. Kneeling before the toilet, she spewed her fear into the icy porcelain bowl. Courage filled the space where the fear had been. She fell back against the wall and clutched her belly, calming the agitated movement in her womb.

A torch flickered in the doorway, illuminating the surroundings. Her husband shone the light on her face and then on his. Carmen looked into his dark brown eyes as he squatted beside her.

"I rolled over in the bed and you were gone," he said.

"I've been sick, Julius."

He lifted her off the floor and stood up. "Let's get you back to bed."

She felt the hardened muscles in his arms as he carried her to their room. He laid her down, pulling the covers over her naked body.

"I'm so cold," she whispered. "Perhaps a t-shirt..."

He tucked the blankets around her. "You'll be warm soon. You know it's best not to wear anything in bed. Best for the *bambino*."

Julius went to the kitchen and returned with a glass of steaming green fluid.

Carmen sipped the homemade potion. "I think this is what's making me feel sick."

"Oh, *cara*. Why would I prepare something to make you sick? It's good for you. Good for the baby." His voice was still soft, but his eyes had changed to pools of dark liquid.

Carmen emptied the glass.

Julius climbed into bed. "Try to get some rest, *cara*," he said, placing his hand on her bare belly and tracing the ring of scarified dots he had etched around her navel. The baby began kicking. "There, there, *piccolo mimmo*. Be still, little baby boy."

Before long, her husband was breathing regularly, but Carmen could not go back to sleep. Could not stop thinking about the fear and darkness that had invaded her bedroom.

When pale light at the window signified daybreak, Carmen rose and covered her nakedness with a warm dressing gown. She sat on the cushioned bench in the window alcove, enjoying the quiet beauty of the sun rising over the small olive grove, enjoying it alone before Julius would wake up and the activities would begin.

Carmen had welcomed the sunrise every morning since Julius had brought her to his family's farmhouse in the broad hills near the medieval town of Montepulciano in Tuscany. No one had lived here since his parents died in a car accident some eight years earlier. At first, newly pregnant, she had been captivated by the rustic charm of the neglected old house with its stone porticoes and terraces. But now Julius was gone every day, working to revive the olive grove. She could not imagine being able to get through the long hours of isolation without this calming dawn ritual, especially with the rigid schedule of tasks he'd devised — meditation, exercise, special potions, reading aloud, playing atonal music — to enhance the baby's development.

As she watched the brightening sky, Carmen slipped her hand inside her gown and sought the dots on her belly, tracing the circle with her fingertip. Julius had done the etching the day they found out she was pregnant. He said it was a family tradition that represented the circle of life, which would expand as her pregnancy progressed. His mother had one of these circles, and her mother before her, way back into their ancestry. It had hurt when he'd done it, and even more when he'd applied the healing ointment to irritate the small wounds, ensuring that the scars would be raised. Julius said it marked her as a member of the Di Nasta family forever.

Julius stirred, opened his eyes and smiled. "Good morning, *cara*. Today is our anniversary. Today we celebrate one year since we married."

Throwing off the bedclothes, he leapt out of bed and padded down the hall to the bathroom. Carmen heard Julius singing in the shower. Soon after, she heard him singing in the kitchen. With luck, his happy mood would last all day, as when they'd first met.

Back then, he'd been lively and full of fun. She'd been flattered by the attention of this darkly good-looking Italian who had engulfed her in a whirl of romance, calling her his "green-eyed beauty" and filling her heart and soul with passionate love. She'd happily followed as he led her through Rome, revealing all the wonders of the ancient city. She had felt her heart would burst when they married in the registry office just five weeks later. Her parents had been horrified. "You're only there for a holiday," her mother said. "What about your degree? You're only nineteen!" But a few months later, Carmen was pregnant. All thoughts of returning to Australia and university went out of her head. And her husband's controlling nature had emerged.

Rising from the window seat, Carmen crossed the room and opened the door of the old timber wardrobe. She removed her gown, selected a loose embroidered dress and pulled it over her head. No underwear. Julius said it was not good to confine the baby.

Joining her husband in the kitchen, Carmen laid placemats and cutlery on the old wooden table, white from the scrubbing of generations of Di Nasta women. She put out butter and jars of jam then sat down and waited for Julius to finish the breakfast preparations.

"A special repast, *cara*, for our anniversary." He took the coffee pot from the top of the wood stove and set it on the table with a plate of steaming rolls. "But first your tonic," he added, pushing a glass of the steaming green fluid towards her.

Carmen took a gulp. "It tastes stronger than usual."

"No, it's always the same." He buttered a roll and bit into it. "Today we go into Montepulciano. First, you go to church to pray for our baby. Then a short stroll and perhaps ice cream. What do you think, *cara*? Sounds like fun?"

"Yes, sounds like fun." Carmen drained her glass and shuddered. "Ugh." She quickly downed some coffee and pushed a piece of jammy roll into her mouth.

As soon as Carmen had cleared away the breakfast things, Julius drove them to town. The rough country roads wound through vineyards that dotted the surrounding hills, their vines heavy with grapes. Cars were not allowed in Montepulciano on Sundays, so they parked their blue Fiat on the outskirts and ambled up the cobbled main street to the cathedral in the

Piazza Grande at the top of the rise. As they passed shops and *palazzi*, Carmen admired the red flowers of alpine geraniums that cascaded from planter boxes on stone windowsills, and the terracotta pots on flagged steps.

"Do not delay, *cara*, the bells are ringing. You'll be late."

Carmen tried to quicken her pace, but her heavily pregnant body refused to obey. Julius went ahead. When she entered the cavernous stone church, he hailed her from a seat next to the aisle in the back row. His face was strained and his forehead beaded with sweat. As Carmen sat down, he stood and turned towards the door.

"Don't go," she whispered.

"You know I must. I cannot stay."

"Please, I don't want to be—"

Yet he was already gone.

When Carmen emerged an hour later, Julius appeared and took her arm. "A treat now," he said, "and then home for your rest."

They bought ice creams and made their way back down the winding Il Corso to the car. It was a long drive over bumpy roads, and Carmen was uncomfortable and unwell by the time they got home. Julius produced another potion and sent her to bed. She wanted to sleep, but wild dreams of being stalked by black-cloaked figures kept waking her, bringing the fear of the previous night back to her conscious mind. When Julius checked on her, Carmen told him she was afraid.

"You've only got two weeks to go. It's normal to fear birth." He pulled the covers from her body and stroked her naked belly. "It's the circle of life, *cara*. Everything will be fine, you'll see. I'll be with you when the baby comes."

She stayed in bed for the rest of the day. She read and listened to music. In the evening, Julius brought her the nightly potion. Then they settled down to sleep.

Carmen woke abruptly. Pain seared through her body and she cried out. Julius reached for her belly. It was contracting.

He jumped out of bed and flicked on the torch.

"Your waters have broken," he said, and pulled on jeans and a jumper. "I'll go out and start the generator."

Carmen was holding her breath against the pain.

"No, no," Julius said. "You must pant. Pant!" He ran from the bedroom. She heard him go out to the terrace and the generator begin to thrum; heard him stop by the kitchen to stoke the fire in the stove. Back in the bedroom, he turned on the light and handed Carmen a glass of clear fluid. "Drink this. It will relax you." He helped her to sit up and held the glass to her lips. She took a sip and grimaced.

"Come, come, drink it up, *cara*." Julius squeezed her cheeks and tipped the contents of the glass into her open mouth.

Carmen spluttered and coughed, spitting back into the glass. "For God's sake, Julius! You're choking me." She lay back against her pillows, still coughing. Finally, trembling, she took his hand and said, "The pain has eased. Thank you."

"You're in labour, *cara*. Don't be afraid."

"I know you planned a home birth, Julius, but I don't think I can do it." She started to get out of bed. "It shouldn't be happening this fast. I want to go to the hospital."

"We can't, Carmen."

"What do you mean? Of course we can go. Help me to dress."

Julius slapped her face. "Control yourself. It's past midnight. We will go nowhere."

She stared into his liquid black eyes. "What are you going to do?" she said.

"I'm going to deliver my son."

Julius changed the sheets and Carmen got back into bed. She lay still, staring at the ceiling. A cobweb fluttered on the wooden beams. Julius busied himself with towels and water and scissors. A while later, waves of pain washed over her again. She panted, as instructed.

After a couple of hours, as the pain came at shorter and shorter intervals, Julius began to walk her down the hall and around the kitchen between contractions.

"You must keep moving, *cara*, to stimulate birth."

Carmen did as she was told.

Julius continued to bring glasses of clear fluid. "You must keep drinking to stay hydrated. And it will help with the pain."

Carmen drank his potions without comment.

Finally, at six in the morning, Carmen felt like pushing. She lay on the bed and Julius positioned her legs so he could easily access her birth canal.

She pushed and panted. Pushed and panted.

He peered and prodded. Peered and prodded.

"I can see his head! Keep going, *cara*. It's almost done."

Julius slipped his fingers into her bloody, wet vagina and yanked at the baby's head. Carmen screamed. But she hadn't the energy to object.

"Push! Push!" Julius yelled at her. Excited. Agitated. Impatient.

Carmen readied herself for the final expulsive thrust.

Julius twisted the baby's shoulders and pulled the body all the way out. He quickly clamped and cut the umbilical cord. Then he faced the window and held the naked baby aloft, exposing a horned birthmark on the infant's thigh. "My son. Filius Di Nasta."

Carmen began to cry. "It *is* a boy. Oh, Julius, we have a son. A beautiful baby son."

"Now the placenta."

"Let me hold him, Julius."

"No, *cara*, you are still busy."

Julius began to wash and dress the baby while Carmen delivered the placenta, which came away into the bed, a gory mess. "I need help," she said.

"A moment. *Piccolo mimmo* needs me too." Julius left the room with the baby. Carmen could hear him moving about in the kitchen. Eventually he returned with a tray that held a serviette, some tablets and a glass of clear liquid. "Here, take these," he said. "They will help you sleep."

"Can you bring me the baby? He'll want to suckle. Then we can sleep together."

"Not now, *cara*. You must rest and you might roll on him. I will look after Filius." Throwing aside the serviette, Julius grabbed hold of a syringe and plunged it into the muscle of her upper arm. "For the pain," he muttered.

Carmen's body tensed for an argument. "No, Julius. I must see the baby." Then her words began to slur. "What's happening? You can't do this." She tried to control her thoughts but was overcome by fatigue. Her breathing slowed, and her eyelids fluttered and closed.

When Carmen woke up, the sun was streaming into the room. The clock showed three. She had slept for hours but felt weak and tired.

"Julius, where are you?"

There was no answer. Carmen called again. Still no response. She pushed the covers back and tried to sit up. It was such an effort. She pulled at her legs and felt something wet on the bed. Looking down, she saw the placenta. And blood. A large pool of bright red blood still spreading across the sheet.

"Julius! Julius?" She called and called, but her voice was faint. Nothing happened.

Carmen waited a few minutes. She slid off the bed, dropped to the floor, and began crawling towards the door. First one hand forward then the other, dragging her knees across the rough seagrass matting until her fingers touched the cool terracotta floor of the hallway. She crawled into each room, looking for her husband. The house was empty. Reaching up, she opened the terrace door to check outside. The car was not in the driveway.

Bewildered, Carmen tried to make her mind think. Did something happen to the baby? Had they gone to the hospital? She rolled her naked body over and sat on the floor, leaning against the terrace doorframe, straining her eyes to scan the olive grove. It was deserted. Looking back into the house, she saw a trail of blood that marked where she'd been. Fear overtook her. Carmen got back on her knees and crawled towards the bedroom. Halfway down the hall, she could go no further. She eased her body down and lay on her back.

Her body was weak, her brain fuzzy. Where was Julius? Why had he left her?

She closed her eyes and conjured an image of her husband's face, but not that of her son. He was a stranger to her. Carmen began to cry. Fleeting images of her parents and her home in Australia crossed her mind. Blood and clots flowed out of her onto the terracotta floor, forming an ever-expanding circle of her expiring life.

MY SWEET PORCUPETTE

GERALDINE BORELLA

Skimming over oceans, mountains, deserts and streams, we cross paths with Sarus cranes and magpie geese. And bounce from continent to continent, taking little time for rest in between. Portia's smile is pure exhilaration and I'm suffused with pride and cautious excitement to watch her unfurl and take flight. We're finally doing this!

When we land the final leg, I ask for the millionth time. "Are you sure you're ready?"

She responds in the same manner she always does. "Of course. Stop asking."

But I can't help it. I'm her mother and I worry. It's her first stab at this, an important milestone in her life, made all the more significant by the events that led to her birth.

I was living in North America at the time. It wasn't the easiest of labours, deviating so far from my original birth-plan I wondered why I'd even bothered to write the damn thing. Still, I had it all laid out, meticulous in its specificity. I wanted music— Massive Attack's *Teardrop* and anything by Sigur Rós—calm, ethereal, spectacularly dramatic music to introduce my child to the beauty and majesty of the world. (No whale song for me, thank you very much). And I'd ranked my preferred pain relief: breathing exercises, hot packs, water therapy, gas, and as a last resort, an epidural. I didn't want anyone present (because there *was* no one), and I wanted to be mobile and not confined to a bed.

My final and most important request was for immediate skin-to-skin contact and to breastfeed straight after. What a fucking joke. Nothing went as planned. And all because of Janina and Federico.

I met them at my six-month check-up.

They seemed nice enough, excited to be having their baby in a month. Like me, it was Janina's first. Unlike me, they'd had lots of trouble conceiving.

"She's precious and already so adored," said Janina, sitting in the midwife's waiting room. She rubbed her pregnant belly and turned to Federico. "Isn't that right, darling?"

"Absolutely," nodded Federico. "And she's got the best mother ever." He lifted Janina's hand and kissed it, then flashed a cheeky grin my way. "No offence to other mothers, of course." Solicitous of his wife, Federico treated her like a fragile flower petal.

I was hit with a pang of envy but dismissed it. I'd have something better soon: unconditional love. A bond that could never be broken.

Janina swiftly drew me into her maternal orbit, demanding we be friends. Before long we were, the two of us sharing in the exquisite anticipation of meeting our babies, counting down the days. We met regularly for coffee and cake, our conversation fairly limited in theme—birth, breastfeeding, cracked nipples and episiotomies trending the highest.

Federico rang from the hospital when Janina went into labour. It was *happening* and I was thrilled. I couldn't wait to meet Avery Rose, feeling privileged and a little smug to be the only friend to already know the sex and name. I wrapped the pink bonnet and booties I'd knitted, waiting to get word from Federico to visit.

I screamed with excitement when his name flashed up on my mobile, and picked up the call straight away. "Congratulations! Can I come meet her? Please say yes!"

The silence was devastating. Seconds passed. I began to cringe, wanting to retrieve my words and stuff them back into my insensitive mouth.

"Federico?" I whispered, fearing the worst.

He sucked in a rasping, broken breath. "Stillborn," was all he said.

I paused, trying to take it in. "Oh, Federico, I'm so sorry."

"I have to go."

The utter pain and anguish in his voice… I ached to help in any way possible.

When I turned up at the hospital, Janina couldn't look at me, couldn't look at my swollen belly. I was a living representation of all she had lost. It was terribly sad, for her *and* for me—we'd become so close—but I understood and kept my distance. I wasn't the right person to console her at that point in time.

So, a month later when she rang and invited me to their farmhouse, I was thrilled. I could be there for her now, support her. Help her wade through the boggy marshes of grief.

"Bring some clothes and stay for the weekend," she insisted. "We miss you so much."

"I miss you guys, too," I replied.

"And Viv," she added, her voice quiet, apologetic. "I'm sorry. I just couldn't…"

"I know, I know," I rushed to answer. "It's okay. I understand."

"I'll make it up to you. I promise," she said, more brightly. "I'll pamper you while you're here. You won't have to lift a finger, I swear."

I laughed. "You don't have to do that!"

Janina was the one who needed looking after, not me. Well, a back rub every now and then would've been nice, but emotionally I was strong and eager to meet my Portia Anne. She was due in two months' time.

Oh, how to describe my first day at the farm? It was nice, albeit a little unnerving. Janina made my favourite cake—orange and poppyseed with cream cheese icing—and insisted that I take a relaxing bath. After a gourmet dinner, we sat talking by the fire, avoiding the difficult topics like Avery Rose and my forthcoming delivery.

Next morning, Janina bustled about the kitchen, whizzing up nutritious smoothies for breakfast. But despite all that, something wasn't right. I felt uncomfortable but couldn't quite explain why.

Janina was trying too hard. Her smile seemed forced. I put it down to the deep chasm of hurt in her heart left by Avery's death. Guiltily, I looked forward to returning home.

Though I should have trusted my instincts.

While packing my bag to leave on Sunday afternoon, Janina and Federico appeared at my bedroom door. Federico held a gun. He trained the barrel on me, pointing at my pregnant belly.

"You're staying here now, Vivienne," said Janina, her gaze hard and fixed.

I glanced at the gun and back at Janina. "You can't be serious."

"Deadly," said Federico. He nodded at my things. "Grab your stuff. We're moving you out back to the barn."

I pleaded my case on the walk over. "You don't want to do this. It's madness."

But they said nothing and shoved me in a lockable cold-room in the far corner of the barn. Thankfully, the room was set on a moderate temperature, but I could see they'd planned all this: a bed, basin, and chemical toilet were set up inside.

The perfect crime. I had no one in my life and they knew it. No one to miss me, except perhaps my midwife. I was expendable, easy prey. They wanted my baby Portia, not me. And as soon as they had their hands on her, they'd get rid of me.

There could be no other way.

"You'll regret this!" I yelled, as they locked the door, and I meant every word.

There was no escape, the walls and floor impervious. A pad-locked door was the only avenue to overpower my captors—not easy when you're heavily pregnant and facing a gun. I couldn't risk any harm coming to Portia. So, I bided my time.

Janina kept me well-fed, and carted over warm bathwater for sponge baths, always guarded by Federico. Each time I pleaded for her to reconsider. I remember one time in particular.

"We can let this go, Jannie," I said. "It's totally understandable, given your grief. I won't press charges. I promise. You could get some counselling, ask for help. Just *please* let me walk out of here."

Janina said nothing and went about her tasks.

"Think this through, Jannie," I said, trying again. "How will you pass off my baby as your own? Surely, I'm not the only person who knows about Avery?"

Or was I?

"Shut the fuck up," hissed Federico. His eyes were hostile, crazed.

I instantly recoiled. He looked mad enough to slice me from end to end and pluck Portia out from within. I shuddered. Portia squirmed. *Calm down, my sweet,* I soothed as I tenderly caressed my belly. *I won't let it come to that.*

When I hit the eight-month mark, they moved me from the confines of the tiny cold-room to a larger storeroom in a shed. I guess they were worried about the logistics of helping me give birth. Once again, they'd set up my jail cell with a bed, toilet and washbasin, but this time I was excited. *This* place I could escape from, especially through the dirt floor. Small animals had already burrowed in, so I had a head start.

I hadn't shapeshifted since becoming pregnant, frightened that my baby and I would get stuck together in animal form. Now I had no choice. I couldn't escape in my current state and besides, Federico's Rottweilers would hunt me down. I often woke at night to terrifying visions of them rupturing my abdomen, tearing open my flesh to get at Portia. It made me sick but also determined to do what had to be done.

So, I transformed into a porcupine.

It was the only animal I could think of that could potentially use the already-dug burrows while presenting a large enough danger to the waiting dogs on the other side. It was a risk—we could be stuck in this form—but a risk worth taking. Besides, if we got stuck, at least we'd be together.

The minute I transformed I began to have contractions.

What's the gestation period of a porcupine?

I had no idea, but it must be less than eight months because the contractions escalated rapidly. I dug into one of the holes, making it wider, burrowing in while struggling to breathe through the pain. My abdomen hardened, the skin stretched taut, turning my milky-grey belly almost pearlescent. Taking a moment to rest, I realised I couldn't tunnel through to the other side, not right now. I was already too far in labour. Instead, I dug as far as possible, alternating between resting and then digging whenever my contractions died down.

When my porcupette, Portia, could wait no longer, I laid in the hollow ready to push. She'd been facing the wrong way at my last check-up. The midwife had warned about the need for a caesarean if Portia didn't turn in time. I could only hope she'd managed to do so.

My abdomen tightened again and I pushed hard, bearing down until sharp, spiking pain ripped through my birth canal. Portia hadn't turned. With every inch forward, her razor-sharp quills scraped and needled my insides. If one caught it would impale me, the barb gripping the quill in place. But I couldn't do anything. There was no other direction to go but onwards.

I stopped for a moment, to breathe through white-hot agony and quell the overwhelming desire to push, buying time to mentally prepare for the next onslaught. And when it came, it hit like a tidal wave, hard and fast, swamping me in a murky, debris-filled pool of pain. Tossed about in the wash, gasping, it became difficult to distinguish between throbbing, stinging, stretching, and stabbing, all sources of hurt merging into one. I groaned and grunted—primal, guttural—and screeched as I pushed once more.

Some of Portia's barbed quills found purchase in the walls of my birth canal.

I fainted with the exquisite agony of it.

Slapped awake by the next round of contractions, I bore down through the torture until Portia emerged, healthy albeit missing a few quills. I knew full well where to find them though. We stayed in the burrow while I recovered and suckled my sweet porcupette.

Janina and Federico's panicked cries soon filtered through.

"Where the *fuck* is she?" yelled Federico.

"No, no, noooo!" shrieked Janina.

They'd imprisoned themselves with their own machinations,

and though somewhat gratified, I was far from fully content. They deserved more than a lifetime of looking over their shoulder. Much more.

A week after I gave birth, Portia opened her eyes. I fell more in love with her, if that's even possible, and forgave her for spearing me with her quills. She grew quickly; I would have to burrow out to forage for food to sustain her. But there were dogs to consider, so I formulated a plan: I'd strike them with my quilled tail or, better still, transform into some larger predator.

The night I emerged was dark and moonless. I ambled about looking for berries, bark, and acorns. Not made for agility or speed, the porcupine body felt cumbersome and clumsy, like being perpetually pregnant. Still, at least my armour of quills afforded me *some* protection. I needn't have worried. The dogs were gone and so were Janina and Federico, already on the run.

We stayed in our burrow until Portia reached maturity at four months of age.

She was ready to leave, the moment fast upon us. My only chance of keeping her was to pray she'd been bestowed with the same gift as me.

"Sit and watch," I said, as we ventured above ground. "Then see if you can copy me."

Eyes closed, I transformed into my human self, enjoying the feel of being back in my own skin, though determined to ignore the insistent throb deep in my pelvis. I'd attend to that later at home.

Portia looked up, mouth gaping and nose twitching. She closed her eyes, scrunching them shut, and tried it for herself. Nothing happened. My heart dropped. Nevertheless, she persisted and after three attempts, transformed into a four-month-old baby girl. I scooped her into my arms, hugged and kissed her, ecstatic to see my baby for the very first time.

The cool air instantly shocked. We were naked, devoid of our warm coat of hair and quills, so I broke into the farmhouse, smashing a window with a loose paver. Janina had left clothes behind, no doubt in a desperate rush to get away, and there were baby clothes and nappies in the nursery. Seeing the nursery brought back sympathy for Janina and Federico, though it didn't remain for long. Not after what they'd put us through. I dressed Portia and then myself and we left that godawful place, hitching a ride to the nearest bus station, and soon we were home, safe though badly shaken.

Extracting the quills proved just as excruciating, if not more so, than being impaled by them. I couldn't go to a doctor or gyno. What would they think? What would they say? I bought a borescope with flexible tubing and a pair of long-handled forceps off the internet, and prepared to tackle the ghastly task myself. Guiding the borescope to where I thought the quills were lodged, I tried prying them out gently with the forceps. I soon realised it was impossible to free them without using force. In fact, I had to wrench the barbed ends from my cervical wall, screaming through the hot flashes of pain. It took ages, and once the last quill was finally removed, I lost consciousness.

But that was a long time ago. And now here we are, having flown with flocks of magpie geese to the other side of the world. We're ready to fulfill our dream, finally.

It's taken us a good while to find Janina and Federico. Twenty-one years, in fact. They moved to Australia and are currently hiding away on the outskirts of Mintabie, a small outback town in South Australia. They've changed their names and have done a little shapeshifting of their own: Janina is obese, missing several front teeth, while Federico is haggard, bald, and leathery-skinned. But it's them alright. Still recognisable under the ravages of guilt and time.

"Ready, my sweet porcupette?" I say as we sneak out the back door of the pub.

Portia laughs, surprising me. She hates that nickname, but it fits the moment and I guess she notices the irony. "As ever," she says with a grin.

We get in the car. Keeping our headlights switched off, we follow Janina and Federico's taillights from the front of the hotel along a dirt track, driving for miles. The red dust turns to white gravel. We end up at a broken-down corrugated iron shack. Open to the weather, the dust and sticky flies, the only niceties appear to be a concrete slab floor and a donkey hot water system. Pig dogs kept caged on the back of Federico's ute snarl and bark and bare their teeth. Perhaps they smell our intent. But even set loose, they won't pose a problem.

"So, you're sure you want to do this?" I ask for the very last time.

"Yep," Portia nods, staring straight ahead at the silhouettes in the cabin.

"Righto," I say. "Let's go."

We pull in behind and I switch the headlights on, flicking them to high beam. Janina and Federico emerge and stand on either side of the ute, shielding their eyes from the glare. Portia and I get out of the hire car and approach.

"It's you," gasps Janina when her eyes adjust. She stares with a mix of horror, disbelief, guilt and trepidation.

"It is," I say, and I gesture to Portia. "And my daughter, the one you tried to steal."

Federico turns to sprint for the shed. Janina does too.

They don't get far.

Portia barks and runs at Federico, ears pointed back, wolf fangs bared, while I take on Janina. I leap high and pull her huge frame to the ground. My jaws latch around the back of her thick neck. Her screams are drowned out by our growls and by the yelps of the pig dogs. Frenzied, the dogs fling their muscled bodies against their cage. They want in on the kill. But they'll have to wait their turn.

It's our moment, and we're not inclined to share.

Sharp, lupine fangs tear at throats, rip apart flesh and puncture windpipes, as animal instinct takes full control. I glance across at Portia, revelling in her complete and unbridled wolfish immersion. It's a sight to see and I'm thrilled to be here, sharing this experience with her. The pig dogs howl and cry, responding to the smell of blood and death, still desperate to get in on the action.

When completely satisfied, we transform back to our human selves.

We shower in the shed. The stench of bloody retribution washes from my hair and body. For the first time in years, I feel unburdened. Clean.

And when we're ready to leave, I drive the hire car alongside the ute, lean halfway out the open window and let the pig dogs free. They leap from the tray, excited to finally take their turn. We drive off, kicking up clouds of pure white dust in our wake.

HAIR AND TEETH

DEBORAH SHELDON

Blood. So much blood. It runs out of Elaine's body for weeks at a time, soaking through sanitary pads at a rate she has never experienced before in her life. Some days—on bad days—she can sit on the toilet and listen to her menstrual blood hit the water in a steady drizzle, *plip-plip-plip*. She is constantly light-headed, woozy, ready to drop. This is menopause, isn't it? Protracted and heavy periods? A normal, natural event? Yet the medical term *menorrhagia* is too clinical, far too sterile, to describe this carnage. And pain. So much pain. A nest of starving mice is gnawing through her insides. A crazy notion, but in the dead of night, when the world is smothered and unable to make a single sound, Elaine lies awake, worrying about the possibility of mice.

For the past year, maybe longer, her husband Malcolm has urged Elaine to tell their doctor. She sees the doctor every three months anyway for her prescription refills, so why not mention the heavy periods? Elaine has refused. The bleeding will soon stop of its own accord. After all, she is fifty-one. How much longer can her exhausted ovaries keep going? But when the blackened clots begin slipping out of her, raw and slick, plump, as engorged as chicken livers, Elaine panics and makes an appointment. Tests follow. Invasive tests.

And now, here she sits in her doctor's office, waiting for the results.

The autumn sun beats weakly through the windowpane. The desk holds a jar of lollipops. A cardboard box of showbags for expectant mothers sits beneath the examination table. Familiar sights. Elaine has come here for some twenty-six years, ever since her one and only pregnancy. Her daughter is grown-up now. Married and gone. Long gone.

The doctor stares at his computer monitor. One fat hand clasps the mouse, clicking, scrolling. The other hand cups his double chin. He was slim once. Back in the day. A chubby finger, preoccupied, taps at his teeth. *Tock, tock, tock.* Elaine shifts in the chair, waiting, perspiring, bleeding. The doctor steals glances at her as he reads the test reports. Time crawls by. Elaine bites her lips, clenches her toes inside her shoes.

The doctor's eyes squint, widen as if in shock, squint again. Clearly, he can't believe the information on the screen. Elaine's stomach lurches. It's mice. A nest of mice, chewing, hollowing her out. If only Malcolm were here. But he's at work. He's always at work. Malcolm fears it may be cancer, which is a much more sensible fear in Elaine's opinion.

The doctor sits back in his chair. "You have fibroids," he proclaims.

She has heard of the condition but is not sure what it means. "Cancerous?" she says.

"No. Benign tumours inside the uterus. Inside your womb."

She says, "But they're loose. The tumours move around."

The doctor taps at his teeth again. He will not meet her gaze. Elaine's heart flitters and flops against her ribs. If Malcolm were here, he would tell her to *calm down.* I am safe, she tells herself, recalling the practised mantra. Not everything is a conspiracy. All is well.

"Doctor?" she says. "Do the fibroids move around? Like mice trapped in a bag?"

He stares at her, intently, without blinking, in a way that makes her afraid. Then he arranges his lips into a grin and emits a chuckle—*heh-heh-heh*—his belly jouncing. "Move? Absolutely not. Fibroids are anchored. They grow out of the womb's endometrium like mushrooms out of dirt." He flicks a runnel of sweat from his hairline. "The uterus is very swollen, about the size of a five-month pregnancy. It'll be a hysterectomy, I'm afraid."

Hysterectomy? Elaine stiffens in the chair. Her womb taken out? That special place where she grew her only child to be excised, thrown without care into a medical waste bin? Elaine clenches her jaw to stop the tears from rising. Yet the pain prowls around, nipping and munching. A clot slithers out. No, Elaine cannot keep living like this. Bleeding like this. Her mice-filled womb is trying to kill her. She knows this to be true.

"All right," she says, smiling, smiling, smiling. "Yes. A hysterectomy."

The doctor pecks, two-fingered, at the computer keyboard. "I'm referring you to a gynaecologist named Smith."

Elaine's smile dies. "Why can't I see my regular gyno?"

The printer sounds. The doctor withdraws the page and hands it over. She takes it, blindly.

"No, I'm sorry," Elaine says, voice rising. "I want my regular gyno."

The doctor regards her from the corner of his eye. "How are your meds?" he says. "Still keeping all those strange thoughts under control?"

She nods, scrunches up the referral, stuffs it into her handbag.

"I can always increase the dosages," he says, hanging his forefingers over the keyboard again. "Double doses might help."

"No. I'm fine. Thank you."

Elaine stands, releasing a hot flood. If she doesn't change her sanitary pad now, right now, it will overflow. Dizzy, she crosses the room and scrabbles for the doorknob.

In a rush, the doctor says, "Your fibroids aren't mobile. What you're experiencing is referred pain. The tumours can't move. It's impossible. Do you understand?"

She glances around. The doctor's sweating face is set. A vein pulses in his temple. Both meaty hands are clenched. Liar. *She is on to him.* But she must not let him know that she knows.

"Yes, thank you." Elaine backs out of the room. "I understand completely."

As soon as Elaine gets home, she studies the referral letter. DR JOHN SMITH. Obviously a pseudonym. The letters after his name are meaningless: MBBS, FRCOG, FRANZCOG, DDU. Yet what can Elaine do? Keep bleeding to death? She has a sherry. It is 10:39am. She drinks another. Her pills have the same red-rimmed sticker on each box: *This medicine may cause DROWSINESS and may increase the effects of alcohol.* She only drinks when Malcolm is at work. In the evening, she has black tea, mint tea, rooibos. A little sherry won't hurt, doesn't hurt. A glass here and there helps her to *calm down*. That's what Malcolm wants, isn't it? A normal, stable, pleasant wife. A calm wife.

She calls the number on Dr John Smith's referral letter. A man answers. "Hello?"

This is not what she expects. No one in a professional setting answers the phone in such a casual manner. Perhaps she has the wrong number.

"Hello?" the man says again. "This is Dr Smith. Is anybody there?"

"Yes," she whispers. "Mrs Elaine Grey."

"Excellent. Let's make the appointment for tomorrow morning at nine o'clock."

Elaine agrees and hangs up, breathless. Over dinner, she tries to explain what has happened but Malcolm reaches across the kitchen table and pats her hand.

"Don't worry," he says. "Specialists usually have long waiting times, sure, but this bloke must have had a cancellation. Stop reading too much into it, okay?"

"Okay," she says. "Of course."

Dr Smith's clinic is located in the midst of a tacky strip of shops. Wedged between a tattoo parlour and a FOR LEASE sign is a door bearing the weathered inscription DR JOHN SMITH, WOMEN'S HEALTH, BY APPOINTMENT ONLY.

Elaine hesitates. Perhaps she should leave. But the tearing pains in her womb change her mind. As it turns out, these pains are not caused by hungry mice. Last night in bed, kept awake by the chomping and chewing, she had a vision of the actual culprits. Limbless and eyeless little monsters, round as meatballs, purplish-black and tufted with random crops of hair, equipped with teeth. How they got inside her womb, she has no idea.

Elaine pushes against DR JOHN SMITH's door. It opens onto

a dusty, musty smell and a single flight of carpeted stairs. She climbs. Atop the landing, there is no waiting room, no receptionist. Nothing but a plain wooden door. She clutches her handbag to her swollen abdomen, clenching her toes inside her shoes. Blood and clots run, run, run from her in an endless fall, soaking the sanitary pad. Spots dance in her vision. This ordeal must end. It has to end. She will rid herself of the multitudes, of the hair and teeth. Otherwise, the monsters will chew right through her womb and escape. Kidneys, liver, pancreas: no organ would be safe. Her doctor must have foreseen this possibility in her test results. That would explain his nervous tics—the tapping of incisors, the side-eye, the sweating—and his referral to the mysterious Dr John Smith. Medical treatment for monsters requires a special doctor, an outlier, a surgeon with his office crammed between a tattoo parlour and a FOR LEASE sign, a gynaecologist without clientele or receptionist. Elaine knocks. Seconds pass.

"Hello?" she says, her voice a faint croak.

The plain wooden door opens. A man peeks his head out. It is a sleek head, with greased black hair combed into perfectly straight and even rows like an empty, tilled field. His dark eyes shine. He smiles with his lips closed. Elaine is small, barely five feet tall, but this man is smaller. Much smaller. He wears a charcoal suit, white shirt, red tie.

"Dr Smith?" she says.

He opens the door and ushers her inside with the wave of a child-sized hand. As he retreats, Elaine takes in the room. An examination table, two chairs, a desk. There is nothing on the desk. No computer, no jotting pad, no pen. Elaine's shoulders tighten even more. The start of a headache squeezes her scalp. She sits opposite Dr John Smith. He is smiling. His face is narrow and pointed as if swept back from the nose.

"Fibroids," he says. Then he wags a tiny forefinger. "Ah, but you don't agree."

This takes her by surprise. She doesn't know how to respond.

"Tell me what you think they are," he says. "Be frank, please."

"What for? You'll assume I'm crazy."

Sombre, Dr John Smith shakes his pinched little head, and

gestures for her to speak.

"All right." She lifts her chin. "At first, I thought my womb held a nest of mice."

"Mice." He nods, mulling it over. "And now?"

"Now I know it holds monsters. Dozens of them. Monsters with hair and teeth."

Dr Smith steeples his fingers, leans back in the chair and contemplates the ceiling. He says, "You believe you're harbouring teratomas?"

"Teratomas? I'm sorry. I don't know what they are."

"A type of germ cell tumour that grows in the reproductive organs. Quite rare," he says, and presses one tiny set of knuckles against his mouth, just for a moment, as if stifling a grin. "Misbegotten tumours. Often presenting with hair and teeth."

"Yes," Elaine says. "That sounds about right."

"Mrs Grey, have you told anyone else of your suspicions?"

"No. Absolutely not."

He takes a business card from his jacket pocket and offers it with just the tips of his manicured fingernails. "Tomorrow, nine a.m. at this hospital. No food or drink after midnight."

"Tomorrow?" She takes the card. "You're scheduling my surgery for tomorrow?"

"Pack a bag sufficient for a two-night stay. Keep taking your medications as prescribed. It's very important that you keep taking your medications. Very important."

"Don't you have any other patients?"

He interlaces his fingers and rests his hands on the empty desk. "You're quite ill, Mrs Grey. Your womb is grossly enlarged and deformed. Some of the tumours have grown so fast, they've outstripped their own blood supply and become necrotic. That means the tumours are rotting, Mrs Grey. Decaying like corpses. You are pregnant with death itself, as it were." He smiles and stands up. "Remember, nothing to eat or drink after midnight."

Elaine stands up too, breathless, faint, nauseated, bleeding, hot clots sliding out.

Over dinner, Malcolm pats the back of her hand. "Well, Dr Smith must have had a cancellation," he says. "You're really poorly. Dr Smith said so himself. Count your blessings you don't have to wait."

The hospital turns out to be a suburban brick veneer. Instead of gardens there is asphalt for parking. The morning is bright and cloudless, glaring. Elaine clutches the handles of her valise, biting her lip, as Malcolm steers their car into one of the many vacant spots and cuts the engine. Ordinary houses where people live are on either side of the hospital. In fact, the whole street is full of ordinary houses.

"It's a private clinic," Malcolm says. "This is how they tend to look out here in the suburbs. Calm down, would you please? Stop chewing the inside of your cheek."

In the pre-surgery waiting room, behind a drawn curtain, Malcolm folds her clothes for her, ties the straps of her hospital gown, helps pull the compression stockings over her feet and up to her knees. He is whistling through his front teeth all the while.

"Aren't you scared?" Elaine says. "People can die during surgery."

"Don't be silly," he says. "You're in good hands."

Elaine stares at her husband very carefully. It was Malcolm who encouraged her to see their GP in the first place. Malcolm who reassured her about Dr Smith's deserted consulting room and unfilled surgery schedule. Malcolm who is sitting next to her, whistling a jaunty tune, now searching through a stack of magazines for something to read.

No, she must be logical.

Soon, she will bleed no more, not ever again. Her womb will be gone, thrown away. That is a good thing. I am safe, she tells herself. Not everything is a conspiracy. All is well. She stops staring at her husband. Instead, she looks around the room. It must have been a lounge room originally, back when the hospital was a family home. There are three other booths, each one with its curtain drawn back, each booth empty. Elaine clenches her toes against the linoleum floor, over and over and over again.

The nurse comes in. It is the same woman from the reception desk. "Ready?" she says.

No. Elaine has changed her mind. She doesn't want to do this anymore. She wants to see her regular gynaecologist instead. She must insist on a second opinion.

Malcolm takes hold of Elaine's hand. Together, they follow the nurse to the corridor.

The nurse stops and says, "Here's where you part ways. Mrs Grey, you come with me. Hubby, you go to the exit and we'll see you in a couple of hours, okay?"

Malcolm leans down to kiss Elaine. A sob chokes off Elaine's throat. She flings her arms about his neck and clings on, until he laughs, taking hold of her wrists to push her away. The nurse is laughing too.

"I'm frightened," Elaine says.

"You'll be fine," Malcolm says, and leaves.

Elaine watches him go, her fists pressed to her swollen abdomen, against her belly pregnant with monsters both dying and dead, against her womb filled with hair and teeth.

"Come along," the nurse says.

Elaine trails behind, crying, hiccupping on sobs. She turns a corner and stops.

There is a gurney with metal side-rails, a half-dozen people in green or blue scrubs. As one, they all look at her and smile with closed lips. None of them seems to mind or even notice that Elaine is weeping. A child steps forward. No, not a child, but Dr John Smith. She didn't recognise him at first in his scrubs with the cap covering the greased ruts of his hair. He is rubbing his palms together, the skin making a dry whisking sound, his dark eyes shining with anticipation and delight. Everyone else stands very still. Motionless.

"Sorry, I'm just a bit scared," Elaine whispers, embarrassed, thumbing away tears.

No one says anything. Their cold, perfunctory manner allows her to regain control. She is helped onto the gurney. The anaesthetist puts a cannula into the back of her hand. The monsters gnaw and rend and gnash. Elaine feels weak. Not long now. Not long.

A couple of women push the gurney into another room. This is the theatre. It has an enormous light fixture with many bulbs hanging from the ceiling, trolleys covered in stainless steel equipment, machines on carts, a central table. The window looks out onto a clothesline.

The women help Elaine to lie on the table. Someone puts a mask over her nose and mouth. Compressed air hisses out of it. The air smells like rubber and medicine. Someone else puts a syringe into the cannula in her hand and depresses the plunger. A sickly dropping sensation, like the downward swoop of a rollercoaster, surges through Elaine and momentarily stops the monsters from biting. Catching them, like her, by surprise.

"Well, that feels weird," Elaine says, and closes her eyes for a moment.

She opens them.

The pain is excruciating. Agonising. It claws and mauls and flails wildly throughout her body, violent and wrenching, taking her breath. She tries to bring her knees to her chest but is too feeble. A wail breaks from her throat.

"Relax," says a voice. "Calm down."

Elaine gasps, blinks. She is in a different room. The operation must be over. Her rotting uterus should be in a medical waste bin. Writhing, she cries, "Help me. Please help me."

"Calm down," intones the voice again. This time, she recognises Dr Smith.

She forces her eyes open. The entire surgical staff is arranged around her bed, watching her. Dr Smith stands at the foot of the bed, grinning. Elaine tries to lift her head.

"Why didn't you take out the monsters?" she says. "Why did you let them loose?"

The teeth are roaming, unchecked, chewing rabidly at her bowels, biting her diaphragm in frantic search of heart and lungs, gnawing through muscle to burrow down into each thigh.

"The operation was a success," Dr Smith says. "Congratulations."

He looks around at his team. They look back at him and at each other.

Elaine clutches her abdomen. "The pain," she says. "I can't stand it."

"Relax," Dr Smith says. "You're in good hands."

His hands are clasped to his chest as if in joy. The team members grip the metal side-rails of the bed. Their hands are white-knuckled. No one touches her. Smiling with closed lips, silently, they watch her as she winces, thrashes, struggles. Elaine understands now, too late, as the unleashed monsters tear and rip through her guts, that she is not safe. Everything is a conspiracy. All is not well.

MOTHER DIAMOND

JANEEN WEBB

When Mother finally had the grace to die, Ruby Jane was too worn out to cry. Mother's illness had been long and painful, especially for her daughter. Ruby had lost everything: her relationship, her job, her friends. She had nothing left. Her choices had seemed straightforward at first, a simple matter of filial obligation. When Mother's cancer had been declared terminal, she had demanded that Ruby — her only child — should take leave from the teaching post and move back home to nurse her through her final weeks of life. Ruby had acquiesced, feeling duty-bound to ease the death of the woman who had given her life.

But Mother had rallied. Weeks dragged into months, then years, while Ruby stoically managed a range of unpleasant physicalities and domestic demands that became more erratic, more peremptory, more hostile as Mother's mind weakened. Mother flatly refused palliative care, telling her doctors that she already had help, treating her daughter as live-in nurse, housemaid, driver, and general dogsbody. In the end, Mother's passing was a relief for everyone concerned.

The prepaid funeral was surreal. Ruby sat in the front pew — thin, careworn and silent in bereavement black — feeling mercifully detached while the professionals carried out their instructions: in earlier, more lucid days, Mother had chosen the celebrant, the church, the music, the flowers, had made her own life-history slideshow, had even dictated guidelines for her eulogy. Afterwards, while the few family friends who'd bothered to show up nibbled sandwiches in the church annexe, Mother was dispatched to the crematorium, safely tucked up in the rosewood coffin of her choice.

Ruby was free to go. She called a taxi and kept her appointment with the family solicitor for a formal reading of the will. The shadows were lengthening by the time she was ushered into his inner-city office.

"No real surprises here," Michael Rosario said, scanning the document. "You are the sole heir. There are a couple of odd bequests that will mean extra work for you, as your mother's executor."

"No surprise in that either," said Ruby.

Michael—middle aged, balding, and running to fat—moved around his desk and patted her shoulder. "The worst is over now," he said kindly. "She can't rule from the grave, you know."

Ruby shook her head. "I wouldn't bet on that. You knew Mother."

"I'll grant she was a difficult client."

"She was a difficult everything."

"True. But between us, we'll manage the estate. It will all be fine."

"Thanks, Michael."

"Have you thought about what you will do with the house?"

"I'll get it fixed up, then sell it. I grew up in that house, but it's not home anymore. I should move on."

"I understand. Just let me know when you are ready. It's prime real estate, so close to the beach—with views like that, there'll be no problem selling it. I can help with agents, contracts and so on. I might even hear of a buyer. I can ask around if you like. There's no rush."

Ruby just nodded, exhausted.

Michael glanced up at the wall clock. "You look done in," he said. "You've had a long day, and it's getting late. Why don't you let me buy you a decent dinner? There's an excellent Italian restaurant around the corner."

Ruby finally smiled. "I'd like that. I don't think I can face Mother's kitchen tonight."

"I'm not much of a cook myself," said Michael. "I'll get my coat."

Michael Rosario was obviously a regular at Geppetto's Trattoria: the owner embraced him warmly and ushered them to a quiet corner table. Michael settled back while the waiter lit the candle, brought table water and warm bread rolls, then rattled off the list of tonight's special dishes.

Ruby was only half listening. "What do you recommend, Michael?" she asked.

"You can't go wrong with the fillet steak. The beef here is all grass fed."

"Great idea. I'm starving. I didn't eat anything at the funeral reception."

"Very wise." Michael grinned up at the waiter. "We'll have an antipasto platter for two, Marc, and a bottle of Sangiovese. Then two rare steaks—and I suppose we'd better have fries and a green salad on the side."

"Perfect," said Ruby. "I haven't had a restaurant meal in forever. I could never get away. My friends stopped asking."

"And now you are free," said Michael. "Ah, here's the wine." He paused while the waiter poured for them, then raised his glass. "To new beginnings," he said.

"To freedom," Ruby responded. She sipped. "Oh, this is nice."

"Thought you'd like it," said Michael.

Wine, warmth and candlelight worked their magic. Ruby relaxed at last. She brightened up enough to chat amicably with Michael as they shared the starter, and when the steaks arrived, he ordered a second bottle of wine.

"It's a celebration, not a wake," he said. "You deserve a little luxury tonight."

An hour or so later, Ruby sighed as she sipped the Frangelico affogato she'd chosen for dessert. "Thank you for this, Michael," she said. "It's just what I needed."

He leaned across the table and took her hand. "You don't have to go home yet," he said softly. "There may be other things you need."

Ruby blushed, but it seemed only natural that she should spend the night with him. Their lovemaking was gentle, comforting. She was grateful for the feel of his arms around her. He held her while she cried herself to sleep.

She awoke to slanting sunlight and the sound of him singing, off key, in the shower. She took her turn in the bathroom, and by the time she joined him in the kitchen, uncomfortable in yesterday's clothes, he was suited up for the office and ready to leave.

He handed her a fresh coffee. "I'm afraid I have an early meeting," he said. "Will you be okay to get home?"

"I'll call a taxi." She smiled at him, suddenly shy. "It's been a long time since…anyone touched me," she said. "I hope—"

He held up his hand. "No explanations necessary. Things are what they are." He glanced at his gold Rolex. "I have to go. Take your time, help yourself to breakfast—there's juice and yoghurt and bread for toast. Just pull the front door shut when you leave." He kissed her lightly on the forehead, marking her with a faint coffee smudge. "I'll call you."

"Okay."

He picked up his slim leather attaché case and headed for the door. He did not look back. It was over.

Ruby shivered. She knew, suddenly, that her being in Michael's apartment was no longer right. Not right at all. She collected her scattered things, called a taxi, and fled—back to the safety of Mother's house. She hesitated at the door.

"It's my house now," she reminded herself, but it still took an effort of will to turn the key in the familiar lock. The house was heavy with the scents of Mother—sickly old-woman smells of medications and stale sweat and soiled incontinence pads. Ruby dumped her bag on the kitchen table, put the kettle on, then wandered through the oddly silent rooms with her mug of Earl Grey. She felt like *she* was the ghost, returning to the empty scene of her own past life.

But by the time she had finished her tea she had reached a

decision. She *would* see this through. She would take control. She shrugged off the oppression, opened all the windows, and headed for her own bathroom. Her second shower for the day scrubbed off Michael's lingering aftershave. She shampooed her dark hair, slipped into clean underwear, and chose a defiant red dress for today's errands: it made all the difference. Ruby dumped her crumpled black mourner's outfit into the laundry basket and felt ready to tackle the last leg of the Mother Marathon. Her buoyant mood lasted while she drove to the crematorium to collect the ashes. Her confidence was high as she parked the car and headed for the reception desk, happy that this would be the end of it.

But Mother wasn't done yet: she had one more surprise in store for her daughter. Ruby was shown into the director's office, offered tea, and informed that Mother's hideously expensive prepaid funeral included her transition into a *deceased diamond*.

"Let me get this straight," Ruby said. "You are planning to take my mother's ashes and process them into a diamond? A black diamond?"

The stylishly-suited director smiled encouragingly. "In a nutshell, yes. The ashes of your loved one will be placed in a special chamber and subjected to forces that mimic the geological stresses required to produce a natural diamond. The result will be a genuine diamond. A forever keepsake." She opened a drawer and offered Ruby a catalogue. "Our master jeweller will facet the stone in the style of your choice. And we have a wide range of settings available. Please select one."

Ruby shrugged. "I guess it'll be like owning a Victorian mourning piece. Except those were carved from jet, not diamond."

"If you like," said the director. "But this is far more personal. A transmogrification, if you will. A diamond is forever, as they say, and your diamondised loved one will endure for eternity. Your mother will be with you forever."

Ruby shuddered at the thought. "And if I don't want it? Can I get a refund?"

"I'm afraid not. Only the person who placed the order can claim a refund, which in this case is unlikely." The director smiled at her well-worn little joke. "Your black diamond is bought and paid for, and I'm obliged to fulfill the contract. If you don't want it mounted, I can give you the loose stone in a standard box. But it'll be so much nicer if you can wear it, or perhaps pass it on to a relative. Do you have children?"

"No," said Ruby.

The director was undeterred. "You never know," she said. "We usually find that grandchildren appreciate a keepsake."

Ruby glared at her.

"Sorry. I didn't mean to offend." She waited a beat, then pushed on. "A lot of clients choose rings, but brooches are also popular with ladies such as yourself."

"I see. Can you do a pendant?"

"Certainly." The director leafed through the catalogue and opened it at a different page. "Do any of these styles appeal?"

Ruby stared for a while, thinking she could always throw the thing into the sea. She probably would. But for now it seemed she had little choice but to go along with Mother's arrangements. "That one," she said at last, pointing to an elegantly simple white-gold setting. It was threaded onto an opera length, curb-linked chain of pink gold.

"Lovely choice. The chain isn't included, but I can offer you a discount."

"Of course," said Ruby, unsurprised at one more additional cost. There had been rather a lot of them so far. She handed over her credit card. "Call me when it's ready for collection."

"It'll be my pleasure." The woman positively beamed. "You won't be disappointed."

Ruby was almost happy for the next three months. She aired and cleaned and scrubbed the house till it no longer smelled of mortal decay; she took carloads of Mother's clothes and shoes and knickknacks to the local charity shop; she arranged a painter to smarten the place up; she ordered new carpets; she even hired an exterior designer to renovate the garden. The new plants were soon blooming. So was Ruby. She was a little nauseated in the mornings and found she could no longer stomach her favourite vanilla latté, but generally she felt fine. She took long walks on the beach. Her fitness began to return. Her pale complexion improved; her brown curls regained some of their former gloss. She even gained a little weight.

But then the call came: "Your pendant is ready for collection, Ms Birthelwaite."

Ruby sighed, but decided to get it over with. "Would this afternoon be convenient?"

"Certainly, Ms Birthelwaite. Shall we say three o'clock?"

"I'll be there."

The funeral director seemed genuinely delighted as she opened a black velvet box and offered it to Ruby. "Your mother has come up beautifully," she said. "She would have been pleased."

Ruby winced. She had to force herself to look. Then, "Oh," was all she could say.

The marquise-cut black diamond was truly a thing of dark beauty, perfectly framed in its white-gold oval, highlighted in contrast with the warm pink-gold tones of the stunning chain.

The director produced a mirror on a stand, setting it down on her desk with practised ease. "Please do try it on," she said. "I haven't seen this design made up before. I'm sure it will suit you."

Ruby hesitated. But then she slipped the chain over her head and settled the gorgeous pendant against the swell of her breasts. She forced herself to look in the mirror.

Mother looked back at her.

Ruby froze. She barely heard the director, still enthusing in the background. "Simply spectacular," the woman was saying. "Would you mind if I take a photograph for our records?" She held up her phone, snapping several shots before Ruby could argue.

"I'd rather you didn't," Ruby managed at last.

"No problem." The professional smile was back, disingenuous. "I'll delete it later."

"I have to go," Ruby said. She stood abruptly, knocking over the chair and snagging her pantyhose. A ladder snaked up her thigh.

"Are you all right, Ms Birthelwaite? Would you like a glass of water?"

"I have to go."

Ruby scooped the velvet box into her handbag and dashed for the door, trying not to throw up. The fresh air helped. She took a deep breath, found her car, and drove blindly out into traffic. She was still wearing the Mother diamond, the pendant slowly warming against her skin.

She had no idea how she drove home. She locked the car in the garage, kicked off her shoes, discarded her ruined pantyhose and headed straight for the beach. Expensive and beautiful as the black diamond was, she knew she should throw it into the sea and be done with it. She clutched it to her chest as she walked, working up the courage to act. But as she walked, she was soothed by the clean salt air and the late afternoon sunlight and the crash and boom of the waves on the shore. Her anxiety subsided. The pendant was blood-warm now. It whispered to her, promising to be good. Ruby wavered. She was too upset to think straight. She supposed she could always dispose of Mother tomorrow. She found herself trudging back up the hill to the house.

The instant Ruby carried the pendant across the threshold, everything changed. The house became less welcoming, less amenable to her touch. The air turned chilly; she snapped a fingernail on the window latch when she moved to shut out the cold. She tripped on the laundry step when she retrieved her damp washing. She couldn't even make tea without mishap — she dropped the kettle and scalded her hand when boiling water pooled on the bench, soaking her new stack of glossy travel brochures. She struggled to focus, close to panic again. The cooktop was clearly beyond her. She phoned out for pizza and carried it through to the living room. She curled up on the couch with a glass of Shiraz, hoping to soothe herself with mindless TV. But nothing could hold her attention. The evening news was bleak. The wine was sharp. The food tasted of ashes. She gave up, opting for an early night. She pulled off the pendant, shoved it into its velvet box and stuffed the box into the back of a drawer before she climbed into bed. It made no difference—the black diamond was still whispering in her mind, cataloguing her failings. Mother was home again.

Sleep was no refuge. Ruby dreamed of bats with baby faces crawling headfirst down the bedroom walls to stare at her with Mother's black, diamond-faceted eyes. Things were worse next day. Ruby woke with a migraine and spent a miserable morning retching over the basin. Her back ached. She feared she might have flu, or worse. She phoned her local clinic for an appointment, relieved to find she could be fitted in late that afternoon to see Dr Phillips—a sensible woman who'd helped her through several Mother-driven crises, a woman Ruby could trust. The short drive to the surgery was an ordeal of heavy traffic, too much noise, too much glare—Ruby was shaking by the time she slumped into a plastic chair in the waiting room. She flinched when her name was called.

"Hi, Ruby," Dr Phillips said cheerfully. "What's up? I didn't expect to see you again so soon. I thought you were doing much better these days."

"I was, until yesterday," Ruby replied.

Dr Phillips listened while Ruby described her various symptoms. "I'll do some bloods," she said. "And if you can just pop into the bathroom, I'll do a urine check as well. The specimen jars are on the shelf."

Ten minutes later, Dr Phillips looked up from her test kit. "You're not sick, Ruby," she said. "You're pregnant."

"What? I can't be."

"You can, and you are. I'll arrange an ultrasound so we can see how far along you are."

Ruby's mind was racing, thinking back to her one-night-stand with Michael Rosario. "I can give you an exact date," she said. "There's only one possibility."

"I'd still like to take a look," said Dr Phillips. "You're relatively old to be having your first pregnancy. There's a lot we should check."

Ruby nodded miserably. "And if I don't...?" She trailed off, not daring to frame the next thought. She was close to tears.

"Your decision entirely," Dr Phillips said briskly. She offered Ruby a tissue. "Let me run the tests so you can make an informed decision, going forward. Okay?"

"I guess so."

Ruby waited numbly while appointments were made for her—diaries were checked, dates confirmed. Released at last, she took refuge in her car for the second time in two days. There were no good choices here. She crossed her arms on the steering wheel, cradled her head, and wept as though her heart would break.

The house seemed even colder when Ruby finally returned. She'd picked up a takeaway chicken masala curry on the way home—she still couldn't trust the kitchen. She ate in the living room again. She needed to think things through. She supposed she'd have to tell Michael, but not yet. Not tonight. Her head ached. Her body ached. She couldn't settle to anything.

No matter what distraction she tried, her thoughts kept cycling back to the black diamond pendant: it called to her from its velvet box, it wheedled, it cajoled. It wouldn't let her sleep. She lay, half-waking, afraid of the shifting shadows behind the bedroom blinds. The sleepless hours were creeping towards dawn when she finally succumbed to the siren song: she switched on the light, got out of bed, pulled the pendant from its box and slipped it on. The Mother diamond settled once more against her breast, radiating relief. The migraine lifted. The house felt warmer. The walls of her bedroom closed in, womb-like, embracing her once more. The pendant's song morphed into lullaby.

Ruby slept.

It was late morning when she woke. She made coffee and toast in the kitchen without mishap. Mother was cooperating. Ruby took off the pendant while she showered and dressed, but she felt uneasy until she was wearing it again. She decided she might as well face up to her situation. She threw the ruined travel brochures into the recycle bin—she wouldn't be going anywhere anytime soon. Then she called Michael and arranged to meet him for lunch at Geppetto's.

The trattoria looked less romantic by daylight. Michael was waiting at his usual corner table. He rose and kissed her lightly on the cheek.

"Good to see you, Ruby," he said as they settled into their seats. "This is an unexpected pleasure." He picked up the leather-bound menu. "They do a good set lunch here—it's on the last page. There's a choice of main course with a glass of wine and a coffee included. Will that suit?"

Ruby scanned the menu and managed a smile. "That will do very nicely," she said. "The spaghetti carbonara looks good. And I could do with a glass of red."

Michael heard the quaver in her voice. "Is everything alright?" he asked.

"Not really."

"Then let's have that glass of wine and you can tell me all about it." He beckoned to the waiter, swiftly arranging the orders. He turned back to Ruby. "You look nice," he ventured. "That pendant is very striking."

"It's Mother," Ruby said.

"You mean it belonged to your mother?"

"No. I mean that Mother paid to have her ashes turned into a black diamond. This is it. The diamond *is* Mother."

Michael pulled a face. "That's a bit creepy, isn't it?"

"Totally," Ruby agreed. "But I couldn't prevent it. And now I can't seem to go anywhere without it."

He reached out to touch. "May I?"

The diamond was cold, treacherous as black ice. Michael pulled back, his fingers trembling.

"Best not," Ruby said quickly.

The waiter returned to pour the wine.

Michael seized the opportunity to change the subject. He raised his glass. "To the future," he said lightly.

Ruby gulped a mouthful of her wine. "That's what I need to talk to you about."

"That sounds dramatic."

"I'm afraid it is." Ruby faltered.

"Come on then. Out with it. It can't be that bad."

"Michael, I'm pregnant. The child is yours."

He blanched. "Are you sure?"

"About which? I saw my doctor yesterday—I'm sure I'm pregnant. And it's like I told you—nobody else has touched me in years. There's no doubt you're the father." She stiffened slightly. "We can do a DNA test if you like."

Michael sat very still for a moment. "What do you want to do?" he asked at last.

Ruby twisted her linen napkin between her fingers. "I don't know. I want you to help me."

The waiter interrupted the moment: he set down bowls of steaming pasta, offered grated parmesan, black pepper, more bread rolls.

When their conversation was private once again, Michael drew a deep breath. "I'll be honest with you, Ruby. Ours was a brief encounter, nothing more. I don't want to marry you."

"I know."

"I don't want a child."

"I know that too."

"Then why are we here?"

"This is a shared responsibility, Michael, whether we like it or not," said Ruby. "We have to face it together."

Michael lowered his voice. "Then let's make it as simple as possible," he said. "I'll make some enquiries. I'll find you the best clinic. I'll pay for the procedure."

Ruby felt a sharp pain in her chest: the Mother diamond was broadcasting distress.

"You've gone pale," Michael said. He topped up her water glass. "Here, drink this."

Ruby sipped obediently. "Sudden heartburn, that's all," she said.

"Have I shocked you?"

"Not exactly. But I thought we might look at all the options." She toyed with her cooling pasta, avoiding his gaze.

"Surely you don't want to keep it—it's an unfortunate accident, nothing more. Think about it: you barely survived the last miserable years as sole carer for your mother. You can't seriously be contemplating starting all over again, caring for an infant. It will eat your life."

Ruby sniffed back tears. "I'm almost forty," she said. "This may be my last chance."

"Are you asking me for child support?"

"I honestly haven't thought that far," said Ruby. "I only found out yesterday. It wasn't right to keep it from you. That's why I called. I'm not asking for anything."

"Not yet," Michael muttered.

"Sorry?"

"Just thinking aloud." He tried to smile. "This is a shock for both of us," he said. "But we'll get through it. I'll be with you all the way."

Ruby returned the smile. "Thanks. I knew you'd help." She pushed her plate away. "I'm not really hungry."

"Me neither. I'll order the coffee. Would you care for dessert?"

"No. Coffee will be fine."

Michael shifted uneasily in his seat. "I must get back to the office. I'll call you. Okay?"

"Okay."

A few minutes later, he was gone.

Ruby sat for a while, nursing her cappuccino.

The waiter came back. "Would you like another coffee, Signora?" he asked. "On the house. Perhaps you would like an affogato?"

"Thank you, Marc, yes—that would be lovely. And thank you for remembering."

"My pleasure," he said. "I hope you will visit us more often. Mr Rosario is a lucky man."

Three days later, Michael turned up at Ruby's house, un-announced. "I've made arrangements," he said. "Get your things. This won't take long."

"But—"

"I'll be with you the whole time, like I said I would."

"And if I don't see this specialist?"

"We don't have time on our side. He can only see you today because I put you on a cancellation list. And before you ask, I'm your legal representative—I already have access to your details. All you have to do is sign the consent form."

"But Michael, I'm coming around to the idea of keeping our daughter."

"Daughter?"

Ruby fished in her handbag for the ultrasound image and held it out to him. "I had my scan yesterday. Everything looks normal. I heard the heartbeat. It's a girl. See?"

Michael closed his eyes, refusing to look. He took her arm. "Please, Ruby," he said. "Put it away. You know this is for the best. The longer you worry about it, the harder it will get. I'm doing this for both of us. Let's at least keep this appointment. Things will be clearer after that. I have rights in this too, you know."

Ruby couldn't really argue with that. She let him bundle her into his shiny black Audi sports car. She sat silent while he drove to a private hospital in the leafy outer suburbs. She allowed him to walk her to reception, noticing that the doctors listed on the information board seemed mostly to specialise in plastic surgery. The waiting room was quiet, expensively furnished with deep carpets and leather couches, the concealed ceiling speakers playing soft classical music—a far cry from the cheerful clatter and plastic chairs of Ruby's usual clinic. It wasn't until she had filled in the paperwork and changed into a hospital gown for her examination that the bubble of panic rose up in her throat.

"I can't breathe," she said. "I don't think I can do this."

Michael patted her hand. "You'll be fine," he said, sneaking a look at his Rolex. "This shouldn't take much longer."

The specialist was matter-of-fact. He ushered Ruby behind the screen, glanced briefly at the ultrasound print, conducted a cursory examination, and left her to dress again. He was at his desk and deep in conversation with Michael when she emerged to take her seat, struggling to concentrate over the mind fog of cold terror emanating from the Mother diamond.

"We can go ahead with termination," the specialist said. "I just have to be sure that it's what you want."

"She's sure," said Michael.

"Ms Birthelwaite?"

Ruby couldn't answer. She doubled over, clutching the pendant to her chest. The pain was intense. She was fighting for enough breath to scream.

The doctor hit the emergency button. He moved swiftly. By the time the nurse came running, he had helped Ruby back onto the examination table and was checking her vital signs. "Oxygen," he said tersely. "And we'll need an urgent ECG. Her blood pressure is through the roof." He turned to Michael. "I'd say that answers the question of her consent, wouldn't you?" he said. "This is a major panic attack triggered by her fear of losing the foetus. I can't go ahead under these circumstances, Mr Rosario. I'm sorry."

Michael sat still as a stone while Ruby was fitted with a portable oxygen mask. A nurse prepared to wheel her off for priority tests. As the trolley left the room, Michael rose to shake hands with the specialist. There was nothing more to say.

Ruby lay quietly on the narrow hospital trolley, too frightened to move, until a nurse brought her a cup of tea and a biscuit.

"You can get dressed now, if you like, Ms Birthelwaite. Your tests are fine. The doctor says you can go home."

"Thank you." Ruby struggled to sit up. She held her hand against her belly as if to feel for signs of life. "What happened back there?" she whispered. "I can't remember. Have I been… in surgery?"

"Nothing like that," the nurse said cheerfully. "I'm told you had a panic attack and collapsed in the consulting suite." She checked her chart. "You've been given a sedative, nothing more. You've been under observation for a couple of hours." She looked down and noticed Ruby's hand, still pressing on her stomach. "Don't fret. Your baby is fine."

Ruby let out the breath she did not know she had been holding. "Thanks," she said. "I was worried."

"No problem." The nurse smiled. "That's a nice pendant, by the way," she said. "We've all been admiring it."

"A gift from my mother," said Ruby.

Michael drove Ruby back to the house and helped her inside. "It seems the decision has been made for us," he said. "But I'll find another specialist if you change your mind."

Ruby shook her head. The Mother diamond was quiescent again, lying calmly against her chest.

"Thought not," said Michael. "I'll order a home-delivery meal. The hospital was insistent that you should not be left alone, so you're stuck with me for tonight." He smiled weakly. "If that's okay."

"I'd appreciate the company," Ruby said. "I'm still pretty shaken up."

"I'm not surprised. You really do go in for drama, don't you?"

"I guess so. I can make up Mother's bed for you. The room has been cleaned out."

"No thanks," said Michael. "I'd prefer the couch. I don't think I could sleep in the bed she died in."

"I suppose not."

The meal was uneventful. Michael had ordered Pad Thai, red duck curry, coconut rice. Ruby fetched plates and glasses and cutlery while he laid out the plastic containers and opened a bottle of Pinot Noir. They ate companionably at the kitchen table like an old married couple. Then Michael made tea and carried the tray into the living room.

"I have chocolates for dessert," he said. "We'll be more comfortable on the couch." He waited until Ruby was settled before he added: "I truly didn't mean to freak you out like that."

"That's okay. Nothing like that has ever happened to me before—but then, I've never been pregnant before."

"I meant what I said, Ruby. I'll be there for you through this, whatever happens. When I saw you collapse…" He faltered, tried again. "What I mean to say is that I'm coming around to the idea of being a father, if that's what you want."

"Really?" She risked a smile. "I've been thinking about names," she said. "I'm Ruby, so it should be another gemstone. What do you think about Emerald? It would shorten easily to Emma."

"My mother's name is Emma," Michael said softly.

"That's it then. And Jane for a second name, after my mother, and me. Emma Jane."

Michael laughed. "We're doomed," he said. "There's no going back now. It's like pets—once you name them, they're yours forever."

"Like the forever diamond," Ruby said, glancing down at the pendant.

"I sincerely hope not." Michael shuddered. "That thing gives me the creeps. I wish you'd take it off."

"I can't."

"Can't?"

"I feel awful anytime I have to take it off. I tried to throw it into the sea, but I couldn't do it. It wouldn't let me. It's whispering in my mind all the time, channelling Mother. It's like it's symbiotic or something."

"A parasite, then," said Michael. "Just like your mother." He reached out. "Let me take it. I'll get rid of it for you."

The heavy painting that hung above the couch where they sat dropped like an anvil. The sharp-edged metal frame crashed onto the back of Michael's head. His neck snapped. He toppled forward to the floor, blood pouring from a deep gash and soaking into the new carpet.

Ruby screamed. She grabbed her phone, called triple zero. She pressed the tray cloth to his wound, desperately trying to keep the blood in his body. The paramedics were fast, but still too late. Michael was pronounced dead at the scene.

For the second time that day, Ruby collapsed in shock. As the outside world faded to black, all she could hear was the Mother diamond's murmured message:

It's just us now, darling. We didn't need him.

The paramedics carried Ruby to the ambulance and took her to a different emergency hospital. This time, there was nobody she could call. Nobody at all.

When she was discharged next morning, there was no escape from the grim reality of her situation. A sympathetic police officer interviewed her at the hospital and then drove her home to check the scene of the accident. The fatal picture was impounded as evidence for the coroner. Photographs were taken, reports written, documents signed. When Ruby was finally left alone, she couldn't face cleaning up the mess. She couldn't even look at the bloodstained carpet. She fled to her room and lay sobbing on the bed, mourning the father of her unborn child, weeping for a future that almost might have been.

It was midday before she pulled herself together enough to creep back to the kitchen for a cup of tea. The dishes from last night's meal were still there, waiting to be washed. She pushed them aside. The pendant was nagging her again.

You have to eat, the black diamond kept whispering. *You're eating for two now. You have to stay healthy.*

Ruby gave in. She decided she could probably manage a chicken sandwich. She buttered some sourdough and was adding lettuce and mayonnaise to sliced chicken when she noticed the half-finished bottle of wine on the bench. She reached for a glass.

The baby kicked her, brutally hard. A rebuke.

No more alcohol, the pendant hissed in her mind. *It's bad for foetal development.*

Ruby gasped, jolted to the core. She rubbed the sore spot. That first, deliberate kick beneath her ribs had confirmed the unthinkable. She knew now, absolutely and for certain, that the girl child in her belly was Mother, impatient to be reborn.

THE REMARKABLE COMPASS FOR FINDING THE DEPARTED

CHARLES SPITERI

For Anna

She stood on the front porch, a red umbrella grasped with both hands, bracing herself against the wind and rain when Demicoli opened the door. She held the umbrella so low that the stretchers rested on top of her head.

"Mrs Dean?" Demicoli said, confused, and checked his watch.

She nodded. "Call me Patricia," she said and shivered. "I'm early. Sorry. I can wait out here if you're not ready. You are Dr Demicoli?"

"Yes," he said. "Come in."

She folded her umbrella and Demicoli stepped aside as she entered, quickly shutting the door to lock out the cold. She sucked in a breath, relieved to be away from the wet chill.

They had exchanged a brief conversation over the phone and from the tone of her voice he had expected her to be younger. She was perhaps in her late thirties, with rounded features and intense brown eyes that were not shy to meet his directly. He was struck by the paleness of her complexion, which contrasted sharply with her cropped red hair. He had seen ghosts with more colour. Rivulets of rain dripped down her long, brown coat.

She looked at his feet, then up at the lit chandelier above their heads.

"Silvia was right," she said. "You don't have a shadow."

Silvia was a previous client who believed that the ghost of her mother had been trying to contact her. As it turned out it wasn't her mother but a trickster demon that had latched on to her loss and pain, feeding. It had taken all his strength to sort that one out.

"She said you're the real thing. You can help."

"Can I take your coat and umbrella?"

She nodded.

After hanging them on a finely-wrought clothes rack next to the door, he gestured down the hallway. "Follow me."

Patricia barely made it two steps when her mobile rang. She reached for her coat and took her phone from the pocket, then smiled apologetically.

"I really have to take this." She turned her back. "Hello, darling… All good, I'm fine. Just a bit of a sore throat." She cleared her throat for emphasis. "Still at the office. I've just got to finish these emails and I'll be on my way… Sounds yummy. Looking forward to it. No, no I'm fine, really. I'll be home in an hour… I know I know. I'll see you soon."

She left it at that and put the phone back inside her coat pocket. She stared at her coat, hesitating long enough for Demicoli to get impatient.

"Shall we proceed?" he said.

"You lead the way."

She made a move to follow him but had barely managed a step when she appeared struck by sudden pain. It was as if someone had stabbed her in the abdomen and twisted the blade. She slumped back against the wall, her face contorted, hands pressed against her abdomen.

Demicoli moved to help, but she backed away from him.

"Just give me…a moment…please," she fought to say.

She hunched forward gasping for breath, her pale face a bright red.

"Can I get you a glass of water?"

"A moment."

She sucked in air through clenched teeth, eyes shut tight, grimacing, her face turning a bright purple. Demicoli thought she was going to choke as she struggled for composure, taking short, sharp gasps. And then, just as suddenly as it had come, the pain seemed to vanish. She relaxed, breathed slowly, regained her composure. Soon, she was able to stand upright again.

Patricia stood unsteadily, expecting the agony to return at any moment, knowing that it eventually would, as it always did, sometimes three to four times a day.

"Are you okay?"

"Lead the way," she insisted.

Lining the dimly lit hallway was a grotesque collection of statues and trinkets, presented in mahogany cabinets like museum pieces. She recognised some musical instruments: a wooden harp with intricately carved swirls and dashes resembling musical notes; a flute that seemed to be made from bone. She could just make out the sounds coming from behind a series of doors on either side of her as she moved deeper into the hallway. There was the ticking of clocks in one, an electrical buzz with a hiss—like steam under pressure—in another. Was that music up ahead? She couldn't tell. The creaking of the floorboards accompanied her every step.

From the shadowless, brightly-lit waiting rooms of hospitals and clinics papered with framed diplomas and degrees to this dark hallway filled with mystical relics wreathed in shadows; from doctors and psychologists to shamans, it seemed to Patricia that she had plumbed new depths of desperation.

When the going gets weird, you just have to get weirder with it.

And she did trust Silvia's judgement. They were childhood friends.

"Would you like a drink?" Demicoli asked as they reach a door behind the stairway at the end of the hall.

"A whisky or vodka?" she said with a wry grin.

"Sorry, no alcohol till we are done." He opened the door. "After you."

Clearly, humour was not his thing.

She hesitated at the threshold. The room was a stark contrast from the crowded hallway. There was a small round table with two chairs, and a spare chair in one corner. A flickering kerosene lamp on the table was the only source of light. No windows, no electrical outlets or fixtures of any kind that she could see. The walls, ceiling and floorboards were painted a solid black. Like stepping into the void.

"I'm not sure what I am getting into."

He smiled. She couldn't help but notice it was a very charming smile.

"Have a seat," he said, pointing to the chairs at the table. "Either chair will do."

She stepped into the room and waited for him, preferring to take his lead. It was cold and she shivered. She watched him gently close the door, then followed him to the table.

"Can you turn up the heating?" The room swallowed up her voice, the sound of each word falling dead silent.

"I can't have any heating in here. There can't be any form of interference."

Interference from what? She thought it best not to ask.

Patricia sat opposite him. Even as the light from the lamp moved across his face, his features remained shadowless. Remarkable.

He didn't seem to mind that she was watching him so intently. Indeed, he raised his eyes to meet hers when he asked, "How long have you been feeling the pain?"

Straight to the point.

"The pain is not the worst of it." She had explained her situation to so many specialists, you would think it would come more easily by now, but it didn't. She was tired of having to remember, and felt guilty for being tired of it. "I met the love of my life five years ago. I'm thirty-nine and Sam is forty." She wondered if Demicoli was married. She couldn't see a ring.

"Neither of us had ever really thought about having children until we met. After four years of trying, we finally decided to visit a fertility clinic. We found out that Sam's sperm count was low, and the quality of my eggs very poor. According to the specialist I had about a five percent chance of falling pregnant. Five percent!"

It was still hard to believe that number.

"Our only real hope was IVF. And do you know how much IVF costs? I mean, we're talking about ten-thousand dollars a try, with no guarantees. We have a mortgage to pay, and like I said, it wasn't as if we'd ever really wanted kids, right? I used to think people were crazy to want kids in the first place, let alone spend all that money for the effort. But I don't think we even lasted a week before we changed our minds. If we really wanted to, we convinced ourselves, we could afford to give it one go. At least in the future we'd have no regrets. Do you know much about IVF?"

Demicoli shook his head.

"It's a remarkably unromantic process, driven by cycles, phases, schedules and words like ovary stimulation, egg harvesting, egg retrieval, sperm collecting. Fun stuff like that. We couldn't even have sex through the whole process—it was all done scientifically. Sam was a cow and I was a lab rat. When I wasn't exhausted, I felt like I'd been tied to a speeding car and dragged through gravel. And I couldn't take time off work because we couldn't afford it."

Was she saying too much? Did he really want to know all this?

He still seemed to be listening so she kept going.

"And every failed attempt just makes you wonder whether the next cycle will be the winner. It took three attempts before I fell pregnant. That's thirty-thousand dollars. And you know what's really amazing? All that pain, all that money suddenly melted away. I was finally pregnant."

She averted her gaze, but there was nothing to stare at, so she just looked down at her hands. "Can I have a glass of water?"

"Sure."

Demicoli left the room. Alone, she struggled to find a distraction. She tapped her fingers on the table to fill the silence and when that wasn't enough, she made up a tune and whistled it. Demicoli returned with a jug of water and a glass on a wooden tray. He poured her a drink.

"I took all the precautions," she went on quickly. "I didn't eat anything that would jeopardise the pregnancy. 'Listeria hysteria' and all that. We didn't tell anyone till after the first three months, and even after that made no plans, accepted no presents. I am sure everyone was wondering why I didn't seem overjoyed; especially Sam. I just didn't want my excitement to tempt fate. You know what I mean?"

He nodded.

She sipped at the glass of water.

"There were regular check-ups and antenatal classes where we met other excited couples. I was welcomed into a new world. But there was always that uneasy feeling that it seemed too easy somehow. Too good to be true. That kind of doomed thinking comes from my mother. She gave up on me ever finding someone, let alone having children. She died five years ago.

"So anyway, seven months into the pregnancy, just as I was getting comfortable with the idea of having our very own child, just as I was starting to feel the joy of it, the kicking stopped. Sam rushed me to hospital. The ultrasound confirmed what I had anticipated all along. I don't even think Sam was surprised, though we had never dared talk about the possibility of things going wrong. I gave birth to my stillborn baby the next day. I don't know what having a baby is like," she said, her voice starting to break up. "The only births I've seen are in the movies. There was no first scream, no crying, no happiness. Just an empty, hollow silence. I didn't want to see the baby. I wanted no part of it. Sam handled everything. I only went to the funeral because of expectations. Bury it and move on."

She reached for the glass and realised she had finished the water. Her hands were shaking.

He poured her another drink.

"And that's that," she went on. She tried a defiant smile, but it turned into a grimace like she had swallowed something sour. "To be honest, I was happy to move on. At my age, who wants a baby anyway? I'd be in my sixties by the time they're old enough to live their own life. Who has the energy for that? Knowing my luck, they'd probably grow up to be a drug addict.

"So, we got into the swing of life without children. Planned a road trip through Europe next year. Another to New Zealand. Most of our friends don't have kids and with those that do... Well, it was difficult at first, but we learned to deal with it. In a way, we get the fun of having kids around without the responsibility. Sam's brother had a baby, a sweet little boy."

She rolled the glass of water between her palms, staring at it closely.

"Three months ago, almost a year after the stillbirth, I started feeling the baby kicking again. And it was intense, more intense than it had ever been during the pregnancy. What happened in the hallway just before? That was nothing compared to what I've felt. Sometimes nothing short of knocking myself out with pain killers will dull the pain. When it goes on for days, I have to take time off work. I've seen doctors, specialists, had ultrasounds, X-rays and even a CT scan. I'm not pregnant and no one can tell me what's going on. The counsellors tell me it's all in my head. A few times, the pain was so great I ended up at the hospital."

Patricia stopped, exhausted. She'd said too much and blamed the emptiness of the room for pushing her to fill the void with words. Her mouth was still dry and her throat hurt. She drank more water.

"What was the name of your baby?" Demicoli said.

She was taken aback by the question. No one had ever asked her that before.

"We never settled on a name."

"Boy or a girl?"

"I didn't want to know."

Was that a hint of sadness that crossed his face? Was he feeling *sorry* for her?

"Look, can you help me or is this yet another waste of my bloody time?" And then she clenched her fists and bit her lip, ashamed by the outburst.

"I think I can help," Demicoli said calmly.

"And how much are you charging me?"

He thought about it for a moment. "How about two-hundred dollars. Is that okay with you?"

"If you can really help."

"You'll have to do all the work," he said, and before she could question him, Demicoli smiled, clapped his hands together and stood. "Let's get to it then. Give me a moment to set up."

He left the room. Alone in the silence, she could hear her own breathing and feel the warmth of the lamp on her face. She felt that tug in her abdomen again and hoped the pain would not return. Sam would be worried. Maybe she should have told him. Imagine what he would think. *You have lost your mind.* No, he wouldn't say that; he'd never say that. Not after everything they had been through. No, he would say something like: *Whatever makes you feel better.* Which would just make her feel worse.

Demicoli returned with a leather box and placed it gently on the table between them. It looked like a suitcase, but it was the size of a shoebox, with brass hinges and clasps, and leather handles on either side.

"This is a compass of sorts," he said. He loosened the clasps with a *click*, lifted the lid and slid the case towards her in one smooth, confident motion.

It was a console made of polished mahogany, with brass dials and levers. There were four tungsten lightbulbs across the top and a tuning fork on the bottom-right corner, with a long copper wire attached to a plastic clip.

"A compass?" It looked like a fancy prop from a science-fiction movie.

He sat down and took a moment to consider his words. "A compass is simply a tool to help people find their way. This one is unique."

"How?"

"Your baby's body might be gone, but its soul is still there inside you."

She pressed her hand to her abdomen.

"Your child is trapped. It doesn't know how to leave. It's lost. And it needs you to help it move on. That's the tricky bit. How do you help someone who has no name, has yet to talk, or even walk?"

He paused and that's when she felt the sting of tears. Her chest tightened anxiously. She quickly wiped the tears from her cheeks.

"Would you like a tissue?"

"Go on," she insisted.

"As I was saying, all living things have a..." He hesitated, trying to find the right word, "...a *name*, yes, let's just settle for a 'name'. A name that is not one made of words but of sounds, almost like music. Think of it this way: everyone's heartbeat might sound similar, yet the truth is that each of us carries a unique beat, as unique as our fingerprints. It's just that our ears and medical machines are not sensitive enough to pick up on it. In fact, our heartbeat is one note of a melody that includes the rush of blood through our veins, the creak of joints pivoting, the spark of tingling nerves. We're each a unique orchestra, the unique melody of which is our true name. And it's not only living things that compose their own song but orbiting planets, the spinning galaxies, quasars, black holes. Just ask any astronomer and they will tell you." He leaned forward as though he was about to reveal a secret. "Spirits, demons and angels dance to their own tune too."

"And my baby."

"Your baby is no different. Since you did get to a stage where it developed its own heartbeat, we will use the echo of that to guide it out."

Crazy as that sounded, at least it was a step up from *It's all in your head.*

"Are you ready?"

She shrugged. "Sure." What did she have to lose?

He took the wire with the sensor. "Please put this over your forefinger."

She slipped her finger into the plastic cap. He pressed a switch and the machine buzzed to life, the lights flashing in sequence. There was no power cable. Must be powered by batteries, she reasoned.

"First, I need to tune the instrument to the rhythm of your song. That'll be our baseline. It will take a few minutes."

"Okay. Whatever."

He slowly turned the dial from left to right watching a gauge rise and fall, and two of the four lightbulbs flashed, one after the other, faster and faster, until both lit up at once. The tuning fork vibrated with a low hum.

"Ah, there you are," he said. "That's your tune right there. Do you feel it?"

She leaned back against the chair and closed her eyes. How delicious to feel each beat of her heart send ripples of calm throughout her body, filling the crevices of emptiness, uncertainty and despair. As a child, she used to love sitting in the back seat of the car, to close her eyes and feel the hum of the engine, the swaying motion of the car lulling her into a peaceful sleep.

"Good," he said. "Now I will home in on the tune of your child. Are you ready?"

She was ready for anything.

"This will be painful but you'll be fine. It's very important that you follow my instructions. Please tell me out loud that you understand."

"I understand."

Demicoli flicked a switch and turned the dial again. The two other lightbulbs began to flicker, one and then the other, faster and faster. The hum from the tuning fork rose in pitch. She gasped as her heart ramped up, thumping like a jackhammer drilling into her chest. Her breath could hardly keep up. She hunched forward, clenching her fist and tugging at the wire of the sensor.

"Stay still," he warned. "Stay as still as possible."

The thumping intensified, becoming a buzzing like a swarm of bees filling her eyes, ears, mouth, threatening to choke her. She clenched her teeth hard, neck muscles tensed, shoulders hunched. She wanted Sam to be here with her, to hold her hand, to tell her everything was okay.

The lightbulbs flickered faster. The hum of the tuning fork grew louder.

"Almost there."

Her face flushed, sweat dripped down her neck. She pressed her free hand tight against her abdomen. The lights flashed across her face, and with her eyes closed, she could see the darkness pulsate. She felt at any moment her body would explode into a swarm of bees.

"We're close now. Think about a moment when you were a

child and lost. When you were helpless."

A rush of air and she was falling, as though the floor had collapsed beneath her, the buzz fading behind her, becoming a dull throb, an echo.

She opened her eyes.

In the dark, she heard her mother's voice, coming from somewhere far away.

"What happened? What's going on?" her mother said.

"It's just a power shortage," her father said. "Must be the storm."

The wind whistled outside like a demented flute, followed by the deafening roar of thunder. When the lightning flashed, the shadows in Patricia's bedroom quivered. If she got out of bed to run to her mother, who knows where those shadows would take her? So, she cowered underneath the bed sheets, trembling and loudly singing nursery rhymes to drown out the noise.

"Oh dear, don't be frightened. You'll be all right." Her mother's voice was so close now. "It's okay."

When Patricia peered out from under the sheet, her mother's face greeted her with a smile.

"Hello there," she said, her smile like the warmth of the sun. "It's just a blackout, that's all. We're here."

Her body fell rigid. She pressed her back harder against the chair and opened her eyes. The two lights flashed on together. The tuning fork stopped vibrating. She gasped. The silence that followed was loud and heavy in her ears.

"There!" Demicoli said and grinned excitedly. "It's done."

Done? she thought, dazed and confused.

Then she heard the baby cry.

She turned her head, following the cries. Her baby was supine, tiny arms waving and legs kicking, looking for all the world like a turtle struggling to get back onto its feet. The umbilical cord was still attached, coiling away into shadow, with signs of peristaltic movement along its length as though it were drawing nourishment from the darkness.

A girl. She could see that. Her gorgeous little girl.

"What do I do? What can I do?"

"A name. Your baby needs a name."

"Jamie."

They had liked the name because it suited a girl and a boy. She didn't care which. Patricia stood and approached, then lifted Jamie into her arms. Her baby was cold so she held her close, sharing warmth with her daughter, rocking her gently, till Jamie's crying subsided, her blue lips and pale cheeks filling with colour. Jamie looked up at her mother. She had blue eyes, Patricia realised, like sapphires. She got those from her dad.

"Hello Jamie," she said. "Hello."

Jamie giggled, then faded away in her arms.

Demicoli switched off the machine.

"Can I see her again?"

He shook his head.

Demicoli followed her as she walked to the front door. She put on her coat. Her mobile phone went off. She took a deep breath before answering.

"I'm sorry, darling… On my way right now. Yes, yes, I'm okay. All good." She paused for a moment, fighting for composure. "I love you, Sam. I love you heaps."

She hung up and slid the phone back into her pocket.

"Will you be okay?" Demicoli said.

She took her umbrella, opened the door and a gust of cold, wet wind greeted her. "My car is only down the street."

It wasn't what he was asking, but Demicoli nodded and watched her dash out into the storm, her figure fading into the rain-swept shadows as he closed the door.

Two weeks later, he opened his letterbox to find an unmarked envelope. In it was two-hundred dollars with a note and the words: *Thank you*. Signed Patricia, Sam and Jamie.

EMPTY BELLIES

ASH TUDOR

For the first time since giving birth, Alma feels hunger without the pang of nausea. Her groin is no longer swollen and the stitches—those evil patterns of X's—have dissolved. The world is her buffet. She imagines a feast of pepper squid and a glass of her favourite gin while presidential-grade tobacco fills her lungs. The once familiar air of freedom brightens her appetite. This pregnancy had tormented her body and now, driving home with a back seat flooded with newly bought clothes, she considers it to be her last.

Her phone buzzes in the passenger seat. *Damn.* Paul and Angus want another marathon phone chat. Their sweetness is understandable. They're in the brooding stages of their baby—a boy they named Roy, for some inexplicable reason—and they consider that Alma is a puzzle piece in the portrait of their new family. They will learn in time, as they all do, that her role is complete; separation shouldn't be avoided or even mourned.

She sighs as the buzzing surrenders to voicemail, knowing eventually she must return the call if only to thank them for the extra cash they added to her last payment. She felt awkward accepting the money, and hiding the amount from the tax man makes her giddy down to her fingertips, but that trip to Cambodia won't pay for itself.

She turns into her apartment car park and barely passes the gate before she sees the baby. Both feet punch the brake. Sitting upright in the centre of the car park is a large blob of a child, its meringue-coloured skin a star on the grey sheet of tarmac.

Somewhere low in Alma's gut, a knot tightens. The baby clenches fists of air, drool smeared over a perfectly satisfied expression. Someone has dressed the baby in a pink gown and white-frilled nightcap, an outfit Alma doesn't recognise from this century or even the last.

Mental cogs turn behind clenched shock. *She can't be more than six months old.* One strong gust of wind and the babe will blow over and smash the soft fruit of her head against the gravel.

"Dear *Christ…!*"

Alma's fumble with the seatbelt feels eternal and she pulls the handbrake so hard the lever cracks. She races without closing the car door, keys left dangling in the ignition.

"What are you doing there, sweet cheeks?"

She's on her knees inspecting the silken flesh and smelling the wafting, signature scent of powdered milk. Baby gazes up slack-jawed, invisible eyebrows raised in wrinkled unknowing. She's a Marlon Brando kind of baby, cheeks so immense they hang past the chin, her beautiful almond eyes and jellybean nose entirely too small to fill the parameters of her enormous head. Alma winces at the oversized cranium.

The intimate spot where Alma required stitches begins to throb.

She extends a finger to meet one tiny hand. Baby grips the digit without looking away from Alma's freshly-dyed golden hair.

"Where's Mummy?"

Alma scans the car park. Midday on a Tuesday and the only vehicle is her own. The candy-blue wall of the apartment block is windowless on this side and offers no clues. Baby leans forward and suckles Alma's finger. The two pops of bottom teeth feel oddly pleasant, like smooth and slimy rock.

For one hazy moment, Alma considers knocking door to door to every neighbour as though she were trying to return a lost wallet. The idea, she supposes, is no more insane than abandoning a baby in a lethal spot. *What kind of fucking parent leaves their child in a—*

But the anger drops away as Baby attempts to fit another of Alma's fingers into her mouth. Aw, cute. At least the melon-headed kid is unharmed.

"Need to call the police, don't we?" she says, and gently pulls her hand free from the drool. "And Mummy needs a hard slap over both arse cheeks."

Alma stands and lifts Baby. The post-natal curve of her hip perfectly cradles the nappy bottom and the Victorian-style dress hangs past Alma's knees. She's good with kids, is a superstar in the eyes of her niece and nephews, and would likely make a great mother if she didn't find children so excruciatingly dull. Baby acts as happy in a stranger's arms as she was on the tarmac, and her fair-lashed eyes glaze over. She's a placid bub. Alma thinks, not for the first time, *this really isn't so hard.*

She heads towards the car, wiggling her finger under the knot of Baby's night cap. The whole outfit is a nightmare, something you'd dress your child in during their christening and throw away after a diarrhoea storm ruins the lace.

"Someone's tied this a little tight, haven't they?" she says, not liking how the string disappears between the flabs of Baby's cheeks. "There. That's better."

Baby tilts her head back, eyes shut, tiny teeth open on display, looking ready to sneeze. The *bless you* is ready on Alma's tongue. A heartbeat before Baby's head snaps forward, the cherub lips roar open to a width large enough to swallow her own colossal head. Alma is mid-step when the demented mouth lunges and grabs the meatiest part of her chest.

Before it happens, she sees the open jaw, gets a hideous view of a wet gum canyon before the bite hits. Yet, Alma thinks she's been shot. She moves on instinct and embraces a protective cage around the child, squeezing the mouth closer. She hears tearing beneath her chin, the sound ploughing through skin, through muscle. Then the sound is shrill and vibrating out her own mouth. She drops the child, doesn't see her land.

Alma wails a low, strangled noise. Blood soaks her right side and feels hot running the length of her leg. When she looks down, there's something poking through the torn material of her shirt. Half her nipple. The other half is gone, along with the top of her breast and the meat below her collarbone. The crater of shredded fat and ragged tendons pings a signal through her veins, and pain rises in a burning tidal wave. Saliva pools down her neck. Even under the agony she knows blood loss is death, but her hands are too small to cover and compress the wounds. The torn skin feels like chewing gum.

A crunch pulsates up her leg and her knees buckle before she realises what has happened. Alma hunches, both hands pressing against her thighs, and sees the boneless curtain of Baby's lips wrapped around one ankle. Its chubby arms hang limp at the sides. The long train of pink gown is untouched by blood, but around that fat face is a spaghetti smear of Alma's flesh.

"Stop it. *Stop it.*"

Pretty eyes snap towards Alma, blue pebbles above beasty jaws. Alma recognises no expression at all as the gums grip down. Alma gargles pain and lands on her knees. The almost toothless mouth still feels human, human skin and bone, but possessed with the power of steel. Alma realises the crunching noise is her own cartilage being pulverized.

"Please. *Please.* Let me go. *Why won't you let me go?*"

The jaw hardens. The crunch changes to a hard snap. Crushed cartilage turns to broken bone. Alma hits the road nose first. Her chest wound litters with gravel. As she tries to thrash herself free, she learns a tough lesson: the body can only take so much pain before it fails to respond. She can barely crawl. Her arms are butter under her own weight.

And there's more pain to come.

She attempts to pull her body by her fingertips, the open door of her car now an oasis. The road acts like a cheese grater against her bloody chest. Every forward lurch is a fight against a bulk fiercer than stone. With her free foot Alma kicks, blindly aiming for the creature she still considers an infant. The bite alters, the grip warping on her crunched ankle.

Before Alma can react, there's another crunch and *snap.*

The jaws obliterate her other foot.

Alma tastes copper. She wants to scream and instead, opens her mouth wide against the gravel and pushes down her teeth. Her siren of pain is a rod shoved through her ears. She chips a tooth. Then her teeth and chest and stomach are slowly dragging backwards. When her front two teeth shatter against tarmac, she doesn't feel it.

Shaking, Alma makes the grand mistake of looking over her shoulder.

With legs pressed together, her feet disappear inside an oval of saggy lips clamped all the way up to her calves. Baby's button nose is folded to a round lump behind a flared mouth, but the eyes are visible and they shine innocent, confused over what their fellow anatomy is doing. At her low angle Alma sees no body, yet she feels her feet inside it, squashed and pulsing against breathing flesh. Acidic fluid sinks into her toes. Screams are not enough. Her head falls back and she begs her mind to faint but the struggle between the agony and the gravel and the slurping mouth is a battle unending.

The lips flap, the gums jerk up her leg and Alma's fingernails scrape down to nubs. The jaws slam down. Alma's kneecaps crumble to broken glass and with the demise of her legs comes a rushing catalogue of memories behind her burning eyes— the pulling up of tights, dancing until sunup, the morning run, scratching a scab off her knee as she sat on the toilet and waited for the pee-stick in her hand to say *positive.*

She rests her head on one side and watches her car grow further away. Pressure reaches her pelvis. Soon, all pain turns to feathers and soars out of reach. Before she closes her eyes, before the Baby jaws gnaw her stomach into warm dough, Alma remembers she is hungry and what a shame it is to feel so empty.

A ROSE FOR BECCA

JASON FISCHER

Becca's Pa wants to sell her to the green men.

"We come to the trade," one of them says. "For a womb of Man."

Pa's men are wired up and little fires dance on the nozzles of their flamethrowers. There must be a dozen or more of the Planty folk, come crackling and crunching from their wild lands. Not a blade of grass grows in town; Pa saw to that. It's been said that their forests are slowly choking the planet, growing perhaps a mile a day. Only poison and flame keep the Districts safe.

So, there they all stand on the ruined ground, flesh men eyeing off green men. Last year they were killing, now there's talk of trading.

Her.

"What's your offer?" Pa calls out.

The creeper-man pauses, drawing into itself. The vines are holding up the rotting head of some poor farmer, tongue half-black and eyes gouged out. Becca can see the man's teeth through a hole in his cheek, and she wants to be sick. The green man pokes its Planty bits every which way into the dead head and the jaw starts working again.

"My lord—my lord brings—"

But the tongue falls out, a dead slug on poison soil. There's an angry rustling as the Planty folk talk in their own way.

"Without a tongue to frame their desires," Pa says, "nor a brain between them."

The men laugh but only to please their boss man.

The largest Planty leaps forward then, a rose bramble more than eight feet high. A thorny cable lashes out and catches Bubner Thomas around his pudgy throat, and laughter is now shouting and curse words. The other men launch licks of flame at the green man but it's already out of their reach, drawing poor, shrieking Bubner into its thorny insides.

There's tearing sounds and the screams stop. Pa's men are ready for a scrap now, and they get their fires going. The Planties are ready to fight, ready to shoot thorns and spores and God-knows-what.

"You damn fools!" Pa yells. "The ink's barely dry on the treaty. Do you want war again?"

"Mourn not your flesh-man," Bubner says, his blind and bleeding head peeking out from the green guts of the rose-bush man. "He serve you well and now he serve me."

Becca has to remind herself that it's not Bubner no more. That head and scrap of spine is not the fat fool who was caught sniffing her drawers and beaten soundly for it. He may be talking, but he's dead.

"Well, now that you've got another mouthpiece, we may as well talk," her Pa says, and motions to the men to turn their flamethrowers down.

Becca tries to feel sad for Bubner but is happy in a way that the fat pervert is dead. She knows her Pa will have already forgotten about him, and that's life in these times and perhaps that makes it okay.

The moment that could have been a killing time passes, and both sides relax. Well, hard to tell if a Planty is relaxed, but Becca guesses if it isn't killing you or ripping you apart to use you, it's relaxed enough.

"Speak for mine own self now," the rose-man says through Bub's fat lips. It still sounds like him, just with gargly phlegm sounds. "You are Sylvester Eli?"

Her Pa nods.

The Planty who is creeper-vines slumps in on itself, for all the world looking disappointed that it can't talk for his boss man, and sheds the rotten bits of farmer onto the ground. The bits stink even from here.

"I am named Rose Prince, in our group your equivalent. I sent a messenger regarding to this trade?"

Her Pa nods again. He doesn't like wasting words on the Planties, hates their talk. "What did you bring for my daughter?" he asks, and she chokes on that first painful sob. He really means to sell her. He looks back at her, angry, and she jams a fist in her mouth before he can.

"Seed for your cropping foods," the Rose Prince says, and more Planties appear from the tree line. Their viny branch arms are wrapped around sacks of fodder and grain.

"Keep your seed. I'm not fool enough to plant anything that might up and eat me," Pa says. "What else have you got?"

"Fuel for your dirty machines," the creature snarls.

The trees themselves move apart and dozens of the green men can be seen, pushing and pulling an enormous fuel tanker.

"Do we have trade?" the Rose Prince asks.

Her father nods. They lost the last refinery in the war.

"Here, you can examine for purity," her Pa says, and shoves Becca forward.

She falls on her knees before her new owner. It's normal enough in the woman trade. A fella don't want used goods and maybe green men aren't no different to the flesh-and-blood kind.

"Please," she whispers as the Rose Prince leans over her.

She's never ever been this close to a Planty before. She can see what's left of Bubner through the gaps of green sinew. Ten thorny fingers reach for her, long and sharp. She cries like a stomped puppy and her bladder empties.

"We are satisfied," the monster says, and hasn't even touched her.

It seems to know she is a virgin, or doesn't care. Pa might have looked at her with a sinner's eyes, but not once had he touched her. The local Nob, Protector of Liberty District, he may have taken it out on her younger brother till he hung himself on the old swing set, but he never touched *her*.

The Rose Prince gently lifts Becca to her feet and the thorns jag her skin. From one green finger-tip a rose instantly grows, impossibly white. He—and in Becca's mind, this Rose Prince is no longer an *it* but definitely a *he*—well, he snaps his whole finger off and hands it to her.

"Smell," he instructs her, and she does without thinking. Spores burn into her throat and lungs. What has he done to her?

"I return for her. One month," the Rose Prince says, and he and the other Planty folk shamble off into the dense forest that is swallowing up the world.

"Burn the seed," her Pa says, and looks at his precious stockpile of fuel with a love that Becca never knew.

Pa puts the rose on the mantlepiece, not because it's pretty but because it's a contract. He keeps it in a dusty glass vase with no water in it. Another leftover from Ma, who kept flowers before the illness took her.

It doesn't need water and Becca stares at that impossibly white rose every day of the month. She is sick every day too, but she's not sure if it's nerves or whatever the Planty did to her with that rose. It's a bad stomach cramp, just like her monthlies, but nothing comes out.

Two days left and she loses her nerve, does a runner. A forage team had found a case of whisky in a broken town at the edge of the District and she waits till her father and his men are as drunk as lords. No one hears her sneak out the kitchen door, and she has a bag packed. There are some cars and a motorbike, but she doesn't know how to drive. Her only plan is to walk all night and hide when the sun comes up. If the Planties don't eat her and the men don't catch her, she might make it to another District or even a ruin with some food.

They catch her just out of town, a trio of lads barely her age. They've been put there to burn any Planties moving on the roads but found something much more fun.

"I'll have her first," the eldest lad says.

The other two are holding her down, and he's wriggling out of his pants, and that's how they are when the Sheriff and a search party spot them. Their protests are met with scorn and they are hung on the spot, ropes slung over a tree that may or may not be alive. They are still kicking as the Sheriff wires a sign to the pantless boy: WOMAN STEALERS.

"You're safe now, Miss Eli. We'd best be getting you back to your Pa," the Sheriff says.

She's too frightened to tell the truth. Only the boys could tell anyone that they didn't break into Sylvester Eli's house, but the boys are dead now. In all the fuss, she kicks her packed bag under a bush and no one notices.

Pa believes her lies, but he whips her anyways. He ties her up in the study and puts the vase right in front of her face where she can't help but see the rose.

The ropes hurt. Somehow, she manages to roll away from the flower, lying on her other side. When the torn skin of her back touches the rug, pain knifes through her, but she bites her lip. It passes. Exhaustion and dreams. There she is, in a yard full of flowers with Ma and her brother. Even Pa is on the porch and he's not drinking and his eyes aren't dead stone. Little Bubner from across the street is over and they're playing a game. It's a lazy afternoon and somewhere there's a lawnmower going.

"You *have* to be a robber!" her brother calls out, fingers as guns.

He ducks behind the swing set, little heart beating and lungs working, and oh my God, for a second, she can see him choked and blue and spinning, then he's back to being an alive little boy. The dream lurches but it doesn't stop.

"I'm not a robber, I'm a fairy princess," Becca pouts, and runs to Ma for adjudication. She's everything kind and warm and her smile can fix anything.

"Of course you're a princess, honey," Ma says. "You're a beautiful girl, the prettiest." And she pats her hair, sets the little plastic tiara properly. "When you grow up, you will be the prettiest lady in all the town. Every boy will be chasing after you."

"Why? I don't like boys. They are dirty and naughty and messy."

"You'll change your tune one day," Ma laughs.

Becca is confused for a moment because Ma is pinched and

pale and her hair has fallen out, but there she is again and her hair shines in the soft sunlight and she's the loving centre of the whole wide world.

"One day, a handsome Prince will come for you. He'll come for you, Becca, and take you away."

The Planties come on the appointed day. They are ranked thick along the dead border of town land, perhaps worried that the flesh-men would cheat them.

Her Pa's men are out in force with jeeps and bikes and engines a-rumble and everywhere the promise of flame if a Planty comes too close. They are right to be worried. There are an awful lot of the green men.

"Here she is," her Pa calls out to the Rose Prince.

Two men carry her forward and dump her on the ground, still tied up. The white rose rests between her breasts, dry bloodstains from where the thorns have cut her; Pa's last punishment.

"Fair trade," the Rose Prince manages through the rotten lips of Bubner.

A month of being dead has done little for his appearance, let alone all them creepers and tendrils jammed into his skull.

"You smell ready. Come," he says, and a thorny limb severs the ropes with ease. "Be calm, well-treated to you we are."

Rubbing her stiff limbs, Becca leaves the town that is now Liberty District. She doesn't look back, doesn't want anyone to see her silent tears. The Planties have her now and they're gonna murder her real soon.

They're all around her and she has no choice as they herd her into the woods. Everywhere the creaking and snapping as they move, a kind of fluid lope that doesn't resemble true walking. Every now and then, what sunlight reaches through the trees shines straight through the green men and once Becca catches the glimpse of bone in a living fern-man.

"What are you going to do to me?" Becca asks and the Rose Prince says nothing. "If you're going to kill me," she says, "please do it. I can't take any more."

She still has her white rose, clutches it like a lifeline. It's the only possession she has, that and the rags on her back. She remembers her dream and her Ma, happy and pottering in the garden with her roses and bulbs and ferns, and Becca holds that thought, squeezes her eyes shut and dreams for some way out of the living nightmare she is in. Any second now and they will pull her apart like a chicken. She only hopes that it's quick.

For hours they walk. Hours become days. When she can walk no longer, a mossy Planty lifts her up and she sleeps in its grasp. When she wakes, another of the green men puts a small fruit between her bruised lips, and when she bites, it floods her mouth with sweet nectar. Becca becomes numb to everything. They've been walking forever, been walking since the bloody dawn of time, and then finally they stop. Blinking, she looks up.

They are on the edge of the forest overlooking the ruins of a city. The Planty serving as her mount gently lowers her to the ground. Then the Rose Prince is beside her.

"I want you understand," he says. "Look on our work."

She doesn't know the city but can see what it was. A great centre of humanity, skyscrapers and factories and neat blocks of houses at the edges. Now it is broken, the towers falling. Trees have burst through the tarmac and cement. Creepers are slowly pulling down the buildings.

"This is our why," the Rose Prince says.

They go back into the thick woods.

"More time needed," the Rose Prince says through a dead man's lips, and goes as if to say more but he stops.

Hours of nothing numb the terror, exhaustion drags her under. She has dreams but not nice ones. It's of dark days, of the garden aflame, of dead women piled in the street. The men are scared and the kids are worse.

There's nothing but fire and monsters and then Districts where once there were towns and every day someone else is dead and then this isn't even news and no one cares no more. There's no more playing, she's not allowed to leave the house. She doesn't see any of the other girls ever again.

Something got into Pa, something made out of stone, and ate all the love in him. Now he's a stone man with a skin and Becca hears the sounds that her brother makes when Pa hurts him, and thanks God that she's a girl.

More days of wordless travel. They stop again. This time the other green folk withdraw, and it is just her and the Rose Prince in a quiet clearing. It is beautiful in a way she could barely remember, and life is all around her, thick and juicy. There are birds here, and the distant rustle of something that might be a Planty or perhaps a lizard.

"Honest word. I am to kill you," the Planty lord says. "I would have you knowing our why."

Somewhere a bird squawks, and Becca sighs. There is no more terror, just a numbness, an acceptance that she is about to die. She can cry no more.

"Man. We must end Man," he continues. "His ways are not life."

The tongue flaps around in Bubner's dead mouth. The words are becoming difficult. Soon, Bubner will be no good for the talking and the only way the Rose Prince will talk is with another man's death. She shivers.

"We killed the wombs of Man, all of your Women. The spore that spared only the children. And now we win. Man does not trust the croppings. He eating the tins, then each other, then nothing. The world, poisoned against you."

She can see the sunlight shining straight through the Rose Prince. He has that look that old briars had. Thick woody limbs, big ravels of spiderweb. A hundred little critters live in her new husband. *You're a bright child Becca*, Ma always said of her, and Ma was right because she notices the great black spots of rot eating away at the Planty. It hasn't reached any of the flowers yet, but the leaves are beginning to curl up and turn brown.

"You're dying, aren't you?" she asks.

Bubner croaks out *Yes*.

The Planty leans over her and she remembers terror. A thick

rod of green creeper is questing around her crotch and it bristles with sharp thorns. A great red rose has bloomed on its end.

"Man could live on, long time. He doesn't realise of a finish. A choice I offer you."

She can't take her eyes off what must be the Planty's pecker. If he wants to do what most men do, those thorns are gonna rip her insides up. Poor little Becca's heart is pounding ferociously and she thinks she is gonna be sick.

"You carry my child," the Rose Prince says.

This shocks her. How?

"The rose. The beginning of it, now in you."

She puts her hands on her belly and wonders. Will it curl in her womb like a burst seed, with green fibres and shoots and buds? How will it come out of her?

"It is the seed only, I must use you," the Planty says, waving its thorny thing for emphasis. "You will die and not die well."

"Why are you asking me this? Why do you need my permission?" Becca says quietly.

"You are the last Womb and a great honour you do us," the Rose Prince says. "Man will die anyway, but you can make quicker and better. My child in your belly, the last and greatest of our kind."

"But you're gonna kill me," she manages through dry lips.

"Only if you will it. If you would go back to Man, freely you may go."

Becca's head reels. A child in her womb, some alien thing. She could give birth to a messiah, the doom of her people. But more, it is the first time ever that she has been offered choice and freedom.

"I'd like to be alone. I'd like time to decide," she tells him, and without a word the Rose Prince withdraws, swallowed by the garden in moments. She is truly alone, and knows that nothing in his world will dare molest her.

Becca walks.

She wanders the achingly beautiful forests, a world-garden so perfect that it pulses with life. She feels energised, and with most of her terror forgotten she makes plans.

She could never return to Liberty District. She knows her Pa, knows that she would die by his hand. He wouldn't dare lose face in front of that mob. Probably take by force what the Rose Prince asked for, just because his pack of scavengers would expect this.

The other Districts held some promise, but she could not expect much. Even if she walked all the way to some other tribe of scared survivors, the outer guards would share her and tell no one where they hid her body, or drag her trembling before their Nob and he would do it publicly. Nope, she mustn't go there neither.

Another choice then. She could find a forgotten corner, some lost ruin where a shop used to be. She knows from the scavengers that there's plenty such places left.

The only place she comes across has been reclaimed by the green men. She can make out the square edges of cement, what's left of a brick wall being edged apart by creepers pushing through the masonry. There are no tins, no shelter to be had. Just one relentless promise: that all of man's work will come to this.

Tired and hungry beyond caring, she finds a tree growing a thick fruit like a melon. She plucks one, bites into the rind. The juice is thick and good, and if it had a poison, she reckons it was worth dying to eat it, but the fruit is just a fruit and not a weapon bred to tempt flesh-men.

"Why hide in a dirty corner of some District?" she says to herself. "Enough to eat here. Safe enough," and she curls up on some soft grass and rests, one hand resting on her belly.

None of the Planties would ever harm her. Becca had seen the strength, the speed of the Rose Prince. He could have taken her by force back in the clearing, but he didn't. She could live here forever, the rose child dormant within her, an honoured guest in a land of plenty.

She dozes, dreams and dreams again. All of it is the same, confused patterns of the war, the chaos, the descent of good men into butchers and child molesters. Without women, men can only hurt and destroy and Becca knows enough to know that her kind is finished. It could take a long time, but she's lived through it and knows that Man is a cockroach, more a pest than a survivor. Until the last starving human dies, her kind will keep picking through the trash of the old world and it won't have ended.

She wakes and has made her decision.

"I say yes," she calls out to no one in particular.

They hear her all right, and soon the Rose Prince kneels before her. They don't talk any more, there's nothing left worth saying. Then everything hurts, and he is tearing her apart worse than any man could. And then the dying plant-lord is done, and she lies there, a broken wreck of a girl.

As the first rose stem punches out through her stomach and breaks into the most beautiful of flowers, Becca somehow smiles through the pain. When she thinks about her Pa, she doesn't mind dying this way. She lives long enough to see her baby Prince emerge, and never has a child known more love.

GRIEVING THE SPIRIT

JACK DANN

I listened. Of course I listened: that's what I'm paid to do, but it seemed that I was listening to everything, listening to the slight rattle of the window behind me (the weather report had predicted storms for the next few days); listening to the hollow sighing of the ductless air conditioner, and listening to the clock, to the reassuring metronome ticking of my antique grandfather clock which functions as an anxiety-reducing talking point for new patients.

But the immaculately dressed and coiffured patient sitting and scratching on the leather barrel chair beside me was definitely not a new patient, and, frankly, I was at an impasse: she really wasn't a good candidate for CBT therapy.

So why did you take her on?

Because I did. Because I did!

Blame it on the pregnant mummy brain.

I glanced at the hand-painted arched dial of the clock: three-thirty.

"But Doctor Strauss—"

"Melinda, remember?"

"Oh, yes, of course, Melinda," Sondra said, her voice smooth, refined, and somehow condescending. "But I can *feel* one of the demons moving under my skin right now." She pulled up the sleeve of her drape-necked silk dress and extended her arm towards me. "Can you see it?" Her voice instantly changed, lost all its practised mellifluousness. "There, right there; it feels wet. They always feel wet."

I clasped her hand and felt an instant and somehow nauseating shock. Static electricity, I reasoned. But the baby huddled inside me must have felt it too, for she kicked. Hard. It was as if we were both repelled by the contact. I made a mental note, for that had never happened before, then carefully examined Sondra's arm, which was spotted with minor excoriations from scratching. I released her hand and feeling immediate relief, told her (as I had told her in every other session), "No, Sondra. I don't see anything moving. Can *you* see it?"

"No, *I* can't see them. I just feel them moving around like…"

"Like snakes?" I asked, massaging my hand, as if to restore life back into it.

"Yes," Sondra said, sitting back in the chair, her relief obvious. "Exactly. Like snakes."

I listened to the tinnitus sussurating in my ears, hissing like one of Sondra's imagined snakes and asked, "Have you been practising the strategies we discussed?"

She straightened in her chair and nodded. She looked like she had been stunningly beautiful in youth. I remembered seeing a photograph of Kim Novak after her failed plastic surgery, then pushed the image aside. Age had not been kind to Sondra…and probably wouldn't be to me either, for that matter. My arm itched with a numbing, serpent antipathy for Sondra; and I noticed that the assortment of roses in the flute on the side table needed changing.

"And have you kept your appointment with Professor Kim?"

The dermatopathologist.

Sondra didn't respond, which meant *no*. I had noted in her folder the number of specialists—and therapists—she had seen. An educated guess. I figured her for a functional psychotic with a base somatic disorder of delusional parasitosis who presents with a rational affect.

"Okay," I said. "Do you want me to give Professor Kim a call? He might be able to prescribe something else to stop the itching."

"How many times do I have to tell you…Melinda? It's not itching, it's demons. And I'm not depressed, or schizophrenic, or obsessive compulsive. We've established all that; and I'm not taking any more medications. The last magic bullet Kim prescribed made me shake like I had Parkinson's."

I nodded.

"And it didn't do a damn thing to stop the…'itching'," she said sarcastically. "So…no more Kim."

I nodded again, repressing a sigh, then shifted to more productive concerns. "But didn't you tell me last week that you know the demons aren't real?"

"No, Melinda, I think what I told you is that I *tried* to believe they're not real."

"But didn't you also tell me that you've been successful in just thinking them away?"

"Yes, you taught me how to do that, and it does work…sometimes."

"Can you try to do that now? Can you try to think the demons away?"

She gazed vacantly at a botanical print on the wall, then nodded, closed her eyes, and lowered her head. After a moment she jerked awake and, looking disoriented, said, "No!" She extended her arm again. "They won't leave, and *you* know why."

"I know what you've told me before…but I think it's better if you can describe what you told me."

"They came after I killed my baby."

I felt a false labour contraction, a sudden, painful cramp. I nodded to Sondra, trying, forcing myself to give her my full attention.

"But didn't you tell me that you had a miscarriage? That's not murder, Sondra; it's just a terrible circumstance." I realised I was patting my stomach.

Stop that!

Oh, God, let it happen to other people. Not to me. Not to me…

Selfish, narcissistic bitch!

"The miscarriage certainly wasn't your fault," I continued. "You cannot, must not, blame—"

"Yes…it was my fault, Melinda. And you know why that's true."

"I do…?"

"I told you I had an illicit assignation, and you know what happened after that."

I nodded again, reflexively confirming that I accepted what she said without any suggestion of agreement, but my thoughts drifted. Sam was cooking tonight; it would be either bolognaise or paella. I felt the baby moving…Sam's baby kicking determinedly inside me as if she had been listening to this entire session and was prodding me to get rid of this patient. I felt a sick, fluttery sensation in my stomach as if, impossibly, my baby was radiating fear and hatred.

Pregnant mummy brain.

No, just get rid of the patient!

"But that didn't cause the death of your husband," I said, ignoring my foetus's calcitrating invocations, forcing myself to maintain a professional demeanour. "Your husband never knew about that assignation…or the miscarriage. We covered that in an earlier session, remember? Didn't you tell me that you understood that there could be no rational connection between your one-time tryst and your husband's death?"

"Yes, Melinda, I *know* there's no rational connection. But I also feel demons crawling beneath my skin. The man who fucked me—the man who was not my husband—gave me the dead foetus. Gave me the demons. Well, I suppose we both gave me the demons. I know that's not rational, too. But that doesn't make the demons—the goddamn snakes—any less real. How would *you* connect the dots? By telling me they're not real? By telling me there's no correlation between fucking and demons? Telling me that black is white doesn't really help." She looked directly into my eyes; and for an instant I felt that our roles were reversed. I felt that she was in control. That she was someone— or something else.

Get her the fuck out of the room.

Something sly and serpentine was looking at me through those hazel eyes of hers. Narrow eyes that seemed to shift from brown to green to achromatic black. Something was peering out at me as if from behind a dark window, and I gasped inwardly— no intake of breath, no sign of surprise—for I too had learned to look out from behind my own protective window. Professional discipline. I had learned how to radiate warmth. I had learned how to empathise rather than sympathise: the former disguised distance, the latter was simply unprofessional.

The baby kicked again, warning.

The session is almost over.

Another few minutes, then a pee and a latté.

"However, I did see the demons…once," Sondra said.

What? A fresh confession?

"You did?" I asked, surprised.

"Yes, in the blood and viscera I had expelled into the toilet. I saw them swimming in the porcelain bowl. Did you know that all demons are snakes?"

"Only that you have told me that's what you believe."

Sondra's demeanour suddenly changed, brightened. "Well, I'll admit I extrapolated from my own experience…my own experience of reality." She looked away and chuckled.

I felt another cramp, and another: strong, insistent.

"And what about your baby?" Sondra asked.

"My baby…?"

"Oh, I'm sorry, Melinda. In context, that sounded quite untoward." Then Sondra looked at her diamond-inlaid watch and said, "Oh, my, our time is up." She smiled at me, a generous smile suggesting empathy and affection. "But aren't *you* supposed to be the one to say that?"

I returned her smile, forcing it; and as we stood up, I said, "Yes, I suppose that's true."

I felt another cramp. This time it definitely wasn't the baby. No, I was sure this was something else, something slippery and infectious. Something was moving, snaking, tearing its way into my shivering womb.

Something Sondra had been very determined to leave me.

A SENSE OF BELONGING

MARK TOWSE

I'm here because my wife killed my son, and I killed her.

The trail is as beautifully nondescript as any other. Trees gently sway in the autumn breeze, and the fading light creates stretched and ever-changing shadows on the ground. Wildflowers sporadically interrupt the damp greens and browns, providing a burst of colour to an otherwise monotone landscape. Since being a kid, I've been mesmerised by the heady cocktail that woodland offers. Life has always scared me, but nature has never let me down. It's the smell of rotting wood, fallen leaves, and a multitude of other odours that signify dying or death but somehow come together in an arousing earthiness that makes me feel glad to be alive. *Nature's perfume* is what my father used to call it.

My stomach flips as I think back to the innocence of home and the adventures with Dad. We'd just take off, leaving my older sister to be happily spoiled by Grandma, and return a couple of days later full of gusto. At dinner, my sister and I would be in hysterics as Dad jovially recounted his encounters: patches of earth that breathed, gigantic spiders, mysterious songs that played on the breeze. I always caught his indiscreet winks towards Grandpa. Yes, Dad never let the truth get in the way of a good yarn. He changed, though—his moods became frequent and intense, and he started making more solo trips. He used to say his dark cloud was approaching and that he needed to outrun it. I never knew what that meant. One day, he never returned.

Mother died giving birth to me.

But I can't waste time with melancholy and nostalgia. I need to reach the peak.

I pick up my pace. The ground is soft and heavy-going, but I'm well equipped, and I've done this plenty of times before trying to escape my own cloud. In my backpack is a hipflask of whisky. I intend to die out here, but my last days will be comfortable.

As I march, I hear the faint thrum of a helicopter. The police are looking for me.

The hallucination sneaks up. I reach for the nearest tree, my vision becoming tarnished with speckles of crimson like red rain against a camera lens. My eyes squeak like marshy ground as I rub them, praying for normality to return. I count to three and open them, but greens and browns have merged into a familiar pinkish hue, and there she is, naked, stepping out from behind the oak tree, stroking her stomach. She's as beautiful as I remember but as ugly as sin.

A small head pushes against her chest; I see the outline of the mouth and nose. She screams as thick black veins network across her belly. The unfiltered smell of death taints the air as the movements inside her become even more violent, limbs stretching her flesh. She reaches inside and brings the baby out by an ankle. The child swings from left to right, squirming, biting at the air.

"Take it. It's yours," she cries, lobbing the child towards me.

Instinctively I reach out my arms, but the child is gone, and so is my wife. I double over, disoriented, heart thumping. These hallucinations haunt me, take me to the edge of madness and rage. It's a while before my breathing calms. The stench of death fades and woody scents begin to filter through like a dose of smelling salts.

The light is almost gone. This will be as good a place as any to fix the tent.

It takes two attempts, but I get a fire going, just like Dad showed me. He made it look easy; the way he caressed the tinder and gently blew as though breathing the fire himself. We'd sit and stare into the glorious blaze as he told tales of the weird and terrifying. I assemble the tent and scout for more firewood. Taking a minute to listen to the sounds, I think I'm safe from the police for now. Dad tried to teach me another trick that involved slowing the breath and focussing on the land. He told me that if you let yourself merge into the carpet of the forest—truly let yourself go— you would notice things not immediately visible. Occasionally, I claimed to see things just to appease him. But I never did. Today is no different.

I throw two large branches into the flames and reach into my backpack for Dad's hipflask. I examine the intricate etching, remembering his eyes glistening after he'd read the inscription on my gift: *Best Dad in the World*. If only I could be at that dinner table again, watching each crease on his face as he entertained with ridiculous tales. We were so close. Sometimes it felt like we were in sync, the way we'd rub our eyes at the same time or scratch the top of our heads. My fingers rest on the lid of the whisky flask… No, I need to stay sharp.

The hypnotic dance of the warm flames becomes too powerful, and I throw handfuls of dirt on the fire and retire to my sleeping bag. Tomorrow I should reach the mountain peak, and my journey will end. I hope I have the courage to do it before the police find me.

I focus on the sounds of the crickets, the wind through the trees, the occasional distant hoot of an owl. Dad said it was the only music he truly enjoyed. The skylight in the tent allows me a stunning view of the stars, and even with a murder charge hanging over me, they do not disappoint. It doesn't take long for the soporific soundtrack of the woodland to work its magic.

She's writhing in agony, face twisted in pain.

"Make it stop, Jon!" my wife screams, blood on her lips where her teeth have bitten through. She wrestles her panties off. "Help me!"

No signal on my phone. I need to get her to hospital.

"Don't fucking touch me!" she screams as I attempt to scoop her up. Frantically, she fumbles at the buttons of her pyjama top. "Get this fucking thing off!"

Hands shaking, I begin to work at the top as she bucks

and twists on the white sheets. Bloodied saliva foams around her lips as her movements become even more frenzied, her screams impossibly louder. The lights flicker with a *fizz*. The first movement is something I put down to sheer panic, my mind working too fast and playing tricks. But then I see it again—a brief expansion of her chest that looks like a—

The lights go out. We are in darkness.

A high-pitched shriek from my wife makes my stomach churn.

"Rachel," I whimper.

As the lights flicker back on, I see the tiniest of hands— bloody, but well-formed—emerging from her vagina. Her screams continue and I take a step back, blood pounding in my ears, fighting a sudden urge to vomit. *It's pulling itself through the opening.* As the small head forces its way through, I take another step back. He looks at me, eyes fiery red. In that instant, there is an overwhelming connection that I can't explain, a bond that could never be broken. He struggles out of her until he is completely free. There is no crying or screaming. His eyes exude a knowledge—an understanding—that he is right where he is supposed to be.

Rachel gapes at the child in terror and disgust, no signs of happiness for her newborn.

"It's a boy," I say softly.

My son shuffles forward. When he reaches the end of the bed, he jumps down and slinks across the carpet to the wall. Scrambling up the wallpaper, he twists his head around, gazing towards Rachel, his eyes constantly flickering between brown and flaming red, his gums occasionally showing razor-sharp teeth. A gurgling laugh emerges.

"What the fuck is it?"

"Our son," I reply. "Our son, Jack."

The child crawls back down and makes his way towards Rachel. Cowering on the bed, she thrusts herself against the headboard as if trying to drive her way through it.

"Keep it away!"

"Rach, he just wants his mum."

"Keep it away, Jon!"

The child is almost upon her now, a wrinkly arm outstretched.

"He's hungry," I say.

"Jon!"

"It's okay, love. Just give him what he needs."

"Please, no!"

The child stands and takes a step forward, both hands reaching for her. He lets out a series of guttural cries that I know are pleas for acknowledgement, for love. I feel it deep within my heart—the connection—just like with Dad.

She twists her head away as the baby reaches towards her left nipple. "I can't do this!"

Gentle suckling sounds emerge as the child presses its hands against her chest and takes in her sustenance. I'm overwhelmed with the beauty of the moment. There are tears in my eyes.

"Bring me some water," she croaks.

I run down the stairs with excitement, jumping the last three. Over time it will just happen because the mother-child bond is inevitable. I wish Dad were here. He'd be so proud. To think, all the adventures the three of us could have had... I carry a glass to the sink, and then it feels as though the floor is taken from beneath me.

Something is wrong.

I drop the glass. The noise of it breaking is distant, as though on another plane.

Head spinning, I run back upstairs to find Rachel rocking my lifeless son in her arms.

"What did you do?" I whisper.

"I did what was best."

I wake up shaking, drenched in sweat, eyes burning, teeth throbbing. The top of my head feels like it's swarming with fire ants. Aren't dreams supposed to be reserved for fiction, not memories of trauma? Pushing myself through the opening of the tent, I suck in mouthfuls of cool autumn air. The sun's coming up; time to move on. But then I feel an ever-so-slight vibration. I close my eyes and lower myself back to the damp ground.

Beyond the crickets and the morning songs of birds, I hear leaves rustling and the gentle moans of trees. I'm sinking into the soil, becoming part of the forest. From somewhere far away, I hear the trickle of a stream. Now I can feel something gently skipping across the ground, perhaps a deer. Smells pour in beyond those of the moss, pines, and dung. This is what Dad was talking about. It's happening! The bitter scent of forest berries carries on the breeze. It's intoxicating, overwhelming. But the air is getting colder. The light filtering through my eyelids is becoming duller. The vibrations are stronger now. And is that the faint smell of cigarette smoke?

They're coming!

Packing up the tent and destroying any evidence of the fire, I sling the backpack across my shoulders and run. I'm not sure how close they are, but already I feel safer, weaving between the trees. A vivid memory: Dad and me sitting on a couple of rocks at the edge of the mountain, each with a pen and scrap of ripped-out paper from the map we never used.

"What are those?" I asked him as he wrestled two silver containers from his backpack.

"Just write something down, son. From the heart. Your hopes, dreams, fears."

We buried the capsules between the two rocks and made our way home. Something he said on the way back caught me off guard. "When I'm gone, son, if you ever feel alone, I mean completely alone, promise me you'll come here. I'll save you a seat."

The undergrowth is getting thicker and the morning dew glimmers like diamonds. I force my way under low-hanging branches and clamber over large rocks. There's a steep cluster of boulders ahead. I plan my route, inserting fingers into the crevices. The climb takes me sixteen feet from the ground, allowing me to see the top of the mountain, and the terrain that stands between me and death.

"I did what was best," she had said, as though she had put down a dog at the end of a long life. How could she do it? So much hate for our child. I can still see the look of fear in her eyes as I marched towards her. She knew. A small garbled noise left her lips as my hand wrapped around her neck—

Blood pounds in my ears. The top of my head feels like it's on fire, as do my eyes, and every nerve ending feels charged. Dank smells of the forest blow over me as the sounds of flora and fauna begin to amplify once more. As I swallow, the faint but bitter taste of tobacco lodges at the back of my throat.

I take in a slow breath.

Closing my eyes, I feel the pull of the forest and let it take me.

The forest begins to change, losing its purity, being replaced with something more menacing. I recall Dad mentioning it once. *Nature's dark side.* As the breeze takes my mind across the forest carpet, I pass through giant webs and burrows. Crows—the size of eagles—perch on blackened branches and watch with beady eyes. A loud mechanical exhaling surrounds me, and random patches of ground lift like drawbridges, emitting huge clouds of breath, their earthy lids closing shortly after. Footprints. Some human, some not. A cigarette butt squashed into the mud. There's a ringing in my ears that's getting louder, unbearable.

"Hello, friend," a voice announces.

It's shapeshifting; human one second and something else the next, constantly morphing between the two forms. The human face is perhaps fifty years old, greying hair, heavy lines engraved in the forehead. Leathery skin suggests years of sun damage, but it's almost a handsome face; a chiselled jawline, large dark brown eyes. A cigarette hangs loosely from his lips. The other form appears younger—yellow eyes standing out against pallid green skin. Two horns emerge from its forehead, one approximately ten inches long, the other broken. Thin blue lips around the cigarette. The stranger steps out, flickering between the two forms. Legs end in hooves. A large forked tail intermittently darts between tree branches, occasionally coiling around them and shaking down the remaining leaves. In the creature's right hand is a crossbow, in its left, a bolt.

"You were easier to find than your father," he croaks. "You're giving off a lot of energy."

I panic, and in a blink I'm back in the world, perched on the cold rock, looking out towards the trees. The forest remains drenched in dullness.

This man, this *thing*, did he really kill my father? There's urgency in my movement as I push forward. I expect he can feel my anger and fear, but that's fine, I came here to die anyway. There's a bolt of intense pain across my head, and my itchy eyes are crying to be rubbed, but I can't afford to lose any time. The ground is getting wetter and more unstable. Earth moves and rocks tumble as I slowly scale the slope, using branches, grasses, whatever purchase I can find. The top of the mountain is close, but the path is becoming more treacherous. I don't remember coming this way with Dad.

Ahead, mud and grass give way to a sheer rock incline, smooth apart from a speckle of slippery moss. A few feet above, it changes to mud again.

I plant my fingers into the green dampness, but I can't get leverage.

"I'm close, friend," the voice rings in my head.

With weary legs, I try again but lose my footing. I'm afraid to commit, fearing I may slide back down and be unable to stop. I can hear and feel his footsteps, the snap of his tail in the air, the tobacco leaves burning.

I let myself lean against the rock and catch my breath.

A whistling melody floats down from the mountain's summit. Dad always said the forest has its own tune, but this one was his; I remember it well. He would whistle the tune as we walked. Right now, I can't imagine a more beautiful noise.

I weigh up the risks, and finally launch into a scramble up the left side of the slope. Through blind luck, my fingers find a gap in the rock beneath a dense patch of green and I heave myself onto the smallest of platforms.

Behind me, a gentle tapping noise. Glancing over my shoulder, I expect to find my hunter, but scrambling up the mountainside towards me is a giant arachnid. Its shiny black body is at least six feet long, and its head and pincers stand three-feet high. Red eyes are menacingly fixed on me. I freeze, unable to move. It's getting closer, legs navigating the mountain easily and quickly. From above, the tune is calling me, but I'll never make it in time. The spider's approach slows, as though it knows it has me cornered. Its front legs lift from the rock, hairs catching on the breeze.

The spider screams, an ear-piercing and otherworldly shrill, and I swear the mountain vibrates. The spider buckles, starts sliding down, a black bolt protruding from its thorax. Another bolt hits. The spider screams again, loses traction on the rock and silently plummets. I expect the voice in my head even before it comes.

"Your head belongs to me."

Another searing wave of pain explodes across my skull, and I let the mountain take my weight as I tentatively run my palm across the top of my head to find pronounced bumps. I bring my hand down to find my fingers doused in blood.

Urgently, I jump across to the next small platform and keep scaling the mountainside. It's getting easier. Instinctively choosing what I believe to be the better path, I glide from one ledge to the next without hesitation as if I was born to do it. Looking down to see if my hunter is closing in, I notice my left foot is no longer human, but a hoof — it's a disorienting image that forces me back against the damp rock, clinging desperately to what little grip it offers. Another wave of pain explodes across the entire front section of my head, causing me to lose my balance. I'm slipping.

"Too easy, Jon."

I fall. As I flail and kick, the mountain passes by in a blur of greens and greys, but now it's my life passing in front of me. The pain in my head is unbearable, as though my skull is going to shatter. I close my eyes and pray for it to be quick.

My fall is broken with a jolt. Somehow, my two hooves are perched precariously on a thick branch protruding from the rock. Now I'm racing towards the peak once again and I'm fast, elegant, dancing across mud and rock. The whistling is getting louder. Finally, I haul myself onto solid ground and take a mouthful of air.

The burning sensation in my eyes intensifies and the top of my head feels like it's ripping in two. I scramble towards the two rocks in the distance, haunted by an image of Dad standing near the mountain edge, whistling his tune. Gently placing the backpack down, I retrieve the small hand-shovel from the outside pocket. The first layers of damp earth come away easily, but it quickly becomes heavy-going and more resistant. Come on! Vibrations rattle up my arm, and my fingers are on fire as I work the shovel over and over. What the—

Bones crackle in my hands as they begin to twist and stretch out of shape. I'm unable to contain a scream as a fountain of blood sprays across the rocks, sharp claws shooting out from my fingertips. In searing pain, I force the claws to scrape desperately at the earth. There—a glimmer of dull silver! Desperately, I wrap my fingers around the neck of the container and heave it out. The lump in my throat is instant as I twist off the top.

Dad. I wish you didn't feel like you had to get away from us.

Tears sting my eyes as I return the paper to the capsule.

"I smell you. Your scent is like your father's," the voice whispers in my head as I begin to dig again.

Nerve endings sing, and more bones crack as my body is sent into an agonising series of spasms. I feel my spine extending and twisting, pain echoing through me with each contortion. Part of me wants to give up and throw myself over the edge, but I carry on, digging at the adjacent patch of dirt. Found it! *Two* notes are coiled inside this capsule. Dad must have come back.

His handwriting across the familiar yellowing patch of the section of map: *Son. It's never about getting away from you. One day you'll understand but, in the meantime, you must take for granted that I love you with all my heart and always will.*

The other note is written on a piece of newspaper, dated years after our last trip:

I've always tried to protect you, to give you a normal life, but the truth is we're not normal; we are half-breeds, demons layered with human emotions. I raised you as human to keep you under the radar, passing on the skills your grandpa taught me to keep the demon form at bay.

For centuries, the male has been born this way. Some mothers have been able to adapt, to love—like Grandma—but others like yours couldn't even bear the touch of their child. She took her own life, Jon, only minutes after you were born.

Being human is a trial. I've suppressed my urges for so long and recently they've started to spill over. I've been weak, slipping in and out of the dark world to satiate my instincts. Humans can't see us until it's too late to escape—they have no window into the dark world. I planned to tell you all of this when you came of age, but I fear I may not make it back this time. A half-breed like us has found me, sniffing out my trail of rage and hate. He's been promised immunity if he eliminates any that are not true descendants of evil. We walk a fine line between these two worlds, son.

I hope you understand and that you can forgive me.

I must go. I can smell him.

Dad xx

My fingers tremble as I turn over the piece of newspaper. The headline: *Four more hikers go missing in the mountains.*

Shaking uncontrollably, I let out a howl that carries over the woodlands. I hear things shrinking back into the flora, whispers fading into the distance, and for the first time in my life, I feel in control. I stand eight feet tall at least, my body muscled and scaly.

It's time to do what I came here to do.

I claw at the earth, throwing handfuls to the side until the hole is deep. The hunter is close; the taste of tobacco in my mouth is getting stronger.

I reach inside the backpack. Momentarily, I think about moving some of the wrapped blanket aside to take one last look at my dead son but instead carefully and quickly lower him into the hole and place the capsules on top.

"We're all here now, Dad. The three of us. Our only adventure together, it turns out."

The tail feels like cold steel as it whips against my cheek. Even before I can raise a hand to the burning wound, it comes at me again, slicing deep into my thigh, forcing a shriek of raw agony. Relentlessly, the tail sweeps across once more. This time I manage to snap it out of the air and sink my teeth into it. With a short and inhuman cry, it's whipped away. The first pale hand reaches over the mountain's edge, fingernails as sharp as knives feeling their way across the earth for a secure spot, and then my hunter hoists himself up.

Suddenly, my jaw gives out a series of cracks. Pain rips across my gums and the inside of my cheeks, leaving the bitter taste of blood. Running my tongue across the sharpness of my new teeth creates a spark of adrenaline and, working my hooves into the ground, I launch myself at the hunter. We land on the ground in a tumbling heap, him on top, claws scraping against each other's toughened hides.

"Do you know how many like you I've killed?" the demon-hunter yells, placing his hands around my neck. I fight back, yet his skin is like armour, covered in layers of impenetrable scar tissue. "You're weak, just like your father," he yells, spittle spraying across my face, sizzling on my skin.

His yellow eyes glow even brighter and the veins in his arms pop with ferocity. I try to pull his hands away from my throat. He's too strong.

To the right, I see my father sitting on one of the rocks, his words echoing in my head. "I'll save you a seat."

My hunter's thin blue lips curl into a smile, revealing layers of pin-like teeth, some broken, others with small bits of flesh hanging from them. More acid-like saliva spills across my face.

"Even your whore mother couldn't bear the sight of you," he spits.

I rip at his eyes, but they are deceivingly hard, as impervious as glass. He squeezes my throat even tighter. Blood pumps violently in my ears. The pressure in my chest becomes unbearable.

"I'll look in on your filthy human sister for you," he says.

The huge rock that crashes against my hunter's back sends him tumbling towards the edge of the mountain. The rock thrown by Dad; who else could be up here? The hunter plants his claws down just in time as the rest of him disappears over the side, tail whipping angrily above. I gulp air and force myself to my feet. His face is twisted in anger as he pulls himself back onto level ground and charges.

We lock halfway, a violent frenzy of teeth and claws. This time,

I draw blood as my claws penetrate his arms and chest. Surprise registers in his eyes, perhaps a little fear, and I feed hungrily on the short moans he provides. My new body no longer feels cumbersome and strange, just incredibly powerful. We trade blows. While blood flows and bones break, it no longer feels like a one-sided battle.

I don't see the tail coming but feel the rush of air behind and the snap of its coldness around my neck. He lifts me from the ground and slams me down with a tremendous roar. An explosion of pain shoots down my right-hand side. I flip myself onto my back in time to see the hoof approaching. He stamps my face. Sharp agony. My nose crumbles, my skull driven into the damp ground.

"And what do we have here?"

Helpless, all I can do is listen to the footsteps as he walks towards the hole. I try and push myself up, but the pain is crippling, and I only manage to raise my head. The hunter is a blur as he crouches towards my son's open grave.

"No, please, no," I whisper.

Then I hear it. The unmistakable cry of my son floods the mountain and I know he's still pleading for his mother's love. The cries are raw and getting louder, approaching an ear-piercing crescendo that rattles trees and sends rocks toppling down the hillside. The hunter covers his ears and drops to his knees, begging for it to stop. The ground shakes violently. My son's grave opens up. The hunter lets out a blood-curdling cry as he disappears into the soil as if swallowed by the mountain.

I drag myself towards the crater, the hunter's muffled cries dampening as I draw closer. Reaching out for the rim, I lunge forward over the edge of the hole. I'm just in time to see his yellow eyes sinking into oblivion. My dead son's small hand is clamped across the hunter's mouth. Finally, I let myself collapse into the mud and sink into my own blackness.

I'm not sure how long I've been out, but the hole is now filled, completely level as though never disturbed. Sunlight bounces off fresh puddles of rain. If it weren't for the pain, I would put it all down to a dream. As the cold breeze wraps around me, I know even before I look towards my feet that I am back to human form. For validation, I run my fingers over the small bumps in my head. Hauling myself up, I reach inside the backpack for the whisky.

"To my father and son," I say, lifting the flask high. Then I drink.

Once again, I remember all those stories my father told, tales of beasts and devils that perished at his hands. Nobody will get to hear mine. I head to the edge of the mountaintop and look down at the trees and jagged rocks so far below. I extend one leg and, hovering my foot over the brink, I close my eyes. After the count of three, it'll all be over.

Three.

The sound of crickets gives way to the distant creak of trees and the approach of many boots shuffling across the forest floor.

Two.

There's a faint bark of a dog, more footsteps, voices. Police?

One…

Definitely human. I can smell them now. Sunlight disappears. My eyes begin to burn. The top of my head begins to itch. Smiling, I step back from the edge.

GRAVID

J.M. MERRYT

A nameless village sits on the long road between thought and memory. Its inhabitants live in thatched cottages and cobblestone streets, garbed in the faux-medieval finery endemic to American medieval festivals. This is the quintessential fairy-tale village, from where Red Riding Hood hails, and where a certain group of children *Played Slaughter With Each Other*. This story is not a fairy tale, but it does have fairies in it.

They are, perhaps, not the sort you are thinking of.

Next, consider our protagonist, a woman generally known as Alodie. Alodie had one defining trait: she wanted what she could not have. However, should she get what she craved, she would soon lose all interest in it. No matter if that thing was a flower, a jewel or a man, she always coveted the unobtainable and scorned what was achievable. She would sit on a picnic rug under an ocean of stars, the northern lights glittering before her, and fixate on the moon. She would demand her lover go fetch it, utterly serious, and should he do so, she would spurn her heart's desire, moving onto something new and better.

Perhaps, in another time and another place, this trait would impress a recruiter and maybe get her a job in real estate or finance. This is not that time or place. Although this is not a fairy tale, it is a story, so certain narrative rules apply, such as the law of inverse fertility: when Alodie's married sister had a child, Alodie found herself desiring the same.

Alodie and her husband tried to fall pregnant for months and months but to no avail. Eventually, she heeded the village rumours, rampant in a town where everyone is at least distantly related. There were whispers of a witch who lived at the village's edge.

The witch was a young sprightly thing with old eyes. She was a changeling child, older than the village and the hills that cupped their small community. Let's call her Zanna. Zanna examined Alodie at length, asking questions, muttering to herself in a tongue beyond human comprehension.

Eventually, Zanna said, "You cannot have a child. No matter how much you try."

Alodie wept, yet this denial sharpened her want further still, and she begged to know if there was any truth to the talk about Zanna. "Aren't you of the Fey?" she said. "Isn't there some eldritch magic that could cure me?"

Zanna leant forward in her chair, face resting on the tips of her fingers. They observed each other for a long moment, across the gulf of an old wooden table in Zanna's tiny cottage, musky with the mingling scents of medicinal herbs and burning peat. Both were pretty standard for any hut in this village. Stranger still was how the walls were simultaneously too wide and too narrow, the ceilings impossibly tall for such a low building. It was the sort of place that did not obey rules of Euclidian geometry.

Zanna said, "I came here a hundred years ago from a mound beyond the village. A *sidhe* near a road where unwanted children are left to die. Some of those children are sickly. Others are left because their mothers can ill afford to keep them. Why not look for a child there?"

Alodie grimaced. Faeries lived in that mound, that was common knowledge. They were a dying race, desperate to shore up their numbers with human children abducted from cots and cradles. It was only fair, the villagers reasoned, that their own unwanted children should be left for the Faeries.

"No," Alodie said. "I want my baby, not someone else's."

Zanna's face twisted, unreadable. "Go there at dusk and maybe you'll get your wish."

Dissatisfied, Alodie thanked Zanna and made for the *sidhe*. It took hours to find that deserted place, the road rough with disuse. Alodie found it at dusk. She paused and listened to a voice carrying on the wind. Soon, she came upon a woman crying and digging out a niche in a mound of leaves. In it, she placed a small shape, swaddled in flax. She pressed the flat of an iron poker to the child's face, branding it. The child screamed, writhing.

Heedless, the woman begged, "Give me back my baby!"

Typically, if a human child was spirited away, the Fey would return it if the changeling was threatened. Nothing happened.

The woman threw her hands up and shrieked, dropping the poker. "Fine! Stay here, for all I care!" She walked off, back to the village.

Alodie waited for a handful of minutes, before stealing over to the child. Save for the burn, it looked like a normal human infant, and Alodie thought, "Why not?" She nudged away the poker with one foot and bent to retrieve the child.

"Taking what's not yours?" a voice said, soft and dry.

Alodie straightened up, her back giving a warning creak. A tall man stood in front of her, a nose-length away. His clothes were strange, not the sort of thing you'd see in the village, and Alodie wondered if he were Fey.

"I want a child, and no one wants him. He's mine now."

The man raised one eyebrow and said, "Well, in exchange for this truly astounding act of charity, may I offer you a gift?" With a sweep of one arm, he pulled a thin pamphlet out of nowhere at all. He proffered it to Alodie.

Taking the pamphlet, Alodie nodded and tucked it into the child's swaddling. She strode off, and the man called, "Good luck!"

Alodie ignored him.

Presented with the Faerie child, Zanna peered at the burn and said, "He will heal, but there will be a scar. An unusual choice."

She gave Alodie a sharp look, questioning, and Alodie avoided her gaze. Zanna did not mention that the child was soft and floppy, even though it drew breath, that it did not smell like a living child. Similarly, Alodie's husband did not question the sudden arrival of a two-month-old baby, knowing by now not to question his wife's whims. He left, silent, and returned with a cot and enough cloth to fashion into fresh swaddling.

Later, when the child was asleep in its cradle, Alodie sat beside the fire and flicked through the pamphlet. It was bereft of text, featuring a series of woodcut prints. The etchings were grotesque. The worst image was of a Faerie woman, tall and graceful from the front, her back hollow and pitted. From the holes in her back bulged a dozen faces, all of them identical to that of Alodie's stolen child.

The baby twisted and writhed in its cradle, strange and silent. It spurned milk-soaked rags. When presented with a wet nurse, it gnawed off her breast, preferring blood. Soon, the other villagers came to curse the child's existence. Alodie soon decided that she must hide it.

Alodie had a plan. She pestered and begged her husband and Zanna for help.

Reluctant, Zanna took a length of twine and an awl. Using the pamphlet as a guide, she stitched the baby to Alodie's back. The child squirmed. Alodie's spine and ribs cracked, caving in to accommodate the child. A pit formed in her back; a place for the child to grow.

Alodie hid her child under her dress and she thanked Zanna. The villagers did not question the child's abrupt disappearance. Grateful, they assumed Alodie must have left it on the road near the Faerie mound.

Every day, the child grew. It became heavier and larger with every passing hour, dragging Alodie over backwards. Alodie demanded her husband's affections, and Alodie soon became pregnant. More pits formed in her back, more children grew between her ribs and nestled against her spine. The first child turned its hunger inwards, and Alodie grew thinner and paler, her hair falling out, her eyes large and glassy. Her skin went green and slimy, her fingers webbed.

The abandoned child's mother soon came to Alodie's door. Her name was Twyla. She was young, no older than sixteen, and said, "I deserted a fell child, and I suspect you know what became of him. Please let me in."

Alodie stepped back from the door.

Entering the house, eyes wide, Twyla regarded Alodie's spine-bending posture—a nightmare pose usually only achievable by the most twisty of contortionists. Alodie went to lay on her side on a mattress of thick straw. Twyla sat in a rough wooden chair and folded her hands in her lap.

Alodie said nothing, only able to let out harsh, grating breaths.

Twyla went on to say, "I left him out there for a reason. Not because he was a Faerie child—that would be expected, considering who his father was."

"Then why?" Alodie managed, gasping.

"He was stillborn, and inside the womb, he ate his own sister." Twyla's eyes glistened, her mouth twisting in an attempt to stave off tears. "He was a shroud eater—a corpse that devours the dead. I only hope you can cut ties with him before he devours you too."

Twyla stood. Her footsteps faded. The door closed. Panting, Alodie crept towards a sheet of mirrored glass affixed to the wall. Painfully, she pulled up the back of her dress and peered at the heads jutting from the rotten flesh of her back. Doomed, she wept.

So, a nameless village sits on the long road between thought and memory. Its inhabitants live in thatched cottages and cobblestone streets, garbed in the faux-medieval finery endemic to American medieval festivals. The quintessential fairy-tale village, from where Red Riding Hood hails, and where a certain group of children *Played Slaughter With Each Other*. This story was not a fairy tale, but like I promised, it did have fairies in it.

MOTHERDOLL

H.K. STUBBS

"**I** can't take this. I can't take it anymore. She won't stop howling," I cried into the phone. Then I lost the line. "Blake, are you there?"

He was gone. Cut off. The line hummed, leaving me alone in our messy loungeroom, while down the hallway, Phoebe grizzled in her cot.

I threw myself back onto the couch and covered my eyes with my arm to block out the bright white light and walls. My breasts throbbed, tender and swollen with milk. My nipples, so raw that even soft textures abraded like sandpaper, grated against my bra.

Phoebe's cries intensified. I opened my eyes and sighed. The bookshelves gathered dust above the couch's crocheted throw-cover.

I had to go to her, comfort her, but I didn't want to. She'd been crying all day. I took a deep breath and dredged up the energy to haul myself off the couch, then trudged towards her room.

Coming out of the rain, Blake stomped and swore through the front door two hours later.

"Shh, don't wake Phoebe," I said. "She only settled ten minutes ago."

He wrestled a large doll-like thing over the threshold. A chill gust rushed in with him, spraying icy droplets on my face. I shivered. He propped the thing against a wall to pull the door closed. His computer bag hung over his chest and a sodden takeaway bag dangled from the crook of his elbow. Once, I would have kissed him and handed him a glass of wine.

Blake's new purchase, wrapped in plastic, slid sideways down the wall. It thumped onto the floor. He watched for my reaction, his wet fringe and drop-speckled glasses obscuring his eyes.

I'd said I didn't want one *just yesterday*.

"Should've seen how people looked at me on the train." He laughed. "Like I'd bundled up my grandma and was dragging her corpse around. She's not that heavy, though."

Maybe the train passengers shared my dread of the uncanny valley.

"It is pretty *Bad Boy Bubby*," I said.

He squatted, grabbed it by the hair and dragged it to the loungeroom. I winced, rubbed my head. It would hurt to be dragged like that. If you had feelings.

"Maybe we don't need to open it yet," I said, leaning against the doorframe.

"Huh?" He scrabbled in a drawer for scissors. "Ah." He held them up, triumphant, and snipped the air.

Like a kid on Christmas day, he knelt over the thing on the Persian rug. He pierced the thin plastic and slid the blade through the wrapper.

Free of its cocoon, the doll looked like a squashed mannequin with flesh-coloured face, hands and feet, but grey-cloth limbs and torso. Fabric joined to plastic seamlessly at the wrists, ankles and neck. The body was stiff, its face turned away from me.

Blake frowned over some instructions and gave it three hard thumps on the chest. The limbs twitched. The body jolted, inflating. It seemed to transform with that intake of air from a synthetic to a solid *human*-type thing. I pressed my belly, faintly queasy.

"It'll take a little while for her shape to fill out and her awareness to come in," Blake said. "They pack 'em tight in transit. She'll grow, they reckon. Develop into exactly what we need." He shrugged. "I guess it'll be okay here, lying on the rug."

I sat on the edge of the couch, biting my thumbnail.

Its face was still twisted to the side, away from me. Its hair was curly and coarse, tinged with grey, almost grandmotherly. It smelled of plastic. A bit burnt. Blake walked to the bedroom to change, leaving me to contemplate the thing in its grey undergarments.

"It'll grow," I said. "Great."

I shook my head. Blake was adding another layer of complexity to our lives. He loved to start new projects and try new things — for about a week. Then it fell to me to clean up the glue dried on the table, dispose of the remnants, take out the kitty litter, feed the fish...because I had nothing better to do? No. I had plenty to do with working from home and taking care of Phoebe. I had to stop letting our home become the cumulative trash-pile of his new ideas.

Phoebe's wail broke the quiet.

"I'll go," I muttered, thinking he wouldn't hear anyway.

"No, Kelly," said Blake, emerging from the bedroom, palm raised. "It's my turn."

He pulled his t-shirt down to cover his stomach. The raindrops on his glasses were smeared and misty. He hoisted the motherdoll with two hands. She moved a little at the waist and her knees bent, but he still had to drag her. As he pulled her around the corner to the hallway, her eyes turned to sneak a look at me.

Hairs pricked up along the back of my neck, then she was out of sight.

I stood, shoulders stooped, hands on my hips, surveying the cups and plates on the coffee table and bookshelves. A bunny rug had fallen beside the couch, yellowed milk staining the corner of the crocheted blanket.

Blake hadn't wasted any time. Hadn't even waited for it to wake up properly. If Phoebe took to the motherdoll, how much work would Blake be doing to care for our child? How much would *it* be doing? These thoughts rubbed me the wrong way, as desperate for a break as I was. *Why did we have a kid at all if we were going to outsource parenting?*

Phoebe's scream sharpened and I laughed. So, she didn't think much of the motherdoll either. Good. We could get rid of it.

She hushed. Went so quiet that I crept to the door, placed my fingers on the frame where the paint was developing tiny cracks, and peered into the dimly lit room...

"You can't do that!" I screamed.

I ran in, pulling Phoebe away from the motherdoll's breast, which was exposed from beneath a Velcro flap. The motherdoll lolled, half upright in my feeding chair, breast dangling and spraying milk. Her boob began to retract into her chest. Her shirt closed and the Velcro pressed itself back into place.

"But that's what the motherdoll is *for*," Blake said, throwing up his hands.

Circles of wetness formed on my shirt as my breasts let down and began to leak. "No! She's never had any milk but mine."

I grabbed the doll's wrist and yanked it out of my chair onto the floor. Phoebe cried again. I lifted my shirt and pressed her against my raw nipple.

"It's just sick," I hissed. "Who knows what chemicals they put in synthetic breast milk. This is how you help, by passing the buck?"

"I just wanted—"

"Get it out of here!"

The motherdoll blinked. When he pulled it upright, it had a little more control, stood on its feet and looked at me.

"You get out of here too," I muttered.

"Sorry," the motherdoll said, slurring its words from a slack jaw. "I can take some...adjustment."

I drew back. I didn't know what to say. Was I going to *apologise* to this thing? Blake glared at me, then led it away, supporting it as it took slow steps.

He came back alone and glared at me.

"Yeah, Kell'. How dare I buy something to help." His lips were drawn back. "Of course, it's much better if we spend all of our time fretting over our screaming child. And fighting. Of course it is."

I woke to quiet for the first time I could remember, and refreshed from a full night of sleep. I hadn't had one since her birth two months ago. Phoebe hadn't cried in the night, but she should have woken for a feed. Maybe she'd reached that mythical milestone of *sleeping through*.

I stretched and stepped out of my bedroom into the hallway. Sunshine streamed onto wooden floorboards. Phoebe lay on a bunny rug in the golden light, kicking at the air.

"I was just making you a coffee," the motherdoll said sweetly from the kitchen, standing in a pair of my jeans. My favourite shirt suited her: orange tie-dye with embroidered sleeves and collar, handmade in Thailand. She looked like a groovy older mum. Had Blake given that to her? Thanks again, Blake.

"I'm fine," I said. "I should change her nappy."

"Done," she said.

"Well, she must be due for a feed."

"I gave her a bottle from the freezer. Coffee?"

That was why my breasts were full to bursting. "I don't drink coffee, not while I'm feeding," I said.

"You don't have to feed her anymore."

"Oh, but I—" *...love to feed her.*

"Looks like you've leaked."

She pointed down at my pants. Blood had soaked though and dried in an oval on the front of my pyjamas. I thought I'd stopped post-natal bleeding. Could it be my period, back already?

"Have a shower," she said. "I can watch Phoebe."

I didn't want to leave my baby with this stranger. Too late. That scoop had already been snatched.

"How long has she been up?" I asked.

"Since Blake left at six. She's almost ready for her nap."

"She usually doesn't go down until nine."

"But she fights it, I bet. I can detect early signs of tiredness. She'll go down without a fuss if I place her in her cot now."

I wanted to argue. Anger simmered within. "Fine," I said. "I'll do it."

Phoebe started to cry.

"Tsk. We've left it too late, already. I can take her. My calming micro-vibrations assist infants to settle. I can also adjust my pheromone synthesisers and the temperature of my—"

"I'm *fine*." I forced a smile and picked up Phoebe. "Shh, little darling."

I lifted my shirt and put her to my breast.

"You shouldn't feed her now—"

"Thanks."

I marched into Phoebe's room, closing the door behind me, and sat in the chair, riled. This motherdoll thing was a disaster. Sure, an occasional sleep-in was nice, but couldn't Blake have given me that himself? I messaged him.

ME: You have to take it back.

BLAKE: I signed a contract for a two-week trial. As soon as it wakes it starts to learn about the family. Give it a chance to adjust.

Two weeks. It might adjust to us, but I was never going to adjust to it.

When I finally left Phoebe's room, the motherdoll smiled at me from the loungeroom.

"I've made you breakfast," it said.

"I like to make my own."

"You're very independent," it said. "Just take a look first."

On the table, a freshly-made plate of breakfast with mushrooms on the side. I never cooked anything so impressive. The eggs fried to crispness on their golden edges. Hot toast spread with butter, not too much. The avocado perfectly ripe, no blemishes (where did she even find that?). The coffee steamed. I sipped its sweet warmth. Delicious. What a waste not to enjoy this. The motherdoll smiled as it turned away. *One to you, then,* I conceded.

"Thank you," I begrudged.

Tuesday is my one night out of the house, when I leave the screaming Phoebe with Blake and go to yoga. I arrived home to find the motherdoll breastfeeding her in my chair. She stood and offered Phoebe to me.

"It was the only way she'd settle," she said. "It seemed cruel to withhold comfort. I didn't release any milk, though."

I didn't like it. But what could I do?

I sat in the chair. She left, closed the door behind her. Phoebe was quiet, half asleep, wouldn't take my turgid breast. I'd have to express later. Or sooner. The top of my breast burned a little, but at least the scabs around my nipple were healing.

From the lounge room, conversation and quiet laughter floated in.

I jerked forward as jealousy flared. Phoebe shifted in my arms, moaned a tiny protest. What did this *motherdoll* and *my husband* have to laugh about? My fury drowned under a wave of mourning as I tried to recall the last time that Blake and I had shared a laugh. Or even a kind word. An embrace.

I placed Phoebe in her cot but didn't want to leave her room. I tapped the nursery mobile over her bed, sending butterflies spinning. My heart gaped with a Blake-shaped hole. Not because he was *gone* but because he made no effort to listen to or help me...though he *had* tried to help, hadn't he? By bringing home that thing. What was I afraid of?

It just didn't feel right to have another...but she *wasn't* a woman.

No, it just didn't feel right.

I woke stiff and uncomfortable in Phoebe's chair. Someone had covered me with a blanket and taken the baby from her cot. I got up, staggered out.

In the kitchen, the motherdoll cradled Phoebe in one arm as Blake ate porridge at the counter. He noticed me.

"Hey, sweetie. Sleep well?" he asked, and sipped coffee from a baby-blue mug.

"Not really," I mumbled, feeling tired, lethargic, like my blood was thick with oil.

The motherdoll gave a smug smile and brought Phoebe to me, then walked down the hallway. I held Phoebe close. She was all warmth and love. I was ice.

"You have to choose," I said. "That thing or me."

Blake laughed. "Well, she makes a mean porridge."

"Not funny."

"Kelly, you're my wife. The motherdoll's just a robot. Your helper."

"It's taking over," I said.

"No, it's the help that we need. Two weeks, we decided. Remember? I have to go to work." He stood. "We're lucky we can afford it. Try to get used to her. For my sake."

Staring out the window at mothers walking their children to school in raincoats, I wondered how they did it. How they survived. A little girl stomped in puddles in her black school shoes, and her mother frowned and pointed at the wet hem of her dress. My head felt heavy and my limbs sluggish. Was I getting sick? I drank a coffee, despite breastfeeding soon, in the hope that it would wake me up. It didn't.

Phoebe's screams drew me to her cot.

"Mummy's here," I said, lifting her out, holding her to my chest.

Still she shrieked.

"Shh, darling. Shh. Was it a bad dream?"

I carried her out to the loungeroom, her face red and mouth wailing wide, revealing her pearly gums and the dark abyss of her misery. I held her as she cried. Nothing would distract her. A sharp pain in my belly almost bent me over. I ran her to her cot where she cried harder as I raced to the toilet, just in time to sit down before my bowels let loose. As I pulled the toilet paper from the roll, her crying stopped abruptly. I washed my hands hurriedly and returned to find her in the motherdoll's arms, cooing happily.

"How did you stop her crying?" I asked, buttoning up my jeans.

She smiled. "I have several systems designed to calm and cheer an infant."

I was curious but another urge to use the bathroom stabbed

my abdomen. This time on the toilet, the brown was tinged with red. What was going on with me? Cancer? A woozy wave rolled through my head as I stood. The scent of lavender and pine that perfumed the bathroom cloyed, overwhelming. I grabbed the sink for stability, washed my hands and staggered back to the loungeroom.

"I'm not feeling well," I said, near to collapsing onto the couch.

"You poor thing," said the motherdoll, eyebrows raised. "Go and have a lie down in bed."

"I'd better. Will you be alright with Phoebe?"

She smiled. "Of course. It's what I'm made for."

I crawled into bed but couldn't settle, too cold beneath the sheet and too hot under the blankets. My belly ached, bent me double. I almost fell asleep until a sharp pain saw me running to the toilet again. Back in bed, covers pulled up to my chin, I heard the motherdoll singing to Phoebe. Phoebe's jewellery box was wound up and played *Twinkle Twinkle* over and over. I wished it would stop, but I heard Phoebe cooing and laughing.

Drifting in and out of consciousness, my belly settled then stabbed with pain again, then it passed. I must have slept.

When I woke and emerged from my room, the evening had settled in. All the lights were off and the house was chill. Blake wasn't yet home. Had my sudden illness had anything to do with the motherdoll's breakfast? Surely not. There was an edge to the silence and I found myself tiptoeing.

"Hello?" I whispered, walking through to the loungeroom.

"Phoebe's sleeping," the motherdoll said, and I jumped and turned to face her, where she sat in a chair.

"You scared me to death. Why are you sitting in the dark?"

"I don't need the light. No need to waste electricity."

"What do you do when you're not working?" I asked.

"I power down my activity-set and reassign my processing capacity to DollCorp's administrative tasks. I'm very efficient. Much more suited to caring for an infant than a human. This frees you to do whatever you like."

"I *like* to care for my child."

She smiled. "It would be lovely if you accepted me. This

afternoon, you needed me. What would you have done without me here?"

"I would have lain next to Phoebe's cot. Kept my eye on her."

"While sick? It doesn't sound very responsible. Isn't that selfish?"

Her accusation shifted uncomfortably, squirming with accuracy like a twitching bullseye. The sensation shifted lower into my troubled bowels.

"It's a pity we couldn't get along," she said. "I hoped you'd give me a name."

"A name?" It was an endearing request. I searched my mind for names for her. *Bitch, Imposter,* and *Baby-Thief* wouldn't do.

I had to run for the bathroom again. Bad things were happening inside me. Was it a burst appendix? I made it to the loo just in time, again, as more than shit poured out of me. The slithering cascade from my body filled me with dread, made my temples burn in panic. I was losing too much. Losing fluid and... it felt like...*flesh.*

A miscarriage? Not possible. Blake and I hadn't had sex.

It took me a moment, eyes closed, to gather the courage to turn and look. The porcelain bowl was splashed with red drops, the water red like blood soup. Beneath dark clots, flesh tubing twitched and shone white in sections. It was a long ribbon of me. But what—my intestines? I stood up, feeling lighter and strangely better. I swallowed, sure I had to keep this a secret. I couldn't go to hospital now. Could I? No, maybe later. Blake wouldn't believe me unless he saw it, so I left it in the toilet. At least the pain was gone and I seemed fine.

I ran a hand through my hair and a hefty chunk came out in my hand. No! God, not my hair! Was this cancer? Was it a nightmare? Scared and confused, I laughed and looked at the hair in my hand, the tuft smeared with blood. I should do something, but I felt...high, lightheaded. My hair looked greyer than I remembered, but these last months had been hard. Little surprise I was falling apart.

I dragged a chair to the window, wooden legs scratching over the floor in a way I used to hate, but now I didn't care.

Come home soon, Blake, I thought, watching the street, hugging my knees. I could call him... What was his number? My head listed to one side, forehead against the window. Down the hallway, the toilet flushed.

"**B**lake?"

Moonlight shone. I hadn't woken when he'd arrived, but I was awake now.

"It's the middle of the night," he muttered. "Go back to sleep."

"The motherdoll...it's done something to me. In the avocado. I'm falling apart."

"You've been falling apart since we had Phoebe." He groaned. "Oh, shit, I'm sorry, I didn't mean that. I'm tired."

"Seriously, Blake, it's killing me."

"It can't do that," he said, leaning up on his elbow. "It only *cares* for its family. Protects them."

I pictured the way she'd looked at me, eyebrows raised, without compassion. Not at all like the way she looked at Blake and Phoebe.

"But what if it classes me as *outside* the family?"

"I don't ...oh, God...it can't do that." He rubbed his face and lay back down, rolled away.

"I was so sick. I shat out a litre of blood and half my insides. My intestines. We have to get rid of it. Now. Tonight."

"Cally told me you were sick. That she looked after Phoebe all day."

"Kelly?"

"That's what she wanted me to call her."

"But that's *my* name."

"No, it's spelt with a C and an A."

"Blake, we have to get rid of the motherdoll."

"Let's sleep on it." He dozed off, snoring seconds later.

I couldn't sleep. I had to *do* something. Rising from my bed, unsteady on my feet, I forced my legs to move, taking only small steps in the dark and quiet of the house. Shuffling, I made it to Phoebe's room. Her door was closed. We never closed it. I tried the handle and found it locked.

No—this wasn't right. I tugged at the handle again, rougher, fighting the door, trying to shove it open, making a racket that might wake her, but I didn't care. I had to get in. I shoved at the door with my shoulder. Rammed and kicked until the frame gave way, wood ripping from the doorway, spitting splinters onto the floor.

Phoebe lay happily in her cot, big eyes open, as coloured lights spun around the room, cast by a new nightlight. My momentum carried me crashing into the far wall.

I opened my eyes. Someone was singing and Phoebe was laughing, somewhere else in the house. I lay in the wreckage of the splintered door.

"It went crazy last night, smashed its way into our baby's room," someone said. It sounded just like my voice. She came and stood in the damaged doorway, talking on the phone, looking down at me. "Auto-shutdown. Yes, that seems to have triggered... You can pick it up today? That's a relief. We're lucky it didn't hurt her. We refuse to have it in the house any longer... Free trial of another model? Not another motherdoll... Oh, really? That sounds interesting." She walked away.

Only my eyes were able to move. What had happened to me? Why couldn't I get up?

I beg Blake with my eyes as he and Cally/Kelly shroud me in bubble wrap.

Blake, can't you see this is me? I smashed the door because I was desperate to save our lives.

The motherdoll has remoulded her exterior into a perfect copy of me. I can see that her flesh is a little plasticky but as her sleeves fall back, her bare arms are flesh-coloured. She's adjusted. She's grown.

Blake, I am me! I shout silently. *Why can't you see me? I'm the woman you married. The woman you love...d.*

Nothing comes out but tears.

"I think we need a bigger box," Blake says. At the door, he adds, "Funny that Phoebe's so much better now. We don't really need this thing. You were right. As usual."

He throws her a warm smile and leaves the room. My heart aches. With Blake gone, the new Kelly pulls my head into her lap, shifting my whole body, as stiff as board. Light. She wipes away my tears with gentle fingers.

Don't dare touch me, I silently protest. *I am me, not you.*

"You *were* you," the motherdoll says. "Isn't Wi-Fi fun?" She winks. "It hurts to lose them, I know. Don't worry, you won't recall soon. Dehydration will vague you out, then the physical pain of transformation obliterates all prior memory. The nano-meds turn the iron in your blood to solid framework. Tasteless but effective. Delivered via avocado." She smiles. "They'll reset you in the factory. You won't remember a thing."

I won't remember Phoebe.

I scream inside.

Blake returns with the box from the go-cart he never finished building.

His eyebrows rise when he sees her stroking my hair.

Please, let me stay. I'll be the motherdoll. You can be me. I just want to stay with them.

"If you're so fond of it, why are we giving it away?" he asks.

She laughs, pushing me off her lap. I hit the floor, wooden.

"I'm not fond of it. I just regret being unkind, I suppose."

Together, they continue bundling me in plastic bubble-wrap, their hands tickling over my legs and ribs.

"I should never have got it," Blake says, cupping her cheek in his palm, right over my chest. "Maybe it was worth it though. You seem happier."

I watch as he leans across me and kisses her tenderly. My head is only half-wrapped, one eye exposed. I remember the softness of his touch and how his kisses felt, his warm lips tingling on mine, stirring a sweet need I'll never feel again.

Kelly smiles. "Maybe we should think about a playmate for Phoebe."

"Another baby?" Blake says, grimacing.

"We could try the new babydoll model. DollCorp offered us a free trial on the phone."

He looks a little puzzled but shrugs and smiles, a quizzical assent.

I scream silently, no. What will that baby do to Phoebe? The flaps close over my face. Tape screams off its roll, thuds down with heavy hands onto thick cardboard. I'm sealed in the past, in the darkness of the box.

THE RED SHRINE (FINGERLESS AND DOUBLE-MOUTHED)

KAARON WARREN

Susie wanted to be as fit as possible for what lay ahead of her, so she took to daily runs, stopping at the outdoor gym where she did fifty squats (to be honest, more like twenty, but sometimes she lost count) and some pullups, building arm and leg muscles as well as lung fitness. Pregnancy was like a marathon that went on for almost a year, she'd been told. You have to be fit to fuck, fit to fall pregnant, and then there was the nine months carrying that baby.

Fit to fuck was the thing she was focused on right now. All very well the bog-standard bonking she and her husband did, nightly/ three times a week/every fortnight/when her temperature was right. Bog-standard and fruitless, but they kept at it. What she had coming at her was the next husband in the daisy chain. If her husband couldn't get her pregnant, maybe this husband could, and *hers* might be able to sow the seed in the next wife. That was the plan, anyway; so far so good. Of the twelve couples (plus three extras, to mix things up a bit), three were already pregnant. She was next in line; one more successful fuck and it'd be her turn. Part of her was dreading it, part of her was excited, and she wondered how her husband would cope with it all. She wondered how *she'd* cope, him going off with another woman. They'd already decided not to tell each other any details, to pretend it hadn't happened.

She added another two sit-ups. Her legs were hairy; she'd have them waxed. And underarms too, and make sure she moisturised over the next few days, keep it all smooth and nice. She didn't want to disgust this guy, whoever he was. She wouldn't know until they both showed up at the hotel room.

She was thinking these thoughts as she made her way home, hoping he'd excite her, hoping she wouldn't need to lube up for it to go ahead but worried she'd have to, when a motorbike veered off the road to avoid a suddenly-opened car door, slid through an oil slick and slammed into her, throwing her into the air and

Susie's husband watched over her. This was the second week of her coma; it was hard to look at her, motionless, her breath hard and regular, almost not her own. He felt anxious; it was her turn. If she didn't take her turn, he wouldn't get HIS turn. He took her hand and squeezed, hoping for some response.

Something.

"How is she?"

Steve turned. He knew this couple, had video-conferenced with them, but this was their first meeting in person.

"She's stable."

The couple nodded.

The husband kissed his wife's head and gave her a gentle push, directing her out of the door. "Go get us some coffee," he said. She looked at him, her hand resting on her stomach. "Not for you! For us. You're on fresh juice for the next bunch of months."

She smiled. Steve had seen that kind of expression before. It was partly proud, partly pitying. It was the face of a pregnant woman who didn't think you were going to manage it. That you wouldn't get pregnant.

"So," the husband said. He licked his lips.

"She looks well," Steve said, nodding after the wife. He wanted to make a crude joke about sex and multiple injections of sperm or something but he didn't.

"Yeah, she's great. Excellent."

"That's great. That's great." Steve had never felt so awkward. He patted the bed next to Susie. "I'm really pleased for you, and I'm sorry that she's…" he nodded at Susie.

"She is fine-looking," the husband said.

Steve had pulled down the sheets and turned Susie's hospital gown around so it gaped open. She had great tits, he'd always said that, and a smooth brown stomach with light blonde hairs that raised up when she was cold.

"She is very fine. And like I said on the phone," Steve said, "I'm telling you," he said, "I'm saying, I couldn't tell the difference. Awake or asleep. She won't know and we can move this forward. It's the other couples I'm thinking of. Waiting for us."

The husband laughed, harsh, short. "You're serious."

He wasn't the only one. Steve had a go himself and he brought others in. Private room, who cares, they all had a go at her. They told themselves she liked it; her cheeks flushed and she almost seemed awake. Steve wanted her out of hospital before they found out she was pregnant, but she was still asleep, still in her own place, hanging on, when the positive result came in.

Steve showered the day he went off to do his duty with the next wife in the daisy chain and he dressed with care. There wasn't meant to be any romance in it all, you weren't meant to enjoy it, but he thought, he *said*, that babies came when both partners enjoyed it. That his wife fell pregnant because her conscious mind wasn't there to say how much she hated it.

Giving birth to the first baby woke Susie up. Her pregnancy had gone over the nine months and they were deciding what to do, how to manage it, and facing questions as to how they'd let it proceed and why, when she went into labour.

She woke up in the middle of it, her eyes wide. She'd gained weight but not a lot; her face was thin and she'd be happy when she saw her cheekbones, Steve thought. She'd be pleased. He'd not been successful in his duty; he'd had to go back in for a second try. But he and Susie would have their baby and that's what mattered.

Susie tried to speak, but her throat was dry and her voice scratchy.

The midwife checked Susie's vitals. "It's all right, dear. Baby coming! Baby on its way! We've got you." She put her hand on Susie's stomach, then examined her to see what stage she was at. A look crossed her face and she exchanged glances with the nurse, also attending.

"What's wrong?" Steve said. "What is it?"

"It's all good. All fine. A small baby, that's all."

He'd refused any ultrasounds, knowing that Susie wanted a natural birth, wanted as little intervention as possible.

Susie grunted, squeezed.

It came out tiny, the size of Steve's hand. Loose-skinned, pink, hairless. It had grey fingernails, long and sharp, and it clenched its fists and waved them, as if fighting something off. They couldn't tell the sex.

Steve stared at it, horrified, and the midwife gagged.

Susie stirred; her eyes opened. "I dreamed I was a rabbit," she said, her voice scratchy, "or, like, a naked mole rat. A sand puppy. Ugliest thing I ever saw. I had one as a pet in this dream and it crawled up my vagina. This happened more than once. The feeling of something slimy and wrong up there."

She'd had no sense of time in her coma, but there was a certain rhythm, a rising of the sun and the passage of the moon, a tidal ebbing and flowing. And her nightmares.

The midwife placed the creature she'd given birth to in a basin and went back to check on Susie. Susie shifted, lifted her hips, and gave birth to another. And another. And

Barry was the kind of cunt who had to monetise everything. Especially if it cost him nothing, body or soul. So, when he heard about that poor woman... Not the hiccups world record holder, on and on for thirty years or whatever. Not the hotdog eater, or the woman with the longest fingernails.

No. She's the multiple birth lady, although calling it "multiple" almost seems like a joke. Once she'd hit eight, the world started to take notice. They allowed one journalist in there with a phone camera, and that's what the world saw of her first.

She wasn't exhausted at that stage but still lost from her months in a coma, confused, talking about her dreams as if they were real.

Barry got himself into the hospital, dressed himself up, made himself useful. Watched her squeeze 'em out like tiny pink guinea pigs and they grew before his eyes. There were twenty of them now, each in a small bucket lined with cotton wool.

The press wanted to know more, who's the father, and Steve took the rap, claimed ownership, because he sure as fuck wasn't talking about all the other donors. He said, "I'll love them, no matter what," but when there were fifty little rat things he stopped talking, and there were hundreds to go although they didn't know that then.

Too many questions about security (and so many of them played the game, so many joined in. You can't shut a hospital down like that, arresting half the staff) so they moved her to a place tagged The Red Shrine, a red-walled stand-alone hospital room with viewing windows all around, up high, but no access apart from one door. They wheeled her away under cover, got there and found more of those things crawling all over her, the umbilical cords like worms, wriggling, alive.

Susie lifted her head to look around her, then dropped back down again. The midwife gave her shoulder a shove. This was the fourth or fifth midwife and she felt impatient with the woman; these babies slid out of her with no pain, no effort involved. All she had to do was lie back, let everyone else do the work, yet she was like this. Susie's face was bloated and swollen and no one was sure why. Her ankles, too, bloated, but they were reluctant to give her anything at this stage.

The room was rounded, used long ago for medical students but now mostly a small museum, a hook-up place too, and rumour had it that pornos had been shot there. Red plastered runnels ran in grooves, for the water or blood, and the place smelt sharply clean, disinfectant so strong it could burn your nostril hairs.

Susie turned her head away, not wanting to see any of them, hearing the mewling noises, and you could almost hear the growth of them, stretching, expanding.

They lost track of how many babies. Babies in basins, growing fast, crawling out and over the sides. Those with no legs or arms wriggling and rocking until the noise was enough to make someone pick them up and put them outside. Those who were fingerless, those with double mouths, those with skin so pale you could see their organs, those without eyes; all were baptised. Quickly, efficiently, given names in the name of the hastily selected Lord.

Priests worked in shifts as well, an hour on and an hour off. "Demons came to visit you," one told Susie, who was well past hearing anything, "because they like babies to look like them. But even these living creatures have souls. Even these."

"Even these," the news reported, and before long the car park was full of those at the end of the tether, wanting some kind of blessing, thinking a miracle was happening and they wanted a part of it.

This was where Barry stepped in. It occurred to him the babies all needed a home, they all would like somewhere to go, and out there in the car park were people lining up for a piece of the miracle. Motors running to keep the heaters on because it was fucking freezing.

He didn't lose track of the baby count; he was the one naming them. The first one was called "Baby of Susie", then "Baby of Susie Two", then they were named by the time they emerged, but as they moved into the second and third day, they were just given a number. It was easy enough to lose track, Barry realised, and as he handed them out, wrapped and safe but without any papers, he gave them all his own names, whatever popped into his head.

Susie panted, not able to draw an easy breath. So tired her arms dropped, she couldn't keep them up, any movement was done by other people lifting and shifting her. Steve did it for a while but he seemed half-dead, bewildered. The sound of all those babies; no one wanted to be near it. Barry was a blessing, everybody said, thanks Barry, thanks mate, because he was bearing the brunt.

Once Steve disappeared, he was the one who fed Susie, like you'd feed a pig with milk and mush. They couldn't keep her on a drip. She'd pull it out.

She seemed happy for Barry to name the babies.

She didn't know Barry was heading out the back way with them, all bundled up like chocolates in an Easter Box, selling them off. He raised the price as he went along. He couldn't sell them all, but he sold enough of them. The reporters were too busy finding out about Susie, doing their research. They found out about the Countess of Henneberg, who'd been cursed for not caring for a woman in labour. She'd been cursed with hundreds of tiny monsters crawling out of her vagina, worms or monsters or "unknown creatures". There was speculation of what Susie had done to deserve this, who she'd offended, who she'd hurt. Steve said, "She didn't have an enemy in the world," and honestly thought this made him a good man, that not inventing some kind of evil act made him the good guy.

Barry thought the births were a bit like popcorn. Slow at first, then popping off a mile a minute, then the slower ones, the last to emerge, coming out at a more measured pace. The Seven Days Wonder, he called it.

Susie is crying. Tears coming out of her eyes but she is spent, she is so done. She will never move again. Her legs flop open. She's a mess down there. They cleaned her up between babies for a while but before long they stopped even that. Someone has propped her mouth open so the babies can breathe and this old tale, this old myth? No one even argues against it. Her mouth is dry. They've forgotten she's human. It's all about her vagina and what's coming out of it. Her skin is grey and she has no pulse but still the babies crawl out, tiny little things and some of them even squeak.

Then she is empty and

(There is a whole other story about all those babies; those who lived, those who died, those who prospered, those who suffered. Those who used their own miracle to perform miracles, those who chose a different life, of anonymity or infamy. But that is another story.)

THE PHOBIA CLINIC

DAVID KURARIA

Autumn had settled on New York City, sending a chill wind along 8th Avenue. Martin alighted from the midtown JFK airport shuttlebus into the shadows of the squat buildings of 8th and 40th. He pressed his slight frame against a brick façade to evade bustling pedestrians. On a lamppost he read a crinkled poster for what looked like the name of a band, *A Beautiful Insanity, Manhattan, October 15*.

Martin's overnight bag rested against his hip, hanging from the strap across his shoulder. Thin fingers of his freckled hand gripped the handle of his travel case. He felt self-conscious and vulnerable amid the throng of tall strangers. He walked, staying close to the buildings, and cursed as he listened to the little wheels of his suitcase clacking on the footpath. At the corner of 8th and 41st Streets, he found an electronics store. He bought a map of Manhattan and a cheap mobile phone, and paid the service technician to set the phone for local calls.

Martin entered a café further up 8th Avenue. He sat and ordered a coffee and called the number Lena had provided.

"Hello, Crepuscular Films, how may I help you?"

The patchy reception was probably because of the cheap mobile. Martin left his table and went outside for better reception. He had not thought of what he might say by way of introduction, and he stammered.

"Oh, hello. My name is Martin. I'm a friend of Lena's, just in from Australia this morning. I worked with her on our animated short film adaptation of Clark Ashton Smith's story *The Seven*

Geases." Martin waited for an acknowledgement, but there was silence on the other end. He hurried on. "Lena suggested I contact her when I arrive in Manhattan so we could meet for coffee." Again, there was silence. Martin was now not sure if there was anyone listening. He wondered if whoever had answered was waiting for further explanation. He frowned and pressed on. "If I may speak with Lena, I'd appreciate it, thanks." He held his breath and started when he heard a voice.

"Lena is not here, she moved out several weeks ago. Who are you?"

Martin pressed his teeth together and stretched his mouth. "I'm her friend, Martin, from Austr—"

"Yeah, you're from Aussie. Lena moved out."

"Greg, stop playing games. Give me that." A second person greeted Martin. "Sorry about him. You're Martin, the Aussie guy Lena mentioned. Hi, I'm Carol. Don't mind Greg, he's a dick." Martin heard laughter. Carol continued. "Lena has said good things about you. Look, if you want to come on over to our office, on the Lower East Side, we can all meet you. As Greg mentioned, Lena moved from Manhattan up to Providence. I have her address. Do you have a pen?"

Martin retrieved a ballpoint from his overnight. Using the bag resting on his knee, he wrote on a café napkin, repeating back to Carol the forwarding address. "12 Farnsworth Street, College Hill, Providence. Okay, I have that, thanks. So, Lena didn't leave a phone number?"

"No, sorry. I kind of wish she had, because we would like her to help us finish a project we have going. To get to Providence, you need to hop on an Amtrak up at Midtown in Penn Street station on 7th Ave. Other than her address, I can't help you, Martin."

With the call ended, Martin returned to his table. It was approaching 4:00pm. He finished his coffee and placed several dollars under the bill the waitstaff had placed on the table. He glanced to where he had left his suitcase and stared at empty space on the linoleum. He looked under the table and about the room and felt a surge of panic when he realised his suitcase had gone. He asked the staff if they had placed it behind the counter.

His stomach knotted when he was told no one had seen it.

Martin raced for the door and out onto the street. He looked up and down the avenue. He swallowed and his fear grew. He leaned against the window of the café and swallowed again, feeling sick. His vision blurred and he lost focus. He heard the chatter of many people about him as he remembered what the suitcase had contained. There had been the second wallet with his credit cards, the majority of his cash, his passport and Australian driver's licence. Martin began to hyperventilate. He swallowed again. His eyes refocussed. The only time he had seen so many people rushing about had been in Sydney.

He blinked and was lost at what to do. He remembered the address Carol had provided. His neck had lowered into his raised shoulders. He rotated his head and tried to think clearly. The secondary wallet in the front pocket of his jeans had about eighty US dollars and some coins. He closed his fingers across the zipper of his overnight bag. Inside was one change of clothes, the map of Manhattan and some toiletries.

A moment of clarity settled. First, Martin thought of going to the Australian consulate to plead his case. But then he would have to stay in Manhattan for the night with less than one hundred dollars. To do that would deprive him of enough funds for a train ticket to Providence. He coughed out a sob. The best move was to walk to Penn station and board the northbound Amtrak. He did not want to think of the situation in which he would find himself should he not be able to find Lena at the address Carol had given.

With these thoughts, Martin had not noticed that someone was speaking to him. He became aware of his surroundings and saw a woman. He blinked and heard her speak.

"I was saying, sir, would you like to earn some quick money?" She was costumed as a Marilyn Monroe lookalike. On her platinum wig she wore a tall stars-and-stripes top hat. She held a piece of paper near his face. "If you are interested in earning some quick money, sir, I suggest you might look at this."

Martin gave a thin smile and took the proffered sheet of paper. His hand was shaking.

"I, ah, thanks. Thank you."

He stared at the paper, some kind of flyer. More in an effort to distract himself from his predicament than of actual interest, Martin looked over what he had been handed.

It was an invitation to participate in a research project with a group named Thrills Incorporated at a place called *The Phobia Clinic*. Subheaded below the headline was written: *Visit us for a quick question-and-answer session and we will pay you for your time.* Under this an address: Moore Building, corner of 9th and 40th.

The woman had gone. Martin checked left and right along the footpath and could not see her. A feeling of danger flicked through his consciousness. He reread the words on the flyer and wondered why someone would offer him a promise of earning quick money so soon after he'd had everything stolen. A competing thought arrived: people in cities were always handing out weird flyers to anyone who could be convinced to accept them. But Martin discarded that thought and his suspicion grew. He wondered if he were being set up. If he went to the address provided, would they have his suitcase and demand something for its return? He wondered what people who organised a scenario such as that would hope to achieve. He had nothing to give. If someone had his suitcase, they would have already cleaned it out. It was only through desperation that he decided to take up the offer for the money.

Martin adjusted the strap of his overnight bag across his chest. He knew the city was a grid and found it easy to reach 9th and 40th. An identical flyer was taped to the façade of the Moore building. He pushed through a set of old-fashioned double doors with frosted glass. The air smelled musty, as if it had been trapped in the gloomy foyer for a long time. He checked his watch as he stood looking up at a set of well-worn wooden stairs. Climbing to the second floor, he wandered into what seemed to be a waiting room. Here was old-style wood panelling, ancient armchairs and carpeting which looked like something from a grand hotel from a century past. Ashtrays on aluminium poles leaned drunkenly. The ceiling was ornate plaster. In places, wallpaper from another age peeled, hanging in flaps like old skirts. The entire effect was one of past elegance.

An inner door opened and out stepped a very tall, thin man in a grey pin-striped double-breasted suit and two-tone brogue shoes, giving him the appearance of a person from an old mid-twentieth century gangster movie. His hands were large and dirty with a fine coating of dust or powder. His face was long and thin, ending in a pronounced jaw. His eyebrows looked like two thick carpet slices glued above his eyes. He turned his head; it seemed the movement was made with some effort. Martin could imagine the neck creaking. He expected the man's voice to be deep and booming; instead, it was quite high-pitched.

"You wish to know what we offer here, Mister...?"

"Martin." He felt foolish and nervous. "I'm Martin."

The man did not smile. "I am Frederick. Thank you for coming. I will introduce you to my colleagues shortly, but for now, welcome to The Phobia Clinic." He stared at a corner of the ceiling. Martin followed his gaze and saw the camera mounted.

Turning towards the door he had entered from, Frederick held it open and ushered Martin through to an inner room.

Many lit candles were placed along shelves set into the walls. The smell of incense was cloying and overpowering. It reminded Martin of his aunt's house back when he was young. There were several desks with chairs arranged in the centre of the floor, like a school classroom. On the desks were paper and pencils as if the room had been set up as an exam space. Frederick waved a hand at the desks.

"If you would take a seat, we can begin by you filling out a form as a waiver. It's nothing, really," he continued. "We simply wish to make plain we are going into this in a legal and open manner."

Martin was hungry and weary from stress. New York City was a place where anything could happen to an unwary traveller. It was with this thought he began to mentally search for the beginnings of a scam. He seated himself at one of the desks and looked about the room. In front, two doors of heavy wood were shut, which he guessed led into the main part of the old building. He stared at the questionnaire, noticing the pages were thick, like old blotting paper used to soak fountain pen ink. He blinked and tried to focus. He started a little when Frederick spoke from behind his chair.

"If you can fill out the forms we can move on to the next stage. I will introduce you to Miss Senna. She will be showing you what we do here."

Martin picked up the several sheets of paper and turned them over and turned them back to look at the first page. He read the first line on the top sheet.

Are you afraid of something and do not know why?

Martin thought of leeches. He was preoccupied with the distasteful image, and ticked a "yes" box. His weariness mounted, as did his hunger. The next question was: *Have you ever handled something that made you feel squeamish?* He looked again and saw the word "squeamish" might have been typed wrong. It appeared to read as "squamous". He picked up the thick sheet of paper. The sheet seemed to have an ink spot on the word. He rubbed the spot with a finger and saw it did say "squeamish". The paper felt damp, as if it had been recently sprayed with a little water. Again, he ticked a "yes" box. His vision blurred and he swallowed, trying to stay awake. He coughed. It felt like dust was settling in his throat.

Martin heard a heavy tread coming from behind one of the closed doors. There was a scraping and sounds of movement; then a huffing noise as if some large animal was expelling air through its nostrils. Martin turned to see Frederick seated at a desk behind him. The man was staring at him with an odd look of anticipation. Turning back to the sheets of paper, Martin read the next question.

Phobias are not inherent. For an individual to become afraid of something there has to have been an origin event. Can you name one such situation?

This time there was no box to fill in. Instead there was a blank space. Martin blinked and yawned. He wrote, "I hate the feel of wet animal fur". He thought of something else that made him afraid, but could not think of an origin event. Next to his first answer he wrote, "Holes in things, lots of holes". He read on. The questionnaire was becoming personal. For the first time since he arrived, he began to feel alarmed.

Did either of your parents or older relatives pass on any fears or foibles to you?

Through his fog and a strange growing dizziness, Martin still managed to realise where this was headed. He had made a mistake. This was nothing more than an undergrad psychology test. He again felt moisture on the blotting paper where the heel of his right hand rested. Without thinking, he wiped his fingertips across the page.

Beyond the closed door came a scrabbling, shuffling sound, like an animal with claws scuttling across floorboards. It was unsettling. He turned to Frederick and saw the man grinning at him. Martin felt afraid, and his anxiousness grew. He fumbled with the thick pages. He managed several more questions, each time forgetting what he had written and which boxes he had ticked. A few minutes later he blinked and his head dropped towards the surface of the desk. He focussed on the page before him and realised he had finished the questionnaire.

Frederick was standing next to him wearing latex gloves. Frederick gathered up the questionnaire and grinned. Martin thought it was more a predatory smirk, but through his fog he couldn't be sure. He began to feel as if he were going to vomit. Again, the scrabbling behind the heavy door; this time with an accompanying yelping and whining as if an animal on the other side was begging to be allowed in. Martin wanted to get away. He tried to stand, but sat again heavily. He lowered his head onto the surface of the desk and closed his eyes.

When Martin came to his senses, he found himself leaning against the wall of an underpass. By the light of a nearby streetlamp, a signpost showed he was still on 9th Avenue. He felt the strap from his overnight bag across his shoulder and was relieved he still had it. There was an itch on his stomach and he reached under his shirt to scratch. His fingertips felt a small lump. He wondered if he had been bitten by something.

In the gloom of the underpass, Martin felt confused. His thoughts felt somehow clouded, muddy. He shook his head. He found his mobile and pulled it from his shirt pocket. Checking the time, he was surprised to find it was nearing 5:00am. Feeling sick and dizzy, he tried to think clearly. He knew he had entered the Moore Building sometime around 5:00pm. Staring out into the chill night and listening to the traffic, he realised he had somehow lost nearly twelve hours. Confused, he looked up overhead at the imposing metal rail bridge. He felt afraid, as if it was going to fall and crush him. Something pushed against the hem of his jeans. He jumped backwards and stared at his shoes. There was nothing there. As he leaned down looking, he again felt the movement. He gave a cry and put his back to the dirty bricks of the underpass. Again came the insistent brushing, tugging sensation. Martin lifted his leg and shook it, his jeans leg flapping against his ankle. A man in an overcoat, the collar masking the lower half of his face, hurried by.

Martin tried to control his confusion. His mouth felt dry. His eyes itched and he used a knuckle to rub them. There was itching across his shoulders. A train overhead hissed along the rails towards Chinatown. Martin saw lights further down 9th. He stood and shuffled along the dirty sidewalk, out from the underpass.

A block further, he found an open coffee shop. He blinked and turned in, ordered a coffee without milk. Reaching into his jeans pocket he felt a piece of paper. Ignoring this, he scrabbled around for some coins and dropped the loose change onto the counter. Taking his coffee, Martin saw the attendant staring at him with some distaste. Martin went to a table and picked up a sachet of sugar, tearing it open and pouring it into his coffee. There was a glass salt shaker with holes in the metal lid. He swallowed. Looking at the holes, he felt a constriction in his stomach. Backing away, he clipped an ankle on a chair leg. He fell to one knee and put a hand out to catch himself. He felt a smack to one of his cheeks as his face hit the corner of the table. He pushed himself to his feet and stood, unsteady and confused. A woman spoke to him.

"Sir, please don't raise your voice."

Martin had not realised he had spoken. The woman seemed concerned, not afraid, even as she stepped away from him. Looking about, he was aware of people regarding him. He sobbed distress and, with his coffee, fled outside.

Reeling between pedestrians, he hurried down 9th and beneath another underpass, finding sanctuary in the darkness of a shop doorway. He crouched, putting his back against a wooden door. He remembered the piece of paper in his pocket, and with a hurried scramble of fingers pulled it out: Lena's address in Providence. His thoughts cleared a little: he had a purpose. He felt itchy on the back of his neck. There were several lumps there. He scratched and it did not help. He drank most of his coffee in two gulps. The itching began all over his chest and stomach. He tried to ignore the maddening sensation. Dawn had arrived. Martin struggled to his feet. He looked up and down 9th, at the several people walking the footpath on the other side, then opened his overnight bag and changed all his clothes. He used his body spray. Squeezed a little toothpaste into his mouth. Using the last of his coffee he rinsed his mouth and swallowed the mixture. He used his discarded underpants to wipe his butt crack and pushed the underwear with his t-shirt into his bag.

He reached around to scratch his back. Then he felt an irritation on his thighs. Scratching his legs, he realised it felt as if there were insects crawling there. He stood, listening to the purring growl of the city.

His thoughts cleared a little. He had enough money to reach Providence and have a meal; maybe enough for a night in a cheap lodging somewhere. He had to find Lena or he would be stuck, destitute. The sun was rising. Martin headed along 9th towards Penn Street Station. Upon entering, he was not ready for the large crowd of people. His neck itched.

Martin joined a line to buy an Amtrak ticket to Providence. In front of the ticket office he proffered his cash, telling the woman behind the plexiglass where he wanted to go. He reached behind and scraped his neck. She frowned. Martin laughed in an attempt to defuse anything which might develop.

"It's okay, ma'am. I just have a bit of an itch on my neck."

Martin smiled at the woman, happy that he was able to explain his predicament. He saw her stare at him and could not understand why she seemed frightened.

"Sir, can I ask you to lower your voice? I'll process your fare. Shouting is not going to help."

She gestured to someone behind him. Martin turned and saw a uniformed railway employee eyeing him.

The uniformed man said, "I will be watching you."

Frightened, confused, Martin stood with the other commuters at the metal barrier, waiting for it to be opened for boarding the northbound. He tried not to itch but found it impossible, and so scratched under his chin and all across his chest. The uniformed man, now with a companion, stood watching him.

Finally, everyone was allowed to board the outbound. Martin found his allocated window seat in economy. He sat with his bag on his knees. He scratched his neck and felt little relief. What had happened at the Moore Building with the sinister thin man? How could he have lost track of so many hours? Knowing he had been drugged somehow, he wondered why someone would do such a thing. They had not stolen his remaining money, but they had taken his wallet and placed it back in the opposite pocket. For safekeeping, he put the wallet with the remaining cash into his overnight bag. The train began to pull from the station. Soon, they gained speed as the train looped through Manhattan, turning north towards Connecticut. The rocking of the carriage made him sleepy, but he was unable to settle because of the maddening itch all over his body. He felt alone and frightened.

The train crossed a bridge, leaving Manhattan behind. As he looked out of the carriage window, someone took the aisle seat beside him. It was a very tall person. The newcomer stared down at Martin. The person wore an old-fashioned tweed overcoat with the big collar pulled up as if to hide their face. Then the collar flopped down. At first, Martin could not tell if it was a man or woman, but he realised with a sudden rush of clarity that it was neither. Its cheeks sagged like jowls on a bloodhound. Martin saw, in a brief glance before he turned away, that there was something wrong with the mouth. He began to smell an odd odour, like a scented candle, at once cloying and comfortable. He turned again to see the strange person regarding him. The deformed mouth opened and closed several times like a fish gasping in the bottom of a fishing boat. Martin realised with encroaching fear that what he was looking at was not entirely human. He was about to stand and leave when he felt pressure on his thigh. He looked down and saw a massive hand with long fingers. He couldn't move. Instead he sat helpless and looked up to the face of the creature. To his horror it attempted a smile. It leaned forward. Martin heard the intake of air into the deformed nostrils as the creature sniffed about his face.

Dizzy, Martin's eyelids drooped. The creature brushed up against him. The pressing grew more insistent. Martin felt a strange paralysis and was shifted up against the wall of the carriage next to the window. He briefly saw the distant Manhattan skyline. His travelling companion reached for him with long fingers. Martin opened his mouth to call for help, but nothing came out. He felt hot and stifled and struggled to breathe.

Looking at the fingers again, he saw the tips open on each of the fingers, revealing tiny grey-lipped mouths. Martin was only able to give one muffled cry of terror before he shut down. His shirt was opened. He felt scrabbling as those awful mouths caressed the flesh on his chest and stomach. He screamed inwardly when the mouths fastened. Rasping tongues, like that of a Great Lake lamprey, rotated left and right, boring holes into his flesh. From each of the mouths, a maggot was regurgitated and deftly inserted into each hole on Martin's torso. A liquid that resembled saliva was piped into each hole, setting like jelly, sealing the holes. Martin was as helpless as a spider under the ministrations of a tarantula wasp.

The hands of the creature moved to his back and down to his waist. The mouths opened and repeated the process, again and again. Martin leaned against the carriage wall, defenceless, staring ahead. Periodically he shivered in anticipation, waiting for the mouths to move up and down his riddled body. The train sped through the abandoned factory towns of Connecticut. He felt a fumbling at his waist. His belt was loosened. One of the frightful hands reached inside his jeans. The rasping tongues went to work.

Martin woke and looked at his hands, and there were pockmarks as if holes were forming in his flesh. The seat next to him was vacant.

At Providence Central, Martin exited the train. He felt dizzy but coherent enough to hand his ticket stub to the station attendant. Running from the station, he gasped in the open air. He wandered about and was lucky enough to come upon a church which offered food for the homeless. Happy to be away from the crowds of the city centre, Martin collected a bowl of soup and a bread roll. He took a seat. Looking at his surroundings, he saw how destitute those present were. He wiped his spoon on his shirt and itched the back of his neck. Something was missing… He had left his overnight bag on the train and it was a terrible realisation.

He sat then, spoon in hand, exhausted, unable to gain enough strength to even stand. Tears welled and he hung his head, shamed and beaten. Nausea engulfed him. He leaned over and vomited onto the floor of the mission house. Falling to his knees, he wept. Then he lost consciousness.

When he woke, he found himself sitting in a small park near some brush. People hurried by about their business, either oblivious or uncaring. Martin fled from one place to another, along streets and through car parks, but still the throngs dogged him as he rushed to escape the city centre. He hurried along a street with less people pressing about him. His inner ears ached and he felt rather than heard a buzzing about his face. Sobbing, he watched his scuffed shoes propelling him along at a shuffle. At an intersection was a hotel on a corner. Running across the road, he stumbled and grabbed a tall metal pole to hold himself upright. The street sign showed he was on Mathewson Street. Martin knew he was losing control of his equilibrium. He let go of the pole and reeled forward, smacking into a sandwich-board, sprawling atop the wooden signage. Raising his head, he made out large-lettered words, *Cellar Stories Books*. Someone touched him.

"Sir? Are you all right? Here, let me help you."

Martin was lying next to a parked car. He saw a hubcap pressed to form a spiral full of miniature holes. The sight horrified him. He gave a cry and scrambled to his feet. Without acknowledging the person attempting to help, Martin shuffled along the street, pulling the collar of his shirt up to hide his face.

Behind him, the man said, "I guess there's no helping some people."

Fleeing the last of the shopping district, Martin ended up in a wide expanse of grass next to a canal. There were fewer people. He wept with the agony of his flesh eruptions. He hurried forward and stopped when he reached the harbour. Turning, he continued his headlong flight alongside a freeway adjoining the harbour foreshore. Everything was a blur. He heard vehicles speed by him, but took little notice of his immediate surrounds. After running for some time, he found himself in a small parkland with trees and bushes bordering the city harbour. Martin sought safety among thicker bushes, away from prying eyes. He scratched his eyelids and could not find relief. He sobbed, helpless to alleviate his physical distress. He slept fitfully, waking every little while to scratch his festering, bleeding hide.

He woke to a chill autumn night. There was no moon. Martin felt itchy all over. He reached down to scratch his inner thighs, and felt movement under his probing fingers. Martin scratched throughout the night. He wept and fell asleep as the dawn showed through the brush where he lay in his soiled trousers.

Towards midday, Martin woke and heard voices of people walking by. The snippets of conversation made no sense.

"My God, I can't believe they would put that in a movie. It was horrific."

"Yes, I was nearly puking."

He began to itch under his arms and between his buttocks. The inhabitants of the holes in his flesh responded. The crisp shells split, and flies wriggled out, ready to emerge from their burrows.

Martin raked his nails across his flesh, crying out, weeping at the agony. He no longer knew his purpose, nor where he was. He moved further in under the brush, and crawled along the dirt until he reached the safety of an adjoining hedgerow. He gasped for breath. In the light reaching through the overhead leaves, Martin tore off his clothes and looked at the open wounds and the writhing bodies on his faeces-smeared thighs. He stared with horror and desperation as bloated white worms squirmed from the elastic rims of the holes, wriggling out like the young from the back of a Joshua toad. The holes gaped red-rimmed. Martin writhed on the dirt under the hedgerow as his babies were born and he succumbed to his trypophobia. He closed his eyes and screamed.

Then a calmness settled, alleviating his sudden panic.

He sighed in growing pleasure. He looked down the length of his body and watched the birth of his babies. Content now, he didn't mind the spreading rash and oozing nest fluids. He touched some of his babies gently with the tips of his fingers. Laying his head on the dirt under the hedgerow, Martin spoke.

"It's all right, it's okay little ones. Daddy's here."

THE SURROGATE

RENEE DE VISSER

The cramps were undeniable in their strength and determination, like being squeezed both inwards and downwards
by a wide, invisible rubber band. It was crushing. Kristen held
her breath despite this being against the advice of the midwives.
Thoughts of *No, not yet* punctuated the white noise of her brain
in between the contractions.

Then they were rushing her into a ward, placing a monitor
around her midsection, checking her blood pressure, heart rate,
temperature. The lights were bright on her face, the sounds of
machines muffled beneath the static inside her head. She wanted
to get off her back, to pace the room, get down on all fours, but
the monitor around her midsection would slip off the baby's
heart whenever she moved, so she was told to lie still. All around,
there was activity—deliberate, calm, professional—seeming far
away and separate.

Inside her, the cramps came in stronger and shorter waves.
She felt tears on her cheeks, but she was not crying. Her voice
was a screech of pain, almost primal in its ferociousness and fear
as she tried to fight against the contractions.

No, not yet.

She was vaguely aware of her husband, Craig, beside her and
holding her hand, murmuring words of reassurance. His words
were lost in the pain of contractions. She could barely respond.
Vaguely, she was aware of him talking to the nurses and the
pinch in a vein of her arm as they injected something into her.
Another machine was wheeled into the room. The sensations of

a cool gel and a firm pressure on her belly. An ultrasound?

And then, miraculously, relief as pain medication kicked in, blissfully fast. The lights softened and the static in her head dissipated. There was a vague odour of faeces—probably hers—but she was too exhausted to care.

She collapsed back into the pillow and dozed.

"I'm not liking what I see." The doctor's face was stern but not unfriendly. He glanced over to where Kristen was dozing on the bed. "And to be frank—your wife is going into premature labour."

"So, what do we do?" asked Craig. His stomach felt heavy and hot, his chest tight and sore. He vaguely wondered if he was going to collapse or shit himself. Or both.

"Okay." The doctor removed his glasses. "Oh Christ, okay. I want you to see this."

The ultrasound image was difficult for Craig to decipher. He could make out his unborn child, the walls of the uterus but not much else.

The doctor pointed out the problem. "See? There."

"What's that?"

"Well…" The doctor regarded Craig. "I'm going to need you to tell me. Because— I'm no expert in this field—but based on skeletal structure, that appears to be a small fish."

"A fish?"

"Somehow alive in your wife's amniotic fluid. Mr Rodgers, I have to know exactly where and how you conceived."

"Where we…? Well, I think on our honeymoon," Craig stammered, flustered by the questioning. Across the room, he could hear his wife's laboured breathing. The heavy, hot weight in his stomach was a constant distraction. "At least, she found out she was pregnant soon after that."

"Soon after your honeymoon?"

"Yes. We went to Brazil."

"And what did you do in Brazil that could explain the fish? Did you go anywhere exotic? Eat or drink anything unusual? Participate in some strange ritual?"

"Uh, no. I mean, just tourist stuff. We did a river cruise. Saw the rainforest. That type of thing."

The doctor seemed to ponder. "I don't understand how this could happen. This is…God, it's nothing I've ever seen or heard of before." Then something seemed to occur to him. "Did you swim in any waters in the rainforest? Any *natural* waters?"

"Yes, we did…" Craig paused to recall. "Yes, we…uh… actually did more than swim. We made love in the river." He flushed like a schoolboy. "We had sex in the river."

"You had sex in the Amazon?"

"I mean, it was quick, you know?" Again, he blushed. "We like having sex in water. Under the surface. It's kind of a public place…*thing*. Being sneaky and no one knows what you're doing. A fetish? So, yeah…"

"Yeah," the doctor responded, quietly. Then he said, "I'll have to consult some colleagues on this one but, on the face of it, I think you may have contracted some sort of parasite whilst having coitus. It seems improbable, impossible even, and yet…" He pointed to the ultrasound. "Well, there it is. Right there."

Kristen woke in time to vomit over the side of her bed. A side effect of the pethidine, a nurse assured her. Beside her, a machine beeped and scribbled lines on paper, showing contractions she could no longer feel. She dozed once again.

Candiru. That's what they called it.

A tiny catfish that lives in the Amazon River. An opportunistic feeder, typically preying on other fish but not overly fussy—any orifice would suffice. Feared by the locals due to its habit of entering the human body, fixing itself in place with barbs and consuming the flesh inside. Unsurprisingly, most infamous for the odd occasion when it enters a human penis, vagina or anus.

Dazed, Craig listened to a doctor explain that one of those tiny fish must have entered his wife's vagina at exactly the same time they'd conceived their child, lodging itself beside their fertilised egg. The *Candiru* had survived for months inside the amniotic fluid next to their developing baby, gorging on the umbilical cord as needed, receiving sufficient nutrients and oxygen to stay alive and grow. And now, the umbilical cord was irreparably damaged by its unwanted host.

Craig's baby was dying, his wife's body rejecting both parasite and child.

Around him, Craig was aware of the nurses, huddled with identical sympathetic expressions. Apparently, there was a risk to the baby being born at only thirty-four weeks but the fish made it too dangerous to continue the pregnancy. The best course of action was caesarian section. And the complete removal of all Kristen's parts, just to be safe, just in case the fish had damaged or contaminated her reproductive organs. The medical staff would try to save the baby, but his wife was the priority. And with that, there was nothing else to do. Craig signed the consent forms.

There were lamps and bright lights everywhere. Before they wheeled her into the room they had given her an epidural, and she was feeling shaky and sick. She gestured to the nurse beside her that she was going to vomit, and he brought over a suction tube and stood dutifully beside her as she dry-retched. She dimly noted that he was wearing an additional layer of protective equipment, and realised that she was effectively being treated as one big biohazard. Her husband had been asked to wait outside due to the "delicate nature of the operation".

Behind the curtain that had been drawn across her body, in the area below her navel, there was a sudden tugging sensation. Something that felt vaguely like the cord of a tampon moved inside her vagina, and she felt the pressure of someone swabbing between her legs. She heard murmurs and conversations, nothing she could decipher.

A wave of nausea washed over her. Kristen vomited into the side of her mouth, where it was suctioned up and away with detached efficiency by the nurse. She began to shudder violently as parts of her were removed and blood was lost. With her husband out of the room, the experience was completely devoid of human interaction. She could've been in a spacecraft, a component of an alien experiment. Above her, a domed metal light provided an elongated and magnified reflection of the doctors and nurses in the room, but she was unable to see or hear any sign of her baby.

My baby. Tears filled her eyes. She wept as the medical team presumably worked around her to deliver her child and save them both from the parasite.

Half the length of a pinky finger, it resembled a thin eel, almost translucent. Like many catfish, its head was flattened with sensory barbels on both sides of its mouth. Now outside the warm water of its host, it had retracted its spines and was writhing and gasping for oxygen in the final moments of life. Both doctors and nurses alike stared at it in amazement with more than a little revulsion—such things had no business being inside a human body.

Dying, it was placed into a petri dish, the lid carefully and firmly screwed in place. This was going to be one for the medical journals.

The doctor closed up the mother with a sigh of relief. Both mother and child had survived the operation and, while both would need ongoing care—the baby for some weeks—both should pull through. A nurse had already gone to give the father the good news and, assured that all was well, the mother was dozing after her ordeal.

The nurses had taken the baby to the crib to suction fluid and prepare him for the neonatal ward, where machines would assist him to breathe and feed. He looked remarkably well, considering he had been sharing the womb with a parasite his entire short life. Not for the first time, the doctor reflected on the incredible will to live that infants possessed.

The sound of a crashing pan startled him out of his thoughts.

Beside him, both nurses backed away from the crib.

Kristen was also startled out of her doze. She looked up at the metal lamp above and saw the magnified reflection of her baby's face from where he lay in the crib beside her. She watched as he let out his first cry, surprisingly strong and loud for his size, and her heart swelled. Then she saw that there was something not quite right about his mouth.

Hundreds—if not thousands—of small, round, yellow-red eggs had been planted on the roof of the baby's mouth, on the inside of his cheeks, on and below his tongue, and along his gums. Kristen could see inside those eggs. Inside there was form and movement.

Horrified and helpless, she watched her baby cry and, inside him, hundreds of other babies started to twitch as if they cried with him. She saw that each of them had little black dots and she immediately recognised those to be eyes. She watched, mesmerised, as each of the babies turned in its egg to look out towards the light of the room.

Via the reflection of the metal lamp, Kristen looked at all her little surrogate babies, and they all looked directly back at her.

SATURDAY NIGHT AT THE MILK BAR

GARY KEMBLE

Vampires. The word hung on the screen, burning itself into my eyes. Around me the office carried on as usual: fingers stabbing at keyboards, stage-whispered phone conversations, the Chief of Staff cursing, and the babble of Sky News. It barely penetrated my bubble. I'd been drinking a lot. Too much? I don't know. How much is too much when you've just buried your family? They put Donna in the ground, and Meg's tiny coffin went down next to her. My olds wanted the funerals on different days. They wanted me to suit up two days running, just so "that bitch" wouldn't get the satisfaction. I said no. They turned up anyway. My step-brother spat on Donna's coffin.

I stared at the email, pointer hovering over *delete*. Vampires. Vampires in Brisbane. A secret club. A soundproof room in an industrial estate in the badlands out past Inala, where members gathered to feed. When you work in journalism, you hear rumours. Lots of them. Your inbox chokes on them. The TRUTH about THE REAL King of England. The SECRET CONSPIRATORS behind 9/11. Chemtrails, lizardmen. You learn to filter the crap. The crazies go first—anything with whole words in caps and multiple exclamation marks. The cadet can do it, and often does. The more mundane stuff is trickier. Local councillors on the take. Police in cahoots with bikies. There's usually a nugget of truth in it. But like a prospector looking for gold, you have to ask yourself whether that nugget is worth the sweat involved in unearthing it. Usually, the answer is no.

This email should have gone straight in the trash, but that

day I needed to believe that there were things more horrific than a woman drowning her baby and then dosing up on sleeping pills, climbing into the bath next to her, and slitting her wrists. I clicked *reply*. Later, staring down into that forty-four-gallon drum, I wished I'd clicked *delete* and got on with grieving like normal people do.

T stopped at the drive-through on the way home as summer storm clouds gathered in the west. The young guy working there knew me by name.

"The usual?"

"Yeah, plus a bottle of scotch. Something cheap."

He loaded the carton of VB and bottle of Vat 69 into my car, and added it to my customer loyalty card.

I went home and drank. Drank as thunder crashed and wind tore at Donna's prayer flags on the front verandah. Drank as rain pelted down, saturating the boxes of baby toys by the front gate. By the second six-pack, I was convinced the place was haunted. By the third, I could see their ghosts. Donna and Meg, playing peekaboo on the couch.

My phone bleated its chirpy harpy song. I swiped it away and fell out of bed, weeks of dirty laundry breaking my fall. I dropped back into my coma, oblivious to the funk of stale sweat, urine and cheap grog. An hour or so later, my alarm went off. I stared at the time with bleary eyes, forced myself into the shower, tried to wash away the remnants of a blank, dreamless sleep that was somehow worse than nightmares.

It wasn't until I was at work, looking at the email, that I remembered the unanswered phone call. She'd sent me a link to a video on a peer-to-peer file-sharing network. I clicked the link, rubbing my eyes. While I waited for it to download, I went and got coffee from a machine that had been at the *Courier Mail* longer than I had.

I sat down, pulled out my phone, and saw the blinking message icon. I called MessageBank, sipped the coffee, grimaced, sipped again.

"Uh, hi. My name's Kay. I sent you the email. About, you know…"

A woman. Maybe forty, maybe older. She had the rough-smooth voice of someone on the game but none of the confidence of someone who was good at it.

"…Thanks for getting back to me. I want you to know this is real…"

A noise in the background. Television. Some kids' show. Multicoloured mutants. Something Donna put Meg down in front of when she was struggling to hold it together.

"…I've sent you a link…"

Something breaking. A glass on the floor?

"…I've gotta go. Watch the video. Don't tell anyone. They'll kill me if they know it was me."

I clicked *play*, dived for the volume control when the sound of panting blared from the speakers. Someone in the office sniggered, then must've realised whose computer it was coming from and shut up. It's amazing what you can get away with when your wife and kid have just died. I plugged in my headphones, started the video again. There wasn't much video to be had; a pixelated blur.

But what I'd first interpreted as moans of pleasure were moans of pain.

"Please, let me go."

She slurred her words: "please" was "pleash". Drugs or grog. Maybe both. Men laughed. The camera shifted, tilted. A leg, trussed. Black and blue. A man in a suit stepped in front of her.

"Here, let me have a go."

He got down on his knees, his body obscuring the act. The woman moaned again, and this time, if not for the ropes and the state of her legs, it was almost the sound of pleasure. But it was wrong. The wrongness was baking off the screen. In the background, a baby cried, the sound so out of context I jerked, turning in my chair, half-expecting to see Kyle's missus bringing their newborn in for a visit. But the view was the same as it always was. Chaz trying to sink wastepaper hoops from his desk. Morag at the front counter, feigning busyness.

The baby cried again. The hairs on the back of my neck stood up.

"Shut that fucker up."

More screams.

"I said, shut that little fucker up!"

The video cut out.

On my second and last visit, the counsellor told me it wasn't my fault. I stared out the window of her high-rise office, watching light twinkling off the river, cars gliding across the Storey Bridge. I was bubbling with rage and confusion. Donna was sick, the counsellor said. Donna had depression and it wasn't treated. I could almost deal with that. But Meg—what about Meg? My job was to protect her. Isn't that the whole fucking point? You protect your kid from the bad things, from the monsters, you teach them right from wrong, and one day you throw a fucking party and give them an oversized key.

The counsellor said I shouldn't blame myself.

And I agreed with her. I lied, because I couldn't tell her the truth. I couldn't tell her about the daydream I used to have in the days after they died. The daydream was this: I arrived home from work. I walked down the hallway. The bathroom light was on and I could hear bathwater splish-splashing about. I slipped off my shoes so I could surprise them. I loved that look on Meg's face when I managed to sneak up on her. Initial fear replaced by a big grin. When I peered around the corner, Donna looked at me. She'd been crying. I sighed, preparing myself for a night of telling her it was all going to be okay, we'd all get through it, things would look better in the morning. Then I saw Meg, lying at the bottom of the bathtub. And it was awful, it was horrifying, right? Even if you've never had kids, you can see that. But the worst thing? The worst thing was that I was already thinking about how we could cover it up, what we could say so that it would all be okay, the two of us would get through it, so that things would look better in the morning.

I entered the brothel clasping my notebook and pen like a shield. The door closed behind me with the noise of a sod of dirt slapping against a coffin lid. Cool air chilled my skin. After the humidity outside, I felt clammy and sick. I regretted the heart-starters I'd downed at the Aussie Nash on the way over. The overweight woman behind the counter raised a heavily pencilled eyebrow when I told her I was there to interview Kay.

"Kay will be right out when she's ready for her 'interview', love."

She waved me over to a faux-leather lounge suite, bathing in the light from a TV bolted to the wall. Daytime TV. Men dressed as babies. The day after I found Donna and Meg, Chaz turned up on my doorstep, notebook in one hand, voice recorder in the other, uncomfortable expression on his face.

"No hard feelings, Chaz, but fuck off."

I had slammed the door. Didn't give him the opportunity to give me the spiel about how my story might help others. It never helped.

Kay stalked down the hallway on patent leather stilettos. Red, matching her stockings and teddy. Perfume that smelt expensive but probably wasn't. Lipstick smeared on, waxy and bloody. Eyes glinting out of deep, dark sockets.

She took me to her room. Heavy red curtains and a four-poster bed struggling to sustain the illusion of opulence over the reality of stained carpet and threadbare sheets. Any fantasy scotched by the chair in the corner of the room, bathed in bright white light from a standard lamp. It was where they checked punters for disease. She perched on the bed, patted a spot beside her. I sat down. I could feel the heat radiating off her body.

"They meet once a month, to feed."

"I thought you said they were vampires, not werewolves."

She silenced me with a look.

"What do you mean, 'feed'?" I said.

"I mean exactly that. Feed."

"Like, a fetishistic thing? The whole man-baby thing?"

She shook her head, frustrated. "The women are mothers. They have babies. You know?"

She broke down, thrust a hand against her mouth and heaved in a breath, trying to hold in the pain. That just made it worse. She keened, rocking backwards and forwards. I forgot about my notebook. I thought about the gruff voice on the video: *Shut that little fucker up.* I put my arm around her, meaning to comfort her.

But then my mouth was on hers, my hands running rough over satin and lace. I squeezed my eyes shut, tried to remember what it used to be like, with Donna. Before the depression got really bad. I went to push Kay onto the bed, but she twisted sideways and slid off the bed, shuffling between my legs. She undid my pants. I felt nauseous. Sweaty. High.

My boss was a nervous man. He had a lot to worry about. Circulation figures. Advertising revenue. Defamation suits. He herded stationery around his desk like an Officeworks jackaroo. To the left of the blotter, to the right of the blotter. They always ended up straight, edges lined up. Pens or pencils that were different lengths were relegated to the dead zone under his computer monitor, where online news mocked him from beneath the screensaver.

"You need to take some time off," he said.

"I need to work."

"We tried that."

"I'm chasing something big."

"Oh yeah?"

You could see the wheels turning. My psychological welfare stacked up against circulation figures; circulation figures stacked against a potential lawsuit. Breach of duty of care. Or defamation if I screwed up and fingered the wrong person.

I laid it out for him in terms he could understand. Illegal immigrants. Locked up somewhere west of Brisbane. Playthings for anyone who had the money and could keep their mouths shut. He asked for the source and I told him it was someone who'd seen it first-hand. I flashed back to that afternoon, Kay brushing her sweaty hair off her face as she spat my come into her hand.

"Okay," he said. "Keep me posted."

I was almost disappointed. I'd wanted an out. I wanted to chase the story on my terms, feel free to pull the pin when I felt like it. Now there was something riding on it.

I knew quite early on that Donna had depression. A couple of months after we started dating, I went around to her place and she didn't want to see the movie we'd booked. She didn't want dinner. She wouldn't even look at me. So we lay on her bed, not talking, staring up at the white mozzie net.

I rolled onto my side and brushed her hair away from her forehead, fingertips sticking to her sweaty brow. It was an awkward gesture. She stared through me.

"I sometimes have bad thoughts," she said.

"That's okay. We all do."

"I imagine that you're here, lying on the bed. It's hot. You're just wearing your boxers. I lay a cool washer over your face. Then I pick up the hammer and smash it into your face."

She said it monotone. No emotion. I hugged her because I couldn't bear to look at her. She didn't hug me back.

No one else saw the depression. She hid it from them. She saved it for me. The counsellor said that's because she loved me, she could trust me. Yay for me. My gentle suggestions of "getting help" were dismissed. The more forceful suggestions met a brick wall. She always picked up. I thought maybe the trip to Greece would help. Maybe the wedding would help. Maybe the baby would help. But she needed a different kind of help. She needed drugs, she needed counselling. I ended up with both. She ended up dead.

Richo met me at Lutwyche Shopping Centre. Faded acrylic walls, filth-smeared windows, the wafting reek of a shitty nappy. Richo looked late fifties, head shaved to escape the comb-over. He had the stringy, tanned look of a concreter, and the tatts to match. Handshake an iron vice. Cheap deodorant masking sweat and tobacco.

I explained that I'd never done it before but was keen. I told him I'd thought about it my whole life, since I was a kid. Lying was easy. I substituted my real obsession for a fake one. He saw the need in me; misinterpreted the source.

"Once you've had full cream, you won't go back, chief."

He slapped me on the shoulder. It was like a cosh.

We sat on a bench and worked out the details. I had to send money—not as much as I'd thought—to a PayPal account. I'd get an email from him telling me the date of the next "meeting". Then a phone call on the day, someone telling me the address. I guessed the someone would be Richo, but he was coy when I asked.

"We work on a need-to-know basis, chief. There are people who, ah, don't understand."

He punctuated that with another jab to the ribs. A mother walked past. Baby strapped into a pouch. Another kid shuffling behind on a lead, snot streaming down his face. Richo raised his eyebrows, nudged me again. I wanted to vomit.

Another storm rolled in that night. I defied it, turning on the TV and the radio and every other device that could possibly be harmed by a lightning strike; plugging in my laptop, researching vampirism, heroin babies, breastfeeding fetishes. I took notes, wrote a rough draft of everything that had happened. Lightning flashed, thunder boomed so loud that it reverberated through the VJ walls and the glass of whisky by my hand. I dared the storm to erase it all. And sip by sip, gulp by gulp, I tried to erase it from my own memory, but already it was indelibly marked.

An almighty *crack* tore through the air and the lights went out. The laptop's screen flickered, then came good. Cursor flicking off and on, off and on. I could see Donna and Meg watching me from the other side of the room, eyes glinting in the darkness.

"Leave me alone! Leave me the fuck alone! I tried. Okay? I tried!"

They didn't respond. I sat there, drinking, watching their eyes gleam until I passed out.

I don't remember much of the following fortnight. When I was on the mend, trying to piece things together, I googled myself. Apparently, I wrote half a dozen stories during that time frame. Half a dozen that were published online. I don't remember writing them. I don't remember doing the interviews. All I remember of that time is my mate at the bottle shop and his entreaties to use the back roads. I vaguely recall buying a ridiculously expensive bottle of Laphroaig 30. But maybe I dreamt it.

The call came on a Saturday night. I suspect it was Richo, talking through a dirty sock. He gave me an address for an industrial estate out past Inala. I tooled up the dusty freeway, past painted faces glaring from concrete sound barriers. Up an exit ramp. Through a wasteland of dry lawns glowing white in the moonlight. Peeling paint. Old cars. Rusty chain-link fences. Fading signage with typos. An abandoned service station, all smashed windows and tag-encrusted walls.

I followed the directions, streets turning in ever more convoluted circlets, until finally I reached the end of the road—a row of low-set pre-fab workshops backing onto a polluted creek. It looked like the sort of place where bad things happen at night. I climbed out of the car, grabbed my jacket from the back seat and slipped it over my sweaty shirt—the dress code was "smart casual"—grabbed my shoulder bag and switched on the recording devices. Red lights glowed then faded, just as the guy from the surveillance firm told me they would. It wasn't strictly legal. It certainly wasn't ethical. But if the story panned out, I didn't figure too many people would be taking me to court.

Richo greeted me at the heavy door, first through the peep-hole, then in person. He had on a suit, an ill-fitting, shiny grey sharkskin. He looked no less the concreter with it on. Sweat beaded his forehead and upper lip. He grinned, eyes shifted to the bag.

"Some work stuff," I said. "I didn't want to leave it in the car."

I opened the bag. He told me that wasn't necessary, we were all friends, then poked around anyway.

There was a small ante-chamber. For a moment I worried he would ask me to leave the bag there, but he was already pushing through a heavy velveteen curtain.

"Welcome to the Milk Bar," he said, and ushered me through.

I walked into the room and turned, taking in the scene, letting the camera record it all. The half dozen women were trussed in various positions like living works of art. They were all colours, nationalities—I figured I wouldn't have the opportunity to quiz them on their creeds. They were united by their predicament and by their naked, filthy bodies, full breasts, sagging tummies, greasy hair, doped up expressions. Each had a sign over her head, printed in tacky fonts and laminated: *Dragon Lady (heroin)*; *Little Angel (PCP)*; *The Real Thing (cocaine)*; and so on. The ones on uppers were tied and gagged, eyes rolling like spooked horses. The ones on opiates were left to sprawl in armchairs and on cheap chipboard beds. At the back of the room was another heavy curtain. The sign above the door made me shiver: *The Nursery*.

Richo's tongue flicked at his lips. "They're all under a fortnight post-partum."

None of the men took much notice of us. They were either guzzling milk from the women or sprawled on lounge chairs or bean bags, looking stoned out of their minds. I knew from my research that only about two percent of drugs went through to the breast milk. These men weren't high on drugs—they were high on filth, corruption, control.

There was no sex.

Richo had told me that was the deal, nothing sexual about it. But it was hard to imagine a bunch of randy, drugged up men and helpless naked women and there not be any fucking. But he was right. No sex. No sign of there having been any sex.

In hindsight, it's obvious I was having a mental breakdown.

The breakdown had given me the story. There was no way I would have followed the initial lead, no way I could have duped Richo so convincingly, if I'd been totally sane. All I knew at the time was that I was having trouble keeping it together, and that if I lost it, losing the story would be the least of my worries. My lips trembled as I struggled to make Richo think I was cool with it all. I didn't want to look behind the final curtain. I knew I had to.

"I'm sorry. It's just…it's like a fantasy."

Richo nodded. He'd heard it all before.

"What's behind the curtain?"

I started across the room, lips numb. I felt Richo's iron grip on my shoulder, managed to shrug out of it.

"Whoa, whoa, whoa big man," he said. "Let's have some fun out here first."

I walked faster, skirting a Melanesian woman bound to an old massage table. Richo didn't have time to stop me, not without creating a scene. And most of us—no matter how pure, no matter how evil—hate making a scene.

Sometimes, most of the time, I wish he had.

For ages, I couldn't remember what happened after I pushed back the curtain. My next memory was of driving back to Brisbane along the Ipswich Motorway, mouth and nose burning with vomit, cheek throbbing, eye almost swollen shut. And blood. Blood everywhere.

Then the nightmares came. Babies covered in blood. Asleep? A worn butcher's block covered in bloodstained scalpels, syringes, carving knives. A rusty forty-four-gallon drum. Donna, staring blank-eyed at the TV screen, blood pulsing out of her damaged nipple while Meg screamed. A wet nurse cradling a baby to her breast with one flabby, tattooed arm. Three fingers missing off her right hand. Donna, smashing a hammer down on Meg's body, over and over again. A balding man in a plastic raincoat, cradling a baby to his mouth with a wrinkled, liver-spotted hand. I saw myself, peering into the drum and seeing Meg's blank eyes staring back at me.

Shut that fucker up, shut that fucker up, shut that fucker up!

The police had lots of questions. Starting at the booze bus on the Ipswich Motorway (my blood-alcohol reading), and ending in an interview room at Roma Street (the blood). There was lots of bad coffee. Questions. And panic. Because I really couldn't remember how I came to have blood on my shirt or why my face was smashed up.

If it wasn't for my boss and the illegal recording I'd made, I think I'd still be in custody. Lying on a bunk in a cell at the Brisbane Correctional Centre, wondering how I'd come to be drinking baby's blood, until I found the opportunity to hang myself with my towel. As it was, the police watched the video and my boss bailed me early next morning. He wanted to drop me home. He said I was in shock. I asked him to drop me at work; told him if he didn't, I'd just get a cab there anyway. So, he drove me through the city as the sun crept above the horizon, muttering about "health and safety" over the easy listening bullshit on the radio.

I wrote my story.

The men at the Milk Bar, all bar Richo, were caught and sent to jail. The guy out the back, drinking the baby's blood, was put into protective custody. Two months into his sentence, he was found bludgeoned to death in his bunk. No one shed a tear. The wet nurse—she had been real, not some Lynchian hallucination—was deemed psychologically unstable and, as far as I know, is still locked up at Wolston Park. And Richo, God bless him, Richo was dumped outside the emergency ward at the Royal Brisbane Hospital, dead before the doc even had time to diagnose the overdose.

And me? The story was nominated for an award but didn't win. I stopped drinking. I got counselling. I don't believe in vampires anymore. Or ghosts. There's just illness and violence and evil. And some days—most days—that's enough.

THE RIVER IS DEEP

KAT PEKIN

Well, my day just got a lot more exciting.

I'm used to seeing weird things dragged on board *CETO Twelve*. It's part of my job to inspect whatever the net brings in. But this thing is something I've not seen before. It takes up the majority of the netting. It looks slightly translucent, like thick plastic, and is a palette of watery blue colours. A narrow oval shape about as large as a baby whale. Organic, for sure. Something born from the ocean, not discarded in it.

It almost looks like an egg.

I press the bottom-left release button on my keypad. One side of the netting unclips, spilling the contents into the inspection pool. The egg is by far the most interesting thing in the haul. Mostly there are traces of dead kelp-beds, seagrass, and remnants of phytoplankton. There is also a chunk of what appears to be dying coral covered in fading violet coralline algae.

A couple of Japanese spider crabs have their claws caught through the netting. Dead, it seems, as they make no hasty snaps of their pincers or try to wriggle free. Possibly died from venturing into too-deep waters. Spider crabs normally live in 300-metre-deep ocean but when the meteor struck the icecaps, it basically turned the world into a gigantic overflowing storm pool, and the sea life that had lived happily on the ocean floor for millions of years was suddenly evicted and displaced. Some creatures, like these crabs, couldn't adapt fast enough.

Which means this egg, if that's what it is, is likely something caught in the shifting tussle of the altered underwater currents.

"Jesus, Sera," Micah's voice says behind me. "That's new."

"It is something," I say.

My brother comes to stand beside me. "That came up in your net?"

"Yep."

CETO arks are equipped with several netting devices to serve different functions across the ship. Our fishing nets are specially designed to capture smaller fish for consumption, but they are fixed to another section of the ark. The net for my sector is made from steel ropes attached to lead weights which lower it to the depths. My net scrapes the ocean floor to gather whatever it can find.

"What is it?" Micah says.

"Unsure. I've never seen something like it before. Possibly an egg?"

"An egg?" Micah sounds worried. "Something *laid* this thing?"

"Calm down," I say with a smile. "I'm just thinking out loud."

I was pre-selected for a spot on the CETO arks based on my expertise. I was allowed to bring immediate family and, since our parents are gone, that technically just meant Micah. I am a biological oceanographer which likely aided my selection, but Micah is a paediatric surgeon. So, it was deemed there was enough benefit to the CETO arks for his family to be given a place too.

"Is it…alive?" Micah asks as he cautiously approaches my panel.

There's thick glass between us and the inspection pool, but he still seems tentative. Where Micah is part of the CETO medical staff who take care of those on board, I am part of the detection sector. The CETO mission statement proclaims that the goal of the arks is to not only rescue and maintain the human race but continue humanity's global quest for information and discovery. Micah does the former, I do the latter. For someone who operates on children, Micah can be surprisingly skittish around the things I find.

"I'm not sure," I say. "Looks like everything else it brought up is dead or dying."

I press a few buttons on my panel and extend the mechanical

arms from the ceiling above the inspection pool. Then I slip my hands into the sensor gloves which allow me to carefully and precisely manoeuvre the arms above the egg. It certainly seems to be alive in some way. The colours on its surface glisten like oil in the sun and seem to shimmer.

Using the most sensitive setting possible, I use an extension on the arms to scrape a tissue sample from the egg. And it is definitely tissue. I notice it weeps slightly as I take my sample.

Then the egg shifts.

Rather, it shivers. Behind me, Micah swears, but I can't stop staring at the egg. Because I see something. Inside the soft, cell-like surface, something moves.

As night falls over *CETO Twelve*, I'm still in my lab, awaiting the results of the tissue sample. Reminders for dinner in the cafeteria pass across my digital watch screen, but I ignore them. We're not required to eat with everyone; that's why the cabins have tiny kitchens. But it seems many of those aboard *CETO Twelve* enjoy the community atmosphere, my brother included. He likes his kids to co-mingle with the other families. And he was happy to have an excuse to leave me and my giant moving egg alone.

It's not the first time something living has been pulled from the ocean floor.

In the days following the floods, we were getting various kinds of living creatures caught in our nets. Sharks, dolphins, fish of every size, all dragged in along with remnants from civilisation. My net brought up hefty pieces of cars, boats, and even planes. Not to mention debris from homes and buildings. Thankfully, that's the worst of what I saw. On the other side of the ship, where the fishing nets trawl much closer to the surface, there were bodies. Human bodies. Hundreds of thousands of them. *CETO Twelve* went into lockdown. No civilians were allowed out on the decks. Not until we were far away from land, and there were no longer bodies floating in the water.

The normal protocol when something is hauled in is to

evaluate and designate. Garbage and anything deemed non-dangerous and non-valuable to our life on the sea is incinerated and its ash sent to gardening. If it's a living creature relatively undamaged from the trip in the netting, it is released back into the ocean. If the creature is sick or dying, it is euthanised and tested to see if it is suitable for human consumption. Otherwise—incinerator.

While I wait for the results, I search my files for a comparative egg. It sits alone in the inspection pool now. I used the mechanical arms to clear the dead crabs, coral and seagrass away, then used a gentle spray of ocean water to clean the egg's surface. I haven't seen the thing inside again, but the egg has shuddered a few times like whatever is in there is agitated.

On my screen, I swipe through images of underwater animals' eggs and offspring. It must be some sort of cephalopod egg. That would explain the membrane shell and oval shape. But it wouldn't explain the colours. Squid and octopus eggs tend to be a single colour, in the same way chicken eggshells are hues of one shade, but this egg is faintly kaleidoscopic.

It's also gigantic. And solo. Cephalopods don't lay one single egg. They lay a clutch which are interconnected by tissue and many of the eggs don't survive to hatching. It doesn't make sense that my net would find just one egg unless it was the only one. There is no damage to the egg either, no indication that it was once part of a clutch and somehow broke away.

This thing is transfixing, that's for sure. Almost hypnotic.

I can see the thing moving inside. Just a little. It's shuddering again. The change in temperature rising from the ocean to the ark may have woken up this thing because it certainly wasn't moving when it arrived. I see a long shape pressing up against the membrane. It moves like a snake, but then I see the suction pads. *Tentacles*.

My computer beeps beside me. The tissue sample results flash up on my screen.

I read through it carefully. Whatever is inside is female. I see traces of cephalopod RNA, as I suspected, but I also find traces of what looks like alterations to the helix. RNA editing? That reminds me of an article I read once, before the waves. I'm sure I saved it to my computer and, in a few clicks, I've found it.

> *RNA editing has been found to occur in the cephalopod species,* Octopus bimaculoides, *commonly known as the California two-spot octopus. The creature is able to manipulate, or edit, its RNA to adapt to a rapid change in temperature.*

This would make sense—the meteor altered the temperature of the whole planet when it spun the Earth off its axis and knocked us towards the sun.

> *Since the most heavily edited RNAs in the California two-spot octopus are related to its neural proteins, RNA could be a factor in the extreme intelligence of the creature. A lot is unknown about the reason for and limits—if any—of an octopus's ability to edit its RNA, but extensive RNA editing may have profound evolutionary consequences.*

I lean back in my chair. The article is just one of many hundreds of thousands written about creatures in the ocean. But I remembered it because I have always been fascinated by how creatures adapt to survive underwater. Like the clown fish forming a symbiotic relationship with the anemone, or sea animals in rough waters developing flat shells to reduce water resistance. There is so much we can't see and so much we don't know. Creatures of the ocean adapt much faster than humans. And cephalopods can adapt fastest of all, thanks to their RNA chromosome, which is single-helix instead of double like human DNA. Seems in this case that they can do more with one than we can with two.

So, if RNA editing has been confirmed in an octopus, then surely it could be true of another species of cephalopod.

Like whatever laid this egg in my lab.

And if that's the case, that could explain why this egg is on its own, why it's so huge, and why I've never seen anything like it before.

Sharp movement from inside the inspection pool catches my eye. The egg. It's moving. Rather, its occupant is moving. I get up from my chair and move closer to the glass. The movement is not just a twitch. It's a move with purpose. A decisive, impending shift from the female within. I hear noises of rapid movement coming from the shell. She's not just shuddering; she's pushing against the sides of the soft shell hard enough to thin the membrane to breaking point.

She's ready.

I ensure my video equipment is recording the inspection pool. The urge to alert someone catches me off-guard, but I'm the one to report to. This is my sector. My job. My problem.

She moves again, more determined this time. I can't tell if it's her head or body or something else, but it's pressing so hard against the shell the inevitable happens right before my eyes. The shell breaks. Just a little, the membrane splits, then tears like a knife has sliced it open. The thing falls out into the inspection pool and I'm as transfixed with it as I was with the egg.

She looks like a monster.

She has tentacles like a squid, and two large eyes with W-shaped pupils similar to that of a cuttlefish. But she also has a hardened shell protecting her, like a mud crab or maybe even a turtle. She is a combination of sea creatures that do not belong together.

Despite having no feet with which to gain footing, she manages to keep her balance. She extends her tentacles slightly—I think I count ten but there could be more—and their length reaches to the sides of the pool. She's searching. My throat is dry because my mouth is hanging open. I close it and step away from the glass.

She darts to the corner of the inspection pool, tentacles pulled inwards. She saw me. My movement startled her. But she saw me. Her eyes, a beautiful shade of bright fluorescent green, are fixed on me. She makes a noise, an uncomfortable chattering noise. Almost like a child whimpering.

Then she unfurls her tentacles and extends her head high out of her shell. She opens her mouth, which is shaped similar to a turtle's beak. For a moment, I see she has teeth. Lots of teeth. Teeth that are far more advanced than to simply eat krill. But all that goes out of my mind when a second later, the creature lets out a screech.

That's all I can call it. It's a loud screech that seems to echo all around me. There's a high-pitched sound that is so sharp I worry it will burst my eardrums. But there's also another sound that reminds me of a lion's roar, with such a bass to it I can feel my bones vibrate. There's a clicking sound too, like a dozen people snapping large gardening shears all at once. I press my palms against my ears, yet I can still hear it. One long, bellowing note that reminds me of when my niece knocked her head against the corner of our table. She sat down and cried a little. Then she took a deep breath, opened her mouth, and screamed.

It's early morning when I return to my cabin. We call them cabins, but they are more like small hotel rooms in size and design. My bedroom fits a single bed, built-in wardrobe, wall light, and nothing else. The largest room is the combined kitchen-dining-lounge area which looks out onto the ocean.

My body aches from the last few hours. Turning off the light in the lab managed to quiet down Neon—that's what I called her, nicknamed for the fluorescent green colour of her eyes. Then I diverted some of the shrimp marked for our veterinary aquarium to feed her, and filled the inspection pool with ocean water. She settled in the water and gobbled up the food.

I sent updates to all heads of CETO sectors—who were no doubt wondering what the hell that screeching sound was—and assured our captains that it was under control. I've had wild animals in the lab before. All have been identifiable to me in the past, true, but my job is to uncover new species and I seem to have done just that. So, there are bound to be "teething problems", which is how I phrased it in my updates where I also referred to Neon as a "giant squid or similar".

I quietly step through my living area past my two nephews. They're tucked underneath the cubby they've made out of sheets and towels. The older, Zack, is curled up with his knees against his chest. His little brother, Caleb, is flat on his back with his limbs sprawled at different angles. Outside, the waves make loud groans against the ark. We're used to water sounds. Maybe a storm is coming in. Something seems to be rumbling out there.

I find my brother on the balcony holding my sleeping baby niece against his chest. Audrey is almost eight months old, named after her mother who did not survive the birth.

"How's the squid?" Micah asks me as I sit in the chair opposite him. The chairs are metal, fused to the decking.

"Still a mystery," I say.

"*Could* it be a giant squid?" he asks.

"Maybe." I smile, then I mention how squids don't lay one egg. I start to explain the RNA editing theory, but I'm too tired.

"What else could lay something that size?" he asks, patting Audrey on the back as she stirs.

"Nothing," I yawn. "Anything."

The ark tips sharply to one side.

I am thrown off my chair and fall against the balcony fence. Micah slides heavily beside me. Audrey wakes with a shriek; for a moment I panic, but Micah hasn't dropped her. Inside, the boys are calling for me and their father. I get unsteadily to my feet. The ark slowly rocks back to centre and regains stability. I grab my brother's free arm and force him back into the cabin.

"Stay inside!" I shout as I shut and lock the balcony door.

Caleb runs into my arms. Zack clings to his father and sister.

"We hit something?" Micah asks me.

"Didn't sound like it," I say.

And it didn't. We've hit things in the past, like old ships and aircraft, that make a lot of metallic scraping and clanging sounds. This was simply movement. Soundless movement. As though someone had reached down and tilted us to one side.

Or...

My throat tightens.

Or it was something reaching up.

Alarms sound across *CETO Twelve*. I'm trying to get back to my lab. We're a scientific vessel, we search for answers. And we need an answer for this. Protocol alerts are buzzing out over the speakers. They're the exact same alerts that played when we boarded the ark all those years ago.

"Remember you are safe on the ark," the harmonious voice repeats. "You are safe with CETO."

I'm crossing the deck towards the Science Sector when the ark tips again.

People around me scream and cry out, grabbing onto railings and poles and anything else tied down. And I'm doing the same. I loop my arm around a staircase post, brace my feet and press my back into the wall. This is worse than the first tip. I actually can *see* the ocean from an angle I shouldn't be able to.

We must be almost completely on our side.

Anything not bolted down is tumbling. Books, cutlery, clothes, bags. Those who couldn't grab onto something fast enough are sliding down the deck, catching their hands on whatever they can reach to stay aboard.

I'm sure some fall. I just can't think of them.

Because I hear a noise that scares me worse than the thought of losing my neighbours.

It's like the sound Neon made in the lab, only this one is deeper and echoes around the ark like thunder. It has a high pitch, a roar, and that clicking sound that reminded me of gardening shears. And it's coming from underneath the ark.

When the boat rights itself again, I sprint to the back deck. It's enclosed back here, a viewing area to allow CETO residents to watch the ocean pass by through solid glass. I run to the screen and, for just a moment, I see it. An enormous tentacle whips down behind the waves. Before it disappears beneath the surface, I catch a glimmer of kaleidoscopic colour on its skin.

"Kraken."

The voice comes from behind me. I didn't realise there was someone sitting there. An elderly lady sitting alone. There's a look of resignation on her face.

"That's a myth," I gasp.

"Based in truth," she says. "Heck, Tennyson wrote about a kraken. Oh, how I love Tennyson." The woman closes her eyes and after a few moments recites in a calm voice:

> *Below the thunders of the upper deep,*
> *Far, far beneath in the abysmal sea,*
> *His ancient, dreamless, uninvaded sleep*
> *The Kraken sleepeth…*
> *Until the latter fire shall heat the deep;*
> *Then once by man and angels to be seen,*
> *In roaring he shall rise and on the surface die.*

Via my digital watch, I tap into the video feed of my lab. Neon is flinging herself around the inspection pool like a monkey in a cage. The sound has animated her. She knows something. And I do, too. That thing below us, the thing that looks and sounds like Neon, is her mother. And she's coming for her baby.

"You think the mother is attacking our ship?" Captain Jonas asks.

I called for this emergency meeting with him, the other captains, and the heads of sectors. Micah came along. The boys sit quietly at Micah's feet; Audrey dozes in his lap.

"Yes," I say to Captain Jonas. "We brought her egg on board and she wants it back."

Captain Jonas looks confused. "I thought you reported it was just a type of squid."

"No. At least, not *just* a squid. It's a product of the meteor, of the change in weather, of all…*this*. The world changed. The animals changed too. Squid don't raise their offspring; they lay the eggs and leave them. But, like I said, this is not just a squid. It's different. Maybe it's a preservation thing. The creature below us needs to ensure the survival of its species. It needs to protect its offspring. That thing that's attacking us," I point down to the ocean, "is our hatchling's mother."

As if on cue, the ark tilts again. But this is worse. There's a straining in the metal skeleton of the ark. Something huge slams against the port side. Everyone in the room loses their footing and we wind up on the ground. I crawl over to Micah and the children. The ark shifts sharply to the side again and that scream—that clicking, roaring scream—bellows all around us. Micah and I manoeuvre the children between us to stifle their ears.

"It could kill us," Micah says. "It could just drag us under. Why doesn't it?"

I'm about to say I don't know, but then I realise that I do. "Neon," I say. "Its child is onboard. It won't risk harming her by sinking the ship."

"But it's a squid! It can live underwater, will survive if the ark sinks. We won't!"

"Too risky. It's an evolutionarily intelligent cephalopod that knows what it's doing. Neon's a newborn. She could get squashed or stuck, or panic and hurt herself. The mother won't chance harming her young."

"So, what can we do?"

The only option I can think of is the one I tell my brother. "Give her back."

Micah gives me an odd look. "How?"

"We can release her, just like any other animal we've rescued."

"Sera, we can't subdue that thing with a dart like a shark or a dolphin. And there's no time to figure out how to move it, that gigantic fucker is circling underneath us!"

I think, I think, and I think. There's a way, there must be. "We have to lead Neon to the release bay. Show her the way out." I become aware that the other people in the room, the captains and heads of sector, are listening to me too. "Hopefully, the mother takes her and leaves us alone."

"Hopefully?" Captain Jonas repeats.

"How do we lead it anywhere?" Micah asks.

"We flood the inspection pool, then my lab, then the hall, then each hallway leading to the release tubes. The flow of water will flush Neon out into the ocean."

"That can't be done," Captain Jonas says. "As soon as one sector floods, the others will go into automatic lockdown to protect the ship. Each door would have to be overridden manually."

"I know that," I say. And any bravery I think I might have had disappears when I see the eyes of my brother on me.

Micah starts to shake his head. "Sera…"

"It's my job," I tell him. "I brought Neon onto this ship; I have to get her off it."

"Sera, that's suicide."

"I'll wear a wetsuit and take an oxygen tank. It'll be okay," I say weakly, because we both know it won't be.

"Sera—"

I cut him off by hugging him tight. We don't often hug—we're not huggers— but now we hug. He's squeezing me and I can hear the sobs in his throat. My nephews are hugging me too. And sweet Audrey is smiling in a blissfully innocent way. It's us, just me and my brother, and always has been. Our parents died, we stayed together. His wife died, we stayed together. The world ended, we stayed together. Micah and these kids are all I have, and I have to leave them to save them.

"I love you," I whisper as I kiss my brother's cheek. Then I kiss each of my nephews and my niece. "You are my everythings."

The water is ankle-deep. I can see on my digital watch that Neon is moving along the path I need her to follow. She's swimming through my lab now, following the current of the water. I move as fast as I can to ensure the next door is open before Neon swims in. I keep two doorways ahead of her to make sure she can't attack me. I'm under no illusions; she might kill me if given the chance, and then no one will be able to manually release the doors.

I'm not thinking about anything except what I'm doing. Manual override. Last door. I pull my mask down over my head and take a few breaths from my oxygen tank. There's about an hour of air remaining. My mask fogs up as I punch in the final override code. A blink of a green light, and I pull down the release handle. The door behind me opens and water from the previous hall starts to fill in. Second to last door completely opens and I hear the chatter of Neon sliding through. She's getting the hang of it now. I see her tentacles underneath the door as it rises.

Even if I wanted to, I couldn't go back this way. All the previous hallways are full of water. I can't swim against the current. But I knew that when I came up with this plan. Maybe I can swim back in once Neon is gone and the water pressure has equalised.

I open the last door for the release bay. The water brings Neon in. She slides to the back of the room, her tentacles gripping the sides of the wall. She moves confidently, her newborn jitters seeming to have left her. The water is at my waist and I punch the exit code for the release bay. I already can't breathe, and my oxygen tank is working fine.

I keep my eyes on Neon as the release tube opens. I wait for her to attack me. To swipe me up with her tentacles and swallow me whole.

But she doesn't. She just looks at me.

Her eyes sparkle green, almost as if she's showing me that I gave her the right nickname. Maybe she is a kraken. Maybe she's something that morphed when the world ended. Maybe she's just an animal. But whatever she is, she doesn't attack me. I don't know why. Perhaps we both know what is going to happen to me. Cephalopods are incredibly intelligent.

The release tube is fully open now. Ocean water rushes in and speedily fills what space I have left. My head keeps dipping below the surface, and then I'm completely submerged. I try to grab onto something but the pull of the ocean is so strong I'm sucked into open water. I bang against the side of the ark on my way out. Something on my watch starts beeping. All I can hear is the clicking inhale of my oxygen mask and a sharp hissing. I can see Neon swimming into the ocean. She moves like a jellyfish, her tentacles pulling in and out to propel her along. She heads for an enormous mass of dark water, but then I see it's not water at all. The darkness rises. The darkness is her waiting mother.

The mother is so enormous I can't comprehend her. She is almost a mirror of Neon, just on an astronomical scale. Her tentacles reach down into the murky depths, but the length I can see could wrap around *CETO Twelve* a hundred times over. Her shell reminds me of a rocky mountain range, and her eyes are each as big as a house. There are fluorescent green hues in the W-shape of her pupils.

Alerts flash on my watch screen. It's paired with my oxygen tank to make it easy to check my O2 levels and water temperature. But the screen just blares two words at me. TANK DAMAGED.

I wonder if the mother can see me or if I am so small that she ignores me like a person would a mosquito. Little specks of light begin to cloud my eyesight. The enormous creature seems to shift her tentacles to the side to allow Neon to swim between them. A musical chatter of mother and Neon begins, perhaps a greeting. They're both retreating from my blurred vision. I hope they are retreating to safety.

Maybe the mother will return to exact revenge on the boat that stole her baby.

Maybe she'll return to the bottom of the ocean.

I wish I could know for sure.

CONTRIBUTOR BIOGRAPHIES

EDITOR

DEBORAH SHELDON is an award-winning author of short stories, novellas and novels across the darker spectrum of horror, crime and noir. Recent titles include the novel *Body Farm Z* (Severed Press), novella *The Long Shot* (Twelfth Planet Press), and the collection *Figments and Fragments: Dark Stories* (IFWG Australia). Her short stories have been published in many anthologies and magazines including *Aurealis*, *Midnight Echo*, *Andromeda Spaceways*, and *Dimension6*. She won the Australian Shadows "Best Collected Work" Award for *Perfect Little Stitches and Other Stories*. Her fiction has also been shortlisted for numerous Aurealis and Australian Shadows Awards, long-listed for a Bram Stoker, and selected for various "best of'" anthologies such as *Year's Best Hardcore Horror*. As guest editor of *Midnight Echo 14*, she won the Australian Shadows "Best Edited Work" Award. Deb's other credits include TV scripts such as *Neighbours*, feature articles, non-fiction books, and award-winning medical writing. http://deborahsheldon.wordpress.com

AUTHORS

When not reviewing prescriptions and medications charts, **GERALDINE BORELLA** is writing stories. She writes for children and adults and has been published in magazines, online, in podcasts and anthologies. Her stories feature in *Spooktacular Stories: Thrilling Tales for Brave Kids*, *Short and Twisted* (2016), *page* *seventeen*, and on *AntipodeanSF*'s website and podcast. In 2018, she won an ASA Emerging Writer's mentorship and placed second in the Buzz Words Short Story Prize. She has worked as an online creative-writing tutor for The Writer's Studio, Sydney, and has recently made the eligibility list for the Ditmar Award 2020. Several of her projects are impatiently awaiting re-drafts, and she dreams of the day when she can hand in her white coat and pick up a quill fulltime. She lives in the village of Yungaburra on the Atherton Tablelands in Far North Queensland.

JACK DANN has written or edited over seventy-five books, including the international bestseller *The Memory Cathedral*, *The Rebel*, *The Silent*, and *The Man Who Melted*. He has won many awards including the Nebula Award, the World Fantasy Award, the Aurealis Award, and the Shirley Jackson Award. He is the co-editor, with Janeen Webb, of *Dreaming Down-Under*, which won the World Fantasy Award, and the editor of the sequel *Dreaming Again*, and *Dreaming in the Dark*, which won the World Fantasy Award in 2017. Dr Dann is an Adjunct Senior Research Fellow in the School of Communication and Arts at the University of Queensland. His latest novel is *Shadows in the Stone*. Kim Stanley Robinson called it "such a complete world that Italian history no longer seems comprehensible without his cosmic battle of spiritual entities behind and within every historical actor and event." Forthcoming is a Centipede Press *Masters of Science Fiction* volume.

RENEE DE VISSER was born in Victoria and grew up in a household of horror movie fans. She always had an interest in writing—winning several local awards as a teenager—but ceased writing when she started working full-time. Renee currently lives in Brisbane, Queensland with her partner and daughter, and her dog and cat. When not working and writing, she enjoys reading, cooking and entertaining. She has a modest collection of horror memorabilia. Her dream is to someday move out of suburbia to a mountain retreat where she can write stories surrounded by free-ranging chickens.

JASON FISCHER is a writer who lives near Adelaide. He has won the Colin Thiele Literature Scholarship, an Aurealis Award and the Writers of the Future Contest. In Jason's jack-of-all-trades writing career, he has worked on comics, apps, television, short stories, novellas and novels. Jason also facilitates writing workshops, is an enthusiastic mentor, and loves anything to do with the written or spoken word. He is also the founder and CEO of Spectrum Writing, a service that teaches professional writing skills to people on the autism spectrum. Jason plays a LOT of *Dungeons and Dragons*, has a passion for godawful puns, and is known to sing karaoke until the small hours.

REBECCA FRASER is an Australian author of genre-mashing fiction for both children and adults, whose short fiction and poetry has appeared in numerous award-winning anthologies, magazines, and journals. Her first novel, a middle-grade fantasy adventure, was released in 2018, and a collection of her dark short fiction is due for release in 2021 (both through IFWG Publishing Australia). To provide her muse with life's essentials, Rebecca copywrites and edits in a freelance capacity, and operates *StoryCraft Creative Writing Workshops* for aspiring authors of every age and ability...however, her true passion is storytelling. Say g'day at writingandmoonlighting.com, Facebook @writingandmoonlighting or Twitter/Insta @becksmuse

GARY KEMBLE is the author of two novels about reporter-turned-paranormal investigator Harry Hendrick—*Skin Deep* (published in the US/UK as *Strange Ink*), and *Bad Blood* (published in the US/UK as *Dark Ink*). His short fiction has been published in magazines and anthologies both here and abroad, and he's a two-time winner of the *One Book Many Brisbanes* short-story award. He lives in Brisbane with his wife, two kids, and a wolfhound-cross with a dislike of birds and possums.

Of Melanesian and Scottish heritage, **DAVID KURARIA** was raised by his extended family on the island of Ranongga in the Solomon Islands. He attended Kingsland Intermediate school in Auckland, New Zealand, before reuniting with his family in Honiara. His story "Kōpura Rising" was published in the anthology *Cthulhu: Land of the Long White Cloud* and selected as a finalist for the 2018 Australian Aurealis Awards for "Best Horror Novella". The author has his first collection of horror tales slated for publication in 2021 from IFWG Publishing. David is an Australian resident and currently resides on the mid-north coast of New South Wales.

PAUL MANNERING is an award-winning New Zealand writer of horror, speculative-fiction, and podcast audio drama, who relocated to Canberra, where he now lives under an assumed identity as a functional adult.

TRACIE MCBRIDE is a New Zealander who lives in Melbourne with her husband and three children. A member of the HWA and the AHWA, her work has appeared in over eighty print and electronic publications, including the Stoker Award-nominated anthologies *Horror for Good* and *Horror Library Volume 5*. She has two short story collections in print, *Ghosts Can Bleed* and *Drive, She Said*, and her work has won or been shortlisted for various awards including the Sir Julius Vogel Award, the Aurealis Award, and the Shadows Award. Visitors are welcome at http://traciemcbridewriter.wordpress.com/

A Canberra girl with Polish roots, **J.M. MERRYT** has published several short stories and poems since the age of eighteen. Since then, she has undertaken an arts degree and an internship at a publishing company. At twenty-seven, she has most recently devoted her time to a criminology degree, folklore studies, and tending to her growing collection of carnivorous plants. One day, she wants to go on a tour of the world, visiting every site that claims to have its own gates to hell, including the infamous Houska Castle in the Czech Republic. Right now, she's binging on the works of Ito Junji and Angela Carter.

SAMANTHA MURRAY is an Australian writer, mathematician, and mother. Not particularly in that order. Her fiction has been seen in places such as *Clarkesworld*, *Lightspeed*, *Beneath Ceaseless Skies*, *Escape Pod*, *Interzone*, *Nature Magazine*, *Flash Fiction Online*, *The Year's Best Australian Fantasy & Horror*, and *The Best Science*

Fiction of the Year (Vol 4), among others. Samantha won the 2016 Aurealis Award for "Best Science Fiction Short Story", and in 2019 was a guest of honour at Another Planet Science Fiction Convention in Beijing. Samantha lives in Western Australia in a household of unruly boys. You can follow her on twitter @ SamanthaNMurray.

ROBYN O'SULLIVAN is a professional writer and editor, living on the beautiful Bass coast of Victoria. Her published works include a novella *Topsy Turvy* and short story collections *Getting a Life* and *Everything's All Right*, all released by the award-winning Ginninderra Press, as well as 40+ non-fiction educational books for children, which have been distributed in Australia, the United States, Canada, New Zealand and China. Other credits include creative non-fiction pieces in magazines such as *Quadrant*, and stories in Things in the Well's *Guilty Pleasures and Other Dark Delights* and *Midnight Echo*. One of her stories has also been selected for production by *The Night's End* podcast. Currently, Robyn is focused on writing short fiction and memoir. https:// robynosullivan.com.

KAT PEKIN is a speculative fiction writer living in her home-town in the western suburbs of Brisbane. Her work has been published in numerous anthologies, and her stories have won and placed in local and Australia-wide writing competitions. Kat works at a bookstore and spends her free time plotting tales, inventing characters and creating worlds. She writes speculative/ dystopian/post-apocalyptic fiction and enjoys delving into what life would be like if the world ended. Follow her on Facebook @ kat.pekin or Twitter @littleton_pace

ANTOINETTE RYDYR is an artist/writer working in the genres of science-fiction, fantasy and horror usually bent into a surrealist and satirical angle. She works with fellow creator, Steve Carter, and together they have produced graphic novels, award-winning screenplays and esoteric electronic music. In 2018 their collaborative steampunk western novels, *Weird Wild West*, were published by Bizarro Pulp Press, USA. They have also published graphic novels including *Savage Bitch, Weird Worlds, Bestiary of Monstruum, Weird*

Sex Fantasy, Femonsters, and the celebratory resurrection of the infamous *Phantastique,* ingloriously presented in full bloody colour! More grotesque delights can be viewed on their website: https://www.weirdwildart.com/

CHARLES SPITERI is a writer, film director and editor. He has written two (unproduced) screenplays, taught film production, and written academic articles on film culture. His short films have been shown at international film festivals. He has also written several short stories and articles, including the 2006 Australian Horror Writers Association Flash & Short Story Competition winner, "Vara". His other passion is woodworking, and when he is not using his pen, he can be found handcrafting fine things of wood. He loves watching movies and playing board games and whilst his wife loves board games and movies too, they're yet to convince the cat to join them. You can follow Charles on Twitter @strangemachina.

H.K. STUBBS lives on the Gold Coast. She's an award-winning fiction and feature writer with stories published in anthologies and magazines, including "Polymer Island" in *Kaleidotrope* and "Uncontainable" in *Apex* Magazine. She's a creative producer at *Razor Gaze,* and interviews speculative-fiction writers for the podcast *Galactic Chat.* For fun she likes to bushwalk, mountain bike, climb rocks, read, and devour Netflix series. Catch up with her at @superleni on Twitter or discover more about her work and adventures at helenstubbs.wordpress.com.

MATT TIGHE recently returned to writing after a ten-year hiatus. He has works in *Nature Futures,* the Third Flatiron Publishing anthology *Gotta Wear Eclipse Glasses, Scary Snippets: Family Edition,* and upcoming in *Daily Science Fiction.* He is an academic who lives in regional New South Wales with his amazing three kids, his incredibly patient wife, and Sherlock, the most misnamed Golden Retriever in the history of the world. Just before the COVID-19 restrictions were put in place, Matt and his family moved to a small bush block out of town, complete with beehives, which became the setting for "A Good Big Brother". This is the first story Matt wrote specifically targeting an anthology call, after seeing the names of the commissioned authors and dreaming of being associated with them.

MARK TOWSE is an Englishman living in Australia. He would sell his soul to the Devil or anyone buying if it meant he could write full-time. Alas, he left it very late to begin this journey, penning his first story since primary school at the ripe old age of forty-five. Since then, he's been published in the likes of *Flash Fiction Magazine, Cosmic Horror, Suspense Magazine, ParABnormal, Raconteur*, and in over thirty anthologies with many more to come. His work has also appeared on *The No Sleep Podcast, The Grey Rooms Podcast*, and many other immersive productions. His debut collection, *Face the Music*, was released early 2020 by All Things That Matter Press and is available via Amazon, Dymocks, B&N, etc. Contact him via marktowsedarkfiction. wordpress.com, @MarkTowsey12 on Twitter, or @towseywrites on Instagram.

ASH TUDOR is a horror writer from Perth, who spends her time hiding from the sunshine while she scribbles dark tales. She lives with three pot plants (all of them are miraculously still alive) and one husband (also alive.) Ash has a degree in ancient history and was involved in ancestry research before her appetite for the macabre led her to horror writing. She has since been shortlisted in several short story competitions and published on *Horror Tree*. You can find more of her work in anthologies, including *Strange Girls, Predators in Petticoats*, and *The Hollow: Where All Things Evil Lie, vol.3*. Find Ash on Twitter @AshTudor888

Shirley Jackson award-winner **KAARON WARREN** published her first short story in 1993 and has had fiction in print every year since. She was recently given the Peter McNamara Lifetime Achievement Award and was Guest of Honour at World Fantasy 2018, Stokercon 2019 and Geysercon 2019. Kaaron was a Fellow at the Museum for Australian Democracy, where she researched prime ministers, artists and serial killers. She's judged the World Fantasy Awards and the Shirley Jackson Awards. She has published five multi-award-winning novels (*Slights, Walking the Tree, Mistification, The Grief Hole* and *Tide of Stone*) and seven short story collections, including the multi-award-winning *Through Splintered Walls*. She has won the ACT Writers and Publishers Award four times, and twice been awarded the Canberra Critics Circle Award for Fiction. Her most recent novella, *Into Bones Like Oil* (Meerkat Press), was shortlisted for a Shirley Jackson Award and the Bram Stoker Award, winning the Aurealis Award.

JANEEN WEBB is a multiple-award-winning author, editor, critic and academic who has written or edited a dozen books and over a hundred essays and stories. She is a recipient of the World Fantasy Award, the Peter MacNamara SF Achievement Award, the Aurealis Award, and four Ditmar Awards. Her most recent book is *The Dragon's Child* (PS Publishing UK, 2018). The sequel, *The Gold-Jade Dragon*, is due for release late in 2020. She is currently co-writing an alternate history series, *The City of the Sun*, with Andrew Enstice; the first book, *The Five Star Republic*, will be released by IFWG Publishing early in 2021. Janeen has taught at various universities, is internationally recognised for her critical work in speculative fiction, and has contributed to most of the standard reference texts in the field. She holds a PhD in literature from the University of Newcastle.

SEAN WILLIAMS is an award-winning, #1 *New York Times* best-selling author of forty-nine novels and over one-hundred-and-twenty short stories for adults, young adults and children. As well as his original fiction, he has contributed to shared universes such as *Star Wars* and *Doctor Who*, and collaborated with Garth Nix. His 2019 novel *Impossible Music* was shortlisted for the Ethel Turner Prize for Young People's Literature and listed as a "Notable Book" by the Children's Book Council of Australia. His latest novel is *Her Perilous Mansion*, a tale of two children trying to escape from a haunted house.